For the Worm, the Bug, and the Spider.

With all my love,
Princy

Table of Contents

PART I: THERE'S DEAD FOLK 1

One 1

Two.. 7

Three... 12

Four 18

Five.. 23

Six.. 25

Part II: THE GAMBLER ON THE TRAIN 29

Seven 30

Eight 37

Nine 44

Ten... 48

PART III: MEN GET TOGETHER 57

Eleven... 58

Twelve.. 64

Thirteen 69

Fourteen... 75

Fifteen.. 78

Sixteen.. 82

Seventeen 87

Eighteen... 92

Through the Perilous Night

By Edward Dobson

Cover design: Safeer Ahmed

Interior design: Nauman Akbar

Printed in the United States of America.

ISBN: 979-8-9943372-0-2

First Edition

Nineteen 97

Twenty.. 105

Twenty one 111

Twenty two.. 116

Twenty three.. 120

Twenty four 129

Twenty five 134

PART IV: CHARLIE RETURNS TO TREMONTON.................. 136

Twenty six 137

Twenty seven.. 142

Twenty eight... 156

Twenty nine 162

Thirty.. 166

Thirty one 177

Thirty two 182

Thirty three 184

PART V: THE MEN EXIT 193

Thirty four 194

Thirty five.. 198

Thirty six 204

Thirty seven... 211

Thirty eight.. 215

Thirty nine 220

POSTSCRIPT.. 231

AFTERWARD 233

Part I

THERE'S DEAD FOLK

One

CHARLES LA RUE HOLMES was like any other red-blooded, thrill-seeking fourteen-year-old American boy in 1950. So when the wailing sirens of an ambulance, a police car, and a fire truck pierced the quiet of his Sunday afternoon in early June, he didn't hesitate. He leapt onto his balloon-tire, knee-action Schwinn bike, his pulse quickening as he pedaled in furious pursuit.

The shrill cries of emergency vehicles were common on the highway skirting the edge of the Holmes's acreage, but this time, the seldom-used frontage road along his father's walnut grove was the stage for the unfolding drama. That was new. That was close.

Legs pumping like pistons, Charlie watched as the vehicles veered east a quarter of a mile ahead. The convoy blurred past the two-room Merchant Creek Grammar School, where he would soon be graduating from the 8th grade. His eyes narrowed as they disappeared from sight. Determination pushed him harder, his bike's tires crunching against the gravel.

He guessed they had turned into old man Heinrick Strub's farmstead. Gripping the handlebars tighter, he picked up speed, the wind messing his hair as he rode. The sirens suddenly died, leaving an eerie silence in their wake. When he banked hard left into the Strub driveway, the fire truck loomed in his path. He swerved just in time, skidding past the ambulance and Tremonton police car before coming to a stop at the edge of the yard. Deputy Singleton Marsh, one of the town's three cops, stepped forward, raising a hand to block him.

"Sorry, Charlie, cain't let you past me."

Charlie's breath came in ragged gasps. "What's happened?"

"Cain't tell you that neither. Chief Borgman and the firemen, they's inside. Ain't said nothin'. 'Cept there's dead folk."

Charlie wasn't about to be stopped. He swung his Schwinn around, determination flashing in his eyes, and pedaled back to the paved road. He knew another way into the Strub farm. He'd gone there to play with ten-year-old Alice Strub and her brother, Hank, and had poked around the farm as he had every other homestead within a day's ride from his house.

The Strub place had once been the heart of a vast thousand-acre wheat farm. But that was before the Foothill Ditch Company brought water year-round to the valley. Within the span of a few years, most of the acreage was planted to permanent tree groves, and wheat farming was forgotten. Today, the Strub farm was only forty acres, twenty-five of them strawberries, with the remainder as peach, plum, and cherry trees. As Charlie bounced down the dirt road leading to the farm, he spotted the old, sagging shed at the end—a relic of the past, where mules once stabled to work the golden wheat fields.

The great Central Valley of California had long shifted from its wheat-growing heyday, a legacy of the Gold Rush when it fed thousands flocking to the state. By 1850, San Francisco's burgeoning population devoured everything grown in the valley, and wheat farming faded into history.

At the far edge of the Strub property, by a winding creek, lived the Go family—a small Japanese immigrant family that worked the berry fields for Heinrick Strub. Charlie often saw them tending the rows of strawberries. Mrs. Go ran a roadside stand where she sold fresh-picked berries and sometimes peaches, plums, and cherries from the orchard near the house.

Further north stood another small shack where the last of the southern Yana Indian tribe, the Heicho family, lived. Once, their people filled the valleys and hills stretching from Sacramento to Redding. But settlers, miners, and disease had dwindled their numbers to a single family. The Gos and the Heichos, side by side, harvested the bounty of the land for the Strubs.

Charlie slipped past the blue Fordson tractor parked near the stable, skidding to a stop inside the shed. Four crumbling stalls stood meagerly in a row, remnants of a time when mules pulled plows through endless wheat fields. The smell of old leather hung in the air, mixing with the musty scent of hay. Beyond the shed, hidden in the tall weeds, lay the rusted hulks of farm machinery—abandoned discs, mowers, and seeders that once clanked and groaned as the mules trudged through the fields.

Charlie leaned his bike against the creaky wooden stall, the old wood groaning under the weight, and walked over to one of the three grimy windows. He rubbed the side of his hand against the glass, smearing away the dust just enough to get a view of the ranch house beyond.

Compared to his five eighth-grade schoolmates—three girls and two boys—Charlie might have seemed unremarkable at first. With his brown hair cut short like all the boys in the '40s and hazel eyes framed by thick lashes, he blended in easily. He stood taller than everyone except Geneva Derrick, who matched him eye to eye. He was faster than all of them by a long shot. He knew he wasn't as smart as the three girls, but Charlie had something else—a sharp instinct that set him apart. He had a knack for sizing up complicated situations in a flash, acting decisively, and often, bravely.

It was this quick, calculating mind that made him the best athlete at school at the tiny school. But more importantly, it had saved his life once. During the war, he and some friends were attacked by rogue air cadets from the nearby army airfield. The cadets, armed with pistols and even a flame-thrower, had come after the school kids. One of Charlie's playmates, a girl, had been killed, and his father, La Rue Holmes, had almost been shot. It was Charlie's fast thinking and quick action that had turned the tide that day.

CHARLIE PEERED ACROSS AT THE OLD HOME PLACE. It looked just like the ranch houses scattered all over the valley, built back in the 1880s. The structure was mainly redwood, with cedar shingles capping the roof. The house stood tall, two stories high, with the ground floor raised on five-foot pilings to fend off the floodwaters that sometimes surged through the valley. A screened veranda wrapped around the bottom floor on all sides except the north, offering shade and a cool retreat in summer. Off to the side, the Strub family's Studebaker Commander was parked under a porte-cochere, its green paint gleaming faintly in the afternoon light.

The upstairs, housing four bedrooms, featured a deep, cantilevered overhang designed to keep the harsh sun off the walls below, a practical touch from an earlier era. Behind the house, on the north side, stood a tank house. Its five-hundred-gallon water tank loomed thirty feet above the ground, maintaining water pressure for the house's bathrooms and kitchen. The tank and its wooden tower were hidden behind siding painted to match the house, blending seamlessly into the landscape. Just beyond it, the pump house crouched with its windmill tower, the fan now still and rusting. Charlie knew Strub had replaced the windmill with an electric motor, one that pumped a steady flow of water into the high tank. He also knew about the galvanized pipe Strub had buried, running from the tank south to the Go family's shack and north to the Heicho place. Strub's accommodations for his workers might have been modest, but he ensured they had access to running water.

Charlie squinted toward the formal entry on the south side, where the porch screens formed a hazy barrier between the outside and the group of men gathered there. They were huddled in conversation, their gestures animated. Charlie figured they were the police. The front of the house opened onto a broad, grassy lawn—two acres wide—worn with a faint trail from the porte-cochere to the old stable. That was his path. Charlie crouched low and sprinted, his heart pounding, hoping the men on the porch were too absorbed in their discussion to catch sight of him.

CHARLIE DASHED PAST THE STUDEBAKER, its chrome trim flashing in the sunlight, and slipped around the front of the house. He pushed through the back door, which he knew was never locked. The familiar scent of bread and spices lingered in the large country kitchen, but there was no sign of the Strub family. Heart pounding, he moved quickly through the swinging door into the formal dining room. The polished mahogany table, perfectly set, awaited its absent diners. Charlie paused, half-expecting to see the family seated there, their voices filling the room. But the silence felt heavy, unnatural.

He tiptoed out the far end of the dining room into the entry hall, peering into the library. The great fireplace stood cold, its mantel lined with trophies and books neatly arranged on the inset shelves. It was empty too. His gaze flicked to a large framed photograph—a younger Mr. Strub in an army uniform, standing proudly beside General Patton. The thought crossed his mind: Strub must have been a hero once, a man of honor in the war. But now, the house felt eerily void of life.

He moved cautiously into the formal living room, but as he stepped inside, he froze. His breath caught in his throat. There, in the middle of the room, lay his ten-year-old friend, Alice Strub. Her pink dress spread neatly around her, black shoes perfectly aligned. Her hands rested by her sides, and her eyes, wide open, stared blankly at the ceiling. Right between those eyes, a tiny, dark hole marked her forehead. Three thin trails of dried blood ran down over her ears, staining her dark, ebony hair.

Stunned, Charlie's eyes darted to Alice's younger brother, Hank, lying next to her. The eight-year-old's body was arranged in the same exact way—his tiny feet perfectly lined up with his sister's. His hands rested at his sides, and the same small, cruel hole marred his forehead.

Next to Hank was Mrs. Strub. She lay face up, her eyes open, her feet aligned with her children's, the same deadly mark on her forehead. The blood had pooled and dried, trailing down to her ears.

Then Charlie's gaze landed on Heinrick Strub. His body lay stiffly beside his family, but unlike the others, he was crumpled, as if he had fallen forward from his knees. His eyes were wide open, and a hole pierced his right temple. Blood had seeped onto the Indian rug, leaving a dark, oily stain—a stain where Charlie and Alice had once played. The glint of a pistol caught Charlie's eye, lying just beside Mr. Strub's hand.

THE HORRIFYING SCENE SUDDENLY CAME INTO SHARP FOCUS. Charlie's stomach churned, and he bolted. He no longer cared if the men on the porch saw him. He sprinted around the car and tore down the path toward the stable. Yanking his bike upright, he swung it around and sped off, racing down the dirt road past the tractor and onto the paved county road. He didn't look back. All he did was pedal—harder than he ever had before. Tears streamed down his cheeks, blurring his vision, but he didn't wipe them away. All he could see was Alice—sweet Alice. Alice of the high, lilting laughter. Alice, whose stories and animated expressions had filled so many of his days. Alice, whom he loved like a sister, was a friend. Now, the image of her still, lifeless face was all that remained, burning in his mind as he rode.

Two

THE NEXT DAY was the last Monday of the school year. Charlie and his four other eighth-grade classmates were set to graduate that Friday. As soon as the final bell rang, he pedaled the four miles into Tremonton, heading straight for the office of the *Tremonton Sun* newspaper. At the front desk, old Mrs. Pease typed away, her fingers dancing over the keys while she managed the phones. To Charlie, she seemed ancient, her face deeply lined with smile creases, her gray hair teased high. The Peases had been friends with the Holmes family for as long as he could remember. He knew they had once owned the Tremonton movie theater, but they had sold it years ago.

"Hi, La Rue. What are you doing in town this afternoon?" Mrs. Pease was the only person who called him by his middle name—his father's first name. Charlie liked it. It made him feel connected to his family's past, like he was tied to the long line of Holmes history.

"Is Mr. Medico here?"

"Of course. Isn't he always?"

"I wonder if I can talk to him."

"What do you have for him, La Rue? Seems like you're always up to something newsworthy." Charlie was perhaps the most well-known kid in the Tremonton area. "I guess there was some excitement out by your school yesterday."

"That's what I want to see him about," said Charlie. "Can I go in?"

"Well, he's not coming out here, that's for sure. Go on, but don't bother him for too long. He's writing up that mess you're interested in, and it's a long story."

"Thank you, Mrs. Pease. How's Norbert?" Charlie asked, knowing her husband had been unwell for some time.

"I think he's getting better. He sits up these days and can even feed himself. Thanks for asking. Oh, you always were a polite boy, La Rue. You should come by the house and visit him sometime."

"I will." Charlie smiled, then headed down the short corridor past the reception desk and into the press room. The room wasn't large, but neither was the *Sun*. It came out every Wednesday. The printing happened in Stockton, but the pages were laid out right here. Along the south wall, two linotype machines sat side by side, and the north wall was lined with tiers of drawers where past editions were stacked by year.

Charlie loved the press room. He had been there when Mr. Joseph Medico interviewed him after that deadly skirmish with soldiers in his backyard during the war. The smell of ink and old paper filled the air, mingling with the warm metallic scent of the machines. Cluttered tables, stacks of papers, and the hum of activity made the space feel alive. But most of all, he loved the idea that from this small room came a complete newspaper, crafted from scratch and sent out to subscribers each week—a labor of love that belonged entirely to Mr. Medico.

Joe was hunched over his desk just inside the room, his fingers flying across the keys of his typewriter. Charlie slid into the chair beside him, but Joe didn't acknowledge him. The man's white hair glowed under the desk lamp, and his thick glasses perched low on his nose. His shirt was buttoned neatly at the neck, a silver and turquoise bolo tie adding a touch of flair. Though age had softened him, Joe still had the look of an athlete—strong and compact. His round face wore a perpetual frown, and an unlit Camel cigarette drooped from his full lips. He had covered Tremonton sports for years, and after returning from the war, he had bought a controlling interest in the paper, making it his life's work.

Charlie waited for a long time as Joe pounded away at the keys, the rhythmic clack of the typewriter filling the room. It was as if Charlie wasn't even there. Finally, Joe looked up, feigning surprise, like he'd only just noticed the boy sitting beside him.

"Well, if it isn't little Charlie La Rue. The fastest kid at Merchant Creek. What can I do you for, son?" Joe greeted him, a hint of a grin beneath his thick glasses. Charlie wasn't surprised that Joe knew he was fast; the man seemed to know everything about everything in that part of California.

"If I could have a minute, sir? I want to know what people are thinking about the Strub incident."

"You were there, Charles," Joe said, peering over the top of his glasses. "I saw you. You were hightailing it out of there like your caboose was on fire. You must've snuck in the back door and saw as much as I did about what happened. You saw that awful room, those wasted lives snuffed out on the floor. How could you stand it?"

"You're right, Mr. Medico." Charlie looked at the floor. "But please don't tell Chief Borgman or the sheriff. I could get into a lot of trouble."

"Hey, your secret's safe with me. I never reveal my sources. Plus, I think I'm the only one who saw you." Mr. Medico looked directly at Charlie. "But tell me, what do *you* think happened out there, son?"

"Well, it's possible Mr. Strub went crazy. He shot his entire family, laid them out in a row, and then turned the gun on himself with his German Luger. I've thought a lot about it, and that seems like the most obvious answer." Charlie looked as if he had more to say.

"That's exactly what I'm writing for the Wednesday edition, Charles. Sheriff Blickenstaff let me into that awful room," Joe paused, taking a deep breath. "I have never seen such a tragic sight. It's a terrible waste. You knew that family, didn't you?"

"I've spent many days over there. Mrs. Strub always gave me fruit from their trees, and I loved listening to little Alice tell her stories. She and I were close friends. I miss her already."

"I bet you do." Joe leaned back in his swivel chair, the leather creaking. "But you don't really think that's what happened, do you, Charles?"

Charlie hesitated. "I don't know. Maybe not. I spent a lot of time with Mr. Strub. He was always kind to me. He talked about his war experiences. That must be where the German Luger came from. But I just can't believe he would do such a thing. I never saw him raise his voice at his kids. He never hit them. He was always there for them." Charlie paused, his brow furrowing as he thought. "I guess you never really know a person... Could be, when the dust settles, you'll find they were all killed by someone else."

"You're crazy, you know that?" Joe was smiling now. "You better not tell that story to anyone. They'll come after you with a butterfly net."

"They'll have to catch me first." Charlie laughed, the sound echoing softly. It was the first time he'd laughed since entering that room in the Strub house.

"Did you know he had a Luger?" Joe asked, his tone suddenly more serious.

"Yeah. He showed it to me once. Said he got it off a dead Nazi. But it didn't have any bullets in it. I checked. I don't think he even had any that would fit. I figured he kept it just as a souvenir of the war. Did you bring back any souvenirs from the war, Mr. Medico?"

"A few. But mostly, they're in my mind. I don't really like to talk about it. War is the worst thing humans have ever invented. I know. I worked for *Stars and Stripes*, the Army newspaper. I saw a lot of what happened. I talked to a lot of guys. I could write a book, but I won't. I just don't like thinking about it."

Charlie nodded, sensing the heaviness in Joe's voice. "Do you think you could find out anything about what happened to Mr. Strub in the war? Maybe that might help us understand why he did it. I'd be happy to help you."

"That's a good idea, Charles." Joe's eyes narrowed in thought. "I know some guys who are still with *Stars and Stripes*. Let me make a few calls. If I find out anything, I'll give you a bang on the pipes. Why don't you get in touch with that base commander over at Beale and see what he can dig up? I'm pretty bogged down here and could use a little help."

"I can do that, but Mom won't let me use the phone for anything but local calls."

"Here, you can use mine." Joe pushed the phone toward Charlie. "But Charlie, I have to warn you. If, as you suspect, that family was murdered, then there's a very dangerous killer out there. And if you start poking around, you might end up in serious trouble. You hear me? You could be putting yourself in great danger. Now, let me finish this story."

Charlie La Rue Holmes then made perhaps the most fateful phone call of his young life.

Three

JUST AFTER THEIR EIGHTH-GRADE GRADUATION, five of Charlie's best friends agreed to meet up at Foothill Ditch to say their goodbyes for the summer. Charlie would be leaving for a summer camp in Vermont the following weekend.

They all knew Charlie's Sunday routine—his mother, Winifred, insisted he attend church every Sunday morning, believing it was an important part of his education. Though neither she nor La Rue went to church, she made sure Charlie and his sister, Carolyn, went to the old wooden Presbyterian Church in Tremonton when they were young. Little Johnny, the youngest, always stayed home with the sitter.

From the start, Charlie enjoyed Sunday School. In the basement of the church, there was a large wooden box filled with sand and tiny biblical characters made from clay. The kids would stand around it, arranging the figures into stories taught by Mrs. Cosart, the Sunday School teacher. Charlie knew that if he placed the tiny sheep, donkey, and camel in front of the manger, with the Christ Child nestled inside, and positioned the two shepherds beside Mary and Joseph while the three wise men knelt alongside, he would earn a gold star by his name on the bulletin board. He was proud of his long line of stars.

As Charlie grew older, he was allowed to attend the regular 11:00 a.m. service in the main sanctuary. He admired the gleaming golden objects adorning the church—the tall candlesticks, the magnificent cross, and the various ritualistic items around the altar. But what he loved most was singing in the choir. Mrs. Stillins, the choir director, didn't mind that Charlie missed the twice-weekly rehearsals. She quickly realized that the new kid had near-perfect pitch, could read music, and could keep up with the others.

It was almost three that Sunday afternoon, and Charlie, fresh from church, was pedaling his bike as fast as he could. He didn't want to be the last one to reach the meeting spot at the base of the hill. The Merchant Creek Highway, the main route into the high Sierras east of Stockton, cut through the foothills where it crossed a river gorge between two hills. To the right of the creek lay the Foothill Ditch, bordering the meeting place. On the left side of the highway, Merchant Creek flowed. Just beyond the gorge, a county road branched off from the north, crossing the creek via an old wooden bridge. Beneath this bridge lay a popular swimming spot known as the Green Hole, where kids from Tremonton and nearby areas would leap off the bridge into the cool, shaded waters below.

Between the highway and the Foothill Ditch stood an old, rusty barbed wire fence. Charlie skidded to a stop, tossed his bike over, and carefully threaded his way between the strands. He wheeled his bike behind a stand of willows that had sprouted along the bank of the irrigation canal.

Don Don, a wiry redhead and one of Charlie's best friends, was already there. Within five minutes, all five eighth-grade friends had arrived, stashing their bicycles behind the willows.

"GUYS, WE'RE GOING TO HAVE TO HURRY," Charlie said. "I've got a lot to tell you, so let's get up to the hideout." They all waded through the Foothill Ditch to reach the base of the hill.

"I want to go swimming," Geneva Derrick complained. "It's damn so hot." Geneva, tall and striking at nearly five foot ten, met Charlie's eyes. God, he thought, she looked beautiful with her long blonde hair and smooth, creamy skin.

"I want to swim, too," Diane Fleming added. She was shorter, only five-three, but athletic and strong. With her nearly black hair, she took after her Portuguese father, who managed a dairy north of Tremonton. Hiking up her skirt, she stepped into the canal's muddy water, which they all knew would be waist-high for her.

"Guys, we have to get up the hill," Charlie urged, feeling like he was losing control of the group.

Then Louise Jackson wadded up her skirt, exposing a touch of white underwear, and waded into the water. A dishwater blonde, Louise was about five-six and easily the smartest of the group, thanks in part to her mother being their teacher. Mrs. Alice Jackson commuted every day from Tremonton, often with Louise in tow. Sometimes Louise rode with her mother, but most days she pedaled her bike to school to blend in with her classmates. Being the teacher's daughter was hard, but by eighth grade, she had become one of them. Her strength was undeniable—Louise was built for speed. She was a natural athlete, Charlie could see it in her superbly muscled legs, especially in their running game, "Fresher." Charlie couldn't help but be impressed by her toned, powerful build.

Louise crossed the ditch and scrambled up the other bank. Geneva followed. The two boys waded in, not worrying about wetting their jeans. They were all finally across except for Diane, who made a point of being last so everyone would watch her as she lifted her skirt well above her panties, exposing a taught, thin waist. Charlie stood in awe. What a moment for a leg man!

On the other side, they took off running through the tall grass to the base of the hill. The spring grass had matured, now brown and crisp, not yet grazed by cattle. The day was close to a hundred degrees, and they ran to dry off, their wet clothes clinging to them. They felt alive, the air filled with laughter and the squeals of friends reveling in the thrill of the day.

They continued their dash, dodging rocks that had tumbled down from the hillside, until the hill's incline forced them to slow. Five abreast, they walked through the treeless, crackling grass, laughing and chatting. Geneva still held her skirt high, letting the sun and breeze dry her off. The moment felt perfect—sun-drenched and full of the joy of being young and free.

They reached the Indian rock—a flat, bare granite table where ancient indigenous women had ground deep, bowl-like impressions while mashing acorns to pulp. The group flopped down, still laughing, catching their breath as they panted like a basketball team after a game.

"What made these holes?" Diane asked, gasping for air. "How many are there?"

"There are seven," Charlie replied, the knowledge instinctive. He had discovered this rock years ago, clearing out the dirt and grass that had filled the impressions. He had swept the granite clean, often wondering about the people who once lived by the creek and came here to prepare their meals. "Indians made these holes. This hill must have been covered with oaks back then."

"He's right," said Louise. "My mom knows about the history of the Indians who lived around here. She's even met some of their descendants. In the winter, they lived down along Merchant Creek, gathering acorns and grinding enough to last through summer. When it got hot, they moved up into the mountains where it was cooler. The women, children, and elders did the gathering while the younger men hunted and performed rituals. There was so much food to gather that these California Indians didn't need to farm like other tribes."

"Jesus, Louise," Don Don said, shaking his head. "Your mom sure knows a lot about California history. I think that's why we moved out here from town." The Deveraux family had relocated from Tremonton to their walnut grove so Don Don could attend the two-room school for his eighth-grade year. His parents had spoken with Charlie's folks and learned about the excellent education and the great teaching of Mrs. Jackson. They'd decided it was better than what he and his sister, Mary, were getting at Lincoln School in town. Don Don had quickly become a part of their group, just like any new kid who joined—no matter their grade.

With only about thirty students, anyone new was welcomed like a long-lost relative. But for some reason, these five had formed a special bond. It was a close-knit friendship that felt like it would last forever—at least until the fall, when they'd move on to Tremonton High School. There, they'd likely meet new people and make new friends. But right now, they basked in the moment, savoring the closeness they shared.

"I think we need to get up to the hideout, I've got something to tell you guys." Charlie was anxious to share the weight of his recent discovery.

"I vote we stay right here," Geneva said.

"Oh, let's," Diane agreed.

"I don't think your hideout is even there anymore," Don Don said. "Have you been up there in the last year? The big earthquake in the Bay Area probably tumbled your rocks."

Charlie realized he hadn't been there in over a year, not since shortly after their run-in with those soldiers.

"Okay. Let's just stay here. I want to talk about the Strub family."

Geneva quickly sat up, holding her knees. "Oh my gosh, I was going to ask you guys if you heard about this. I used to babysit for them. I loved little Alice and Hank. I just can't believe Mr. Strub would do something like that. I saw him give Mrs. Strub hugs and kisses all the time." Tears welled up in her eyes. Charlie could feel the depth of her sorrow, and the group's mood turned somber.

"So, you don't think he did it?" Diane asked.

"Not in a million years," Geneva pressed. Silence settled over the rock, and Charlie listened to the gentle breeze whispering through the bushes along the cliff. He felt as if the wind was trying to tell him something.

"He must have done it," Don Don said. "Who else would? They found his gun right there."

"All I know is I wouldn't go near that place," Diane said. "Too many ghosts. And if someone else killed them, like you said, what's stopping him from coming back for the Heichos, don't they live right there?"

"I heard they had all the bodies lined up in a row," Louise added. "How creepy is that?"

"They did," Charlie confirmed.

"Chuckles, *you were there?*" Don Don asked incredulously. "That's why you called this meeting, isn't it?"

"Well, yeah, I guess."

"Unbelievable. Of course you were there. You always just kind of stumble into this stuff." Geneva was shaking her head.

"So...what did you see?" Diane winced as she asked.

"I snuck in while the police were out on the front porch. You're right, Louise—they were all lined up, except Mr. Strub, who was collapsed off to the side. I couldn't believe it. I'm pretty sure it was staged to make it look like he killed his family and then himself."

"Well, didn't he?" Diane pressed. "The cops and the papers can't all be wrong."

"I think they're wrong, dead wrong," Charlie insisted. "I think Geneva's right. Mr. Strub would never have done that. There's another explanation."

"Okay, smarty pants. What's your theory?" Diane's voice echoed off the cliff, carrying up the hillside.

"I think a guy named Jackson Overstreet did it," Charlie said. "And I'll tell you why."

Four

CHARLIE HAD USED JOE MEDICO'S PHONE to call Beale Air Force Base. They connected him to Major General Gerald Boccioni, the base commander.

Charlie stated his name and asked, "Do you remember me, sir?"

"I sure do, son. What was it, maybe one, two years ago? If I recall, you killed one of my soldiers."

"Yes, but—"

"I know, son, you had to, and you found our stolen payroll. Did I ever thank you for that?"

"You did, sir."

"Well, not enough. What can I do for you?" You could hear the grateful tone of Boccioni's voice.

"Did you read about the killings over here near Tremonton, sir?" Charlie asked.

"Yes, I did. It was in the *San Francisco Chronicle*. What a tragedy."

"Well, the father was Heinrick Strub. He was a soldier in the war. I think he was in Germany. Could you check the records and tell me anything about him?"

"I don't need to check the records. I know all about him," the general said.

"Can you tell me?"

"Of course. It's not classified—at least, I don't think so."

MAJOR GENERAL GERALD BOCCIONI told Charlie that he had been Strub's commanding officer after the war. They were stationed outside Berchtesgaden, Germany, near Hitler's residence, the Berghof. Their mission was similar to other detachments across Germany: to locate and monitor returning Nazi soldiers, especially SS members, and catalog their whereabouts. They were also tasked with collecting and destroying war materials—guns, tanks, ammunition, and the like.

Boccioni commanded about fifty men, mostly noncommissioned officers and soldiers. They set up in barracks that once housed Hitler's elite guards at the Wolf's Lair. The soldiers patrolled in groups of three, combing the area. Boccioni remembered Strub well because he spoke fluent German, allowing him to question villagers about SS members and hidden weapon caches.

The general mentioned that Strub had received a medal for his work around Berchtesgaden. "He was an incredible soldier, son. But that's about all I know about that poor man."

"THAT'S NOT MUCH INFORMATION for a soldier in the General's unit," Louise said. "If Strub got a medal, you'd think he'd remember more."

"I know," said Charlie. "I told Joe Medico about that, and he said the same thing. But there's more."

"Get on with it, Bucko," Don Don urged. "It's getting close to dinner time."

"Shut up," Diane snapped. "I want to hear the rest, and we've got plenty of time."

"Okay," Charlie said. "It was almost dinner that Monday night when Joe called me back. My sister Carolyn answered. She thinks the phone is her personal possession. She spends an hour on it every evening. Mom is always fit to be tied, and Dad just throws up his hands, saying, 'What do those kids have to say to each other that they didn't say in eight hours at school?' Carolyn handed me the phone and gave me a dirty look. 'Don't talk too long,' she said. 'Greg is going to call.'"

"Is that Greg Hampton?" Geneva asked. "Doesn't your mom hate him?"

"She sure does. She hates how he speaks, and I think he's got my sister smoking in secret. I stay out of it. I kind of like the guy."

"My mom says the same thing as your dad when I'm on the phone," Diane added. "It drives me crazy."

"Jesus, guys," Don Don groaned. "Can we get back to the story? What did Joe say?"

"Joe said he made a long-distance call to Maryland to his old buddy who works for *Stars and Stripes*."

"What's *Stars and Stripes*?" Geneva interrupted.

"It's the army newspaper, dummy," Don Don said.

"Oh," Geneva replied.

"Joe said Corporal Strub and privates Jackson Overstreet and Wilson Carter all got Unit Citations. That's a medal when a group does something good. His friend read Joe the article from *Stars and Stripes*. It said the three of them discovered a secret tunnel near a town called Mindenhoff, where they found about ten million dollars in hidden Nazi gold bars. It was gold taken from Jews in concentration camps—melted down from eyeglasses, watches, rings, jewelry, *even gold teeth*."

"God damn those Nazi bastards," Louise whispered, her voice tight with anger.

"Wow, our Heinrick Strub was kind of famous," Geneva said, sounding a bit in awe.

"Will y'all shut up?" Don Don snapped.

"Now, here's the kicker," Charlie continued. "Joe said the name Wilson Carter rang a bell. Then he remembered something he read in the paper—Wilson Carter used to live over by Orosi, just south of Sacramento." Charlie paused for effect. "He killed his wife and young daughter and then himself, just like Heinrick Strub did."

SILENCE FELL OVER THE ROCK as everyone processed what Charlie had just said. They each seemed to be putting the pieces together in their minds. Charlie had already done the math. Finally, Geneva spoke up.

"Did Mr. Medico know all this before he wrote his piece for Wednesday's paper?"

"There's more. I found out something that might blow the lid off these killings. Joe said he added it to his article at the last minute, just before it went to press."

"Come on, kiddo," Diane urged. "Give us the straight scoop."

"Yeah," Don Don added. "Quit dragging it out like some big drama."

"If you guys would quit interrupting, maybe he'd tell us everything," Geneva shot back.

"That's okay, guys," Charlie said with a grin. "This is front-page news, and I want to make the most of it. Here goes. Tuesday morning, I pedaled back out to the Strub place. It was deserted—no cops. I heard David Heicho was taking care of the place so I expected to find him. The back door was still open, so I called out for David, but no one answered. I took my chance and went in. I went through the whole house. I looked everywhere—even tried lifting floorboards."

"What the hell were you looking for?" Don Don asked, eyebrows raised.

"Gold."

"Gold?" Geneva repeated, eyes widening.

"Yep. Gold. I figured there had to be a reason for killing those two families. Those three soldiers found Nazi gold. *What if they stole some of it?* How about that, sports fans?"

"What's going through your wild little mind?" Don Don said. "You're crazier than a shithouse rat. You know that?"

"You're going to eat those words," Geneva countered. "When Charlie figures something out, he usually knows what he's talking about."

"Thanks, Geneva. And as for you, Don Don, you ding-a-ling— take a look at this."

With a triumphant grin, Charlie pulled out a twenty-dollar gold piece and tossed it down on the rock.

Five

THE GOLD COIN BOUNCED off the granite rock and rolled right between Diane's bare legs.

"I'll get it," Don Don said, reaching out to grab it.

"Get your cooties away from me!" Diane roared, swatting his hand away.

"I've never seen such a big gold coin," Geneva said. "Can I hold it?" Diane reached down, plucked the coin from between her thighs, and handed it to Geneva. She held it up, turning it in the sunlight. It gleamed as only gold could—brilliant and beautiful.

"Okay, Chuckles, what's the story?" Don Don asked.

"When I was in the Strub stable last Sunday, I noticed the dirt floor looked like it had been dug up and smoothed over. I found an old shovel and decided to dig around. That's when I found this coin buried about five inches down."

"What does that mean?" Louise asked. "That coin could have been buried there fifty years ago."

Charlie smirked and tossed down three more coins. They bounced and rolled across the rock.

"One for each of you. Yes, you guessed it—I found a bunch."

"One for me?" Diane said, delighted. "Thank you, thank you!"

"How many?" Louise asked, curiosity lighting up her eyes.

"I saw a small, broken wooden box—like an old cigar box—tossed into one of the horse stalls. When I dug down, I hit something solid. It was another box, the same kind, and it was full of these gold coins. I won't tell you how many, and you have to swear not to tell a soul."

"But—" Don Don started.

"No buts. Remember, seven people have already been killed over these coins. Jackson Overstreet, the third guy who found the gold, is still out there. If you talk, he might come after me—or even you. So, mum's the word. I want you all to raise your right hands and swear. This has to be our secret."

One by one, they all gave their word.

Yet, for some, the temptation to flash the bright yellow Golden Eagle proved irresistible.

Six

"HOW ABOUT A KISS?" said Geneva. At least five different times that spring, the friends had met after school over at Diane Fleming's house when her parents were away at work. They had lain on the grass lawn and had kissed. Don Don had kissed Diane, and Charlie had kissed Geneva. Louise merely sat and watched. The session lasted maybe fifteen minutes.

High up on the hillside, Charlie, who had yet to go through puberty, was still aroused by this activity. Now, he found his body was pressed along the length of Geneva, feeling her perfect leg rubbing against his, their lips wet and warm, their tongues tenderly exploring, not coming up for air the entire expected fifteen minutes.

It was joyous and exhilarating and experimental and innocent, and for those minutes each couple was eternally in love. For a while, they were more than just best friends; they were as one, with one thought and one emotion.

Louise looked on as usual. None of the boys would consider kissing the daughter of their teacher for the last four years. She didn't expect it, but each suspected she longed to do it. Someday, she knew she would be kissed. But for now, she just waited and watched.

Suddenly, Geneva pulled Charlie over on the rock so that he lay against her side. She took his hand and placed it under her skirt so he was holding the top of her thigh.

He didn't dare move his hand up or even away. All he did during those fifteen minutes was feel the smoothness and when he gently squeezed, the erotic resistance of her warm flesh and muscle made him feel a flush of excitement. For the rest of his life, that moment would live to be remembered with regret. Why didn't he do what he knew the most beautiful Geneva wanted him to do? He would rationalize that if he had, he would have ruined that perfect moment, that lovely innocent happening. But later, when he did experience puberty, his thoughts were of that time there on the Indian rock.

"OK, BREAK IT UP," said Charlie. "If I'm late for dinner, my mom will kill me." They came up for air, rolled over, and got up.

"Did I tell you all?" asked Charlie. "I leave early tomorrow for summer camp in Vermont. This is goodbye for the summer." They knew he always went to camp. But each felt his going more this time because of the pending events.

"What do you think we ought to do about this gold thing and the murders?" asked Diane.

"I've spent all week thinking about it all," said Charlie. They started walking off the rock and heading down the hill through the high grass. "The danger has to come from that guy Jackson Overstreet. He's the third one in the group who found the gold. Maybe someone should go out to his place and try to see what he looks like so you can be on the lookout."

"I can do that," said Louise. "I have to ride everywhere I go anyway. Mom is just too busy to take me anywhere."

"Okay, but be sneaky, kiddo," said Charlie. "We are playing with fire here."

"Got ya!" she said. "Last one to the ditch is a brass baboon."

They ran then, yelling and screaming and laughing. Louise was first as expected, but Geneva was right behind, and she didn't stop when she came to the edge of the ditch. She actually made a shallow dive into the water, clothes and all. What guts, thought Charlie. He took off his shoes and pants and shirt and dove in after Geneva, grabbing her and ducking her under water. She came up sputtering, hair dripping down, and eyes full of ditch water, but laughing and fighting back.

Diane slid to a stop at the edge. Then shucking her dress and her bra and panties, and saying something about having dried off her undies already, why get them wet again, jumped in. Her well-developed breasts bobbed as her feet slammed into the muddy bottom. Charlie had glimpsed her nakedness and was astounded at how much hair she had between her legs. He had almost none. He thought it was beautiful.

Then a real fight started. Everyone was in the water in various stages of undress. Even Louise had shucked all her clothes and had joined in. They were ducking each other and splashing and pushing and shoving and it all was great fun and Charlie, for one, was having the time of his life.

"Hey Don, old buddy, stand on me, I want to practice holding my breath." Everyone knew Charlie had this idea that he could set a record for holding his breath underwater and he practiced every time he went swimming. Don Don waded over. Charlie had learned he could hold his breath longer if he didn't exert himself in any way. In the Holmes pool or in the Deveraux pool he would have Don Don put a foot on top of him as he lay on the bottom. He could then freeze, not using any muscle to keep himself down.

Now he lay squished into the muddy bottom of the ditch. Don Don stood on him and counted off the minutes and seconds using his waterproof watch. At two minutes and twenty-five seconds Charlie wriggled and Don Don moved his foot. Up came Charlie gasping and blowing.

"You son of a gun, Charlie," said Diane. "I thought Deveraux here was drowning you. It seemed like you were down there forever. You scared the dickens out of me."

"It's jake," said Charlie, "Don't worry about it. If I hadn't just run down the hill I could have made it another fifteen seconds. One of these days I am going to get to three minutes. Hide and watch."

"I'm not hiding and waiting for you, you piece of mud," said Geneva laughing. "Look at you. You've got hair full of ditch muck. What a mess you are Charlie Holmes." He ducked under water and swirled his hands through his hair to get most of the mud out.

Then he waded over and retrieved his clothes and waded across and climbed out to put them on. He had to get home. But not before he saw a completely naked Geneva coming across carrying her dress and her things and looking like a Greek goddess. He truly marveled at how beautiful she was. He fell in love all over again.

They said their goodbyes and mounted their bikes. It would be the last time they were all together. Or even *all alive.*

Part II

THE GAMBLER ON THE TRAIN

Seven

IT TOOK SIX DAYS AND NIGHTS by train for Charlie and his little brother, Johnny, to reach the camp on Lake Dunmore near Middlebury, Vermont. Their trunks had been shipped a week ahead, so both boys traveled with small suitcases lovingly packed by their mother, Winifred. Inside were six polo shirts, pants, socks, underwear, and their toilet kits. For Charlie, she included a selection of his favorite *Walt Disney Comics and Stories* along with *A Tale of Two Cities*. As she suspected, he never opened the book.

The view from their Pullman car window was far too captivating for reading. Charlie and Johnny loved watching the passing scenery, and they adored the Pullman porters and dining car waiters.

Every night, while the boys dined in the dining car, their porter transformed their seating area into an upper and lower bunk. Charlie always took the upper bunk, enjoying the small reading light that shone over his shoulder. It was his favorite time—lying there, listening to the rhythmic click-clack of the train wheels while reading his comics over and over.

Back in 1947, the boys had been driven by their parents, La Rue and Winifred, in the family's Lincoln Continental to Sacramento, where they boarded the Southern Pacific train. After an emotional farewell, they settled in just in time for their first meal in the dining car. To reach it, they walked through four sleeping cars, quickly learning to enjoy the swaying walk and the heavy doors between each car. During the six-day journey, they would explore the train many times, taking in every detail.

Their first lunch was an eye-opener. When they arrived in the dining car, they were seated with another couple already at the table. The couple kindly showed them how to read the menu and fill out their selection card. After lunch, they were presented with the bill. Charlie was surprised at how expensive things were, but La Rue had given him a generous amount of money to cover their meals. That first lunch totaled two dollars and eighty-five cents. Charlie put a five-dollar bill with the tab, and the waiter picked it up.

Then they waited. And waited. The couple left, and the dining car slowly emptied. Finally, the waiter passed by on his way to the kitchen.

"Excuse me, sir," Charlie said. "Can we have our change?"

The waiter's face broke into a wide grin. "Oh, I thought you boys wanted me to keep it for a tip."

"Oh," Charlie replied, embarrassed.

With their two-fifteen in change lying on the table, the boys debated how much to tip. On one hand, the waiter had been attentive and friendly, always refilling their water glasses. On the other hand, he had tried to take advantage of them, assuming they were too young to know better.

They finally decided to leave him a penny. They placed it on the table, got up, and returned to their car.

As luck would have it, they got the same man as their waiter for dinner. When he saw them, he broke into a wide grin, almost laughing. Seated near the door to the tiny kitchen, Charlie and Johnny could hear their waiter telling everyone inside about how the two boys had tipped him a penny. The laughter from the kitchen was loud and infectious. Somehow, Charlie sensed there was no animosity in their laughter, and he and Johnny couldn't help but join in. Needless to say, they tipped generously for the rest of the trip.

AFTER FIVE DAYS, THEIR PULLMAN CAR pulled into Grand Central Station. That summer of 1950, the boys were met by Jackie Haas, a counselor and chaperone, who escorted them to the northbound Rutland Railroad train. The train was packed with about fifty boys, mostly from the East—New York, Philadelphia, and Washington, along with a few from Chicago, St. Louis, and Kansas City. Charlie and Johnny were the only ones from California. They had two Pullman cars filled with boys, many of whom Charlie and Johnny already knew.

No one really slept that night on the run up to Vermont. There was endless chatter, pranks, and comic book exchanges. By midnight, most of the older boys were telling dirty jokes, while the younger ones listened in awe. Hans Houser, an old German counselor, and Jackie Haas were in charge. They wisely let the boys be boys, only ensuring no one got off the train at its many stops.

By mid-morning on the sixth day, Saturday, the train pulled into Brandon, Vermont. The boys piled off and climbed onto the Dodge flatbed truck with wooden slat sides, the main transport for Camp Keewaydin. The rest loaded into cars, creating a honking parade as they made their way into the campgrounds at the north end of Lake Dunmore.

Charlie found a bunk in one of the three cabins up the side of Mount Moosalamoo, the area designated for the older boys. Johnny was down below by the lake, in a tent with the younger kids. All 150 boys gathered in the dining hall for their first lunch, and during the rest hour that followed, Charlie found a letter from his mom waiting for him.

He recognized the familiar "Dear Son" at the top of the letter. His mom began her note just as she had the past three summers, telling him how sad she felt seeing him off at the train, but how happy she was that he and Johnny would have a great summer. She mentioned that his friend Weezie, as his parents called Louise Jackson, had stopped by on her bike. Weezie had said she was going to do what Charlie had suggested when they were up on the hill. His mom admitted she had no clue what that meant, but lightly admonished him for getting Weezie into possible trouble. Charlie chuckled; he did have a habit of getting his friends into mischief, often being the one with new ideas and plans.

Charlie noticed that tucked into the envelope was a newspaper clipping. It was the article Joe Medico had written about the Strub killings. The piece detailed everything the police had permitted him to share—the approximate time of the crime, the caliber of the pistol, the positioning of the bodies, and the official conclusion that it was a murder-suicide. However, Joe had also mentioned that an unnamed source questioned the evidence, suggesting that someone from outside the family might have committed the crime. The source believed the motive could have been to steal some gold coins owned by Strub.

At the bottom of the article, his mother had scribbled a note in pencil. She asked if perhaps he was the unnamed source.

Charlie felt a jolt of alarm. Why did Joe add that last line about speculation? If his mother could connect the dots and suspect that he had spoken to the *Tremonton Sun*, then maybe the killer could, too.

The thought made his stomach tighten. What if the murderer figured it out and went after him—or, worse, Louise, who was out on her bike, scouting the Overstreet farm? She could be in real danger.

That evening, Charlie couldn't sleep. Nor the next night. He worried about it for weeks, the thought gnawing at him. Even when he was practicing holding his breath underwater in the lake—his favorite escape—he couldn't shake the fear that his friend might be in serious trouble.

IT WAS AT THE BEGINNING OF THE SECOND MONTH of
camp that Winifred sent Charlie another, deeply disturbing letter.
Charlie opened it at rest hour.

Dear Charles,

*I have terrible news... Your dear friend, Weezie
Jackson, is dead. I'm so, so sorry, Charles.*

*Last Saturday, Alice said Weezie didn't come home
for dinner, and she never returned. Her father went out
searching for her, and Alice asked all her friends if they
knew anything. She spoke with Geneva Derrick, Diane
Fleming, and Donald Deveraux, but they knew nothing,
except that Louise had been interested in the Strub case.*

*Late Tuesday afternoon, a trout fisherman found her
body in Merchant Creek, just below the little bridge near
the Green Hole where you kids swim. He went to town
and alerted the Sheriff, and they brought her to
Waterman's Mortuary.*

*The Sheriff believes she somehow ran her bike off the
bridge and crashed onto the rocks below. They found her
bike upstream. He said if she'd fallen off the downstream
side, she would have landed in Green Hole and likely
been alright...This is just devastating. I'm so sorry,
Charlie.*

*The whole town is in mourning. The funeral will be
this Saturday. Members of our card club will serve as
pallbearers—your father, Mr. Wheeler, Mr. Bill Cosart,
Dr. Wallace, Mr. Redford, and Jim Pogue will all attend.*

*LaRue suspects that Louise's death might have been
more than just an accident, especially since your friends
mentioned she was poking around the Strub story. He
went to the County Sheriff and asked for an autopsy,*

suspecting that she might have been dead before hitting the water and rocks. The Sheriff, however, refused to overrule his detectives, who are convinced it was an accident. Your father also spoke with Joe Borgman, our police chief, but he said it was beyond his jurisdiction.

Your teacher Alice and her family are beyond words. Weezie was such a wonderful girl. I'm sure you'll miss her terribly. We all will. Sending you a hug, Charlie. We will make sure to honor Louise properly when you return.

Love,
Winifred

Charlie read the letter during rest hour, and he buried his face in his pillow, crying quietly. He didn't want his fellow campers to see him like that. He had truly loved Louise; he'd known her all his life. He remembered spending a summer with the Jacksons at their cabin in the Sierras back in 1944. Weezie and her sisters had staged a play they'd written, and he and Johnny had been given parts. Her mother had brought Louise with her to Merchant Creek School all eight years, and they often sat at desks next to each other.

By the end of rest hour, he had written a letter back to his mother. In it, he expressed his sorrow over the heartbreaking news, but his words also carried a sense of urgency. Something about Louise's death didn't sit right with him, and as he wrote, a growing sense of alarm took hold.

I know that bridge, he wrote. *There's a low railing on each side, but it's too high for a bike to launch over and end up in the river. Someone must have taken Louise there and thrown her and her bike into the water. Dad is right about this. Besides, she would never ride up into those hills alone. We were just there on my favorite hill, and she told me she'd never been there before. That bridge is close to where we parked our bikes.*

You have to warn Dad that because he went to the Sheriff, he might have drawn attention to himself. Whoever killed Louise, the Strub family, and the Wilson Carter family might be aware of him now. Louise planned to investigate Mr. Jackson Overstreet's place to see what she could find. I think he's the killer. Please tell Father to be very careful. Give my love to my teacher and hug my eighth-grade friends for me.

He handed the letter to the secretary in the camp office that afternoon.

THE DAY BEFORE CHARLIE AND JOHNNY were set to take the train home, Charlie received another letter from Winifred. This one was short.

"You were right, Charles," Winifred wrote. "Someone took a shot at your father."

Eight

ALL THE WAY across the United States, Charlie's mind raced. He worried about the news—about someone taking a shot at his father, about the death of his friend Louise, and about the gold coins he had hidden in his possession. Those coins, he realized, were likely the reason behind Louise's death and the danger his father now faced. He desperately wanted to confide in someone, but he kept it all to himself, not wanting to burden Johnny.

That someone appeared in Chicago. An intriguing man boarded the train and took the seat across the aisle from them. He was an older man, likely in his sixties, with white hair, glasses, and a neatly trimmed mustache and goatee. He wore a tweed coat and tie, and his fingers were adorned with rings—four in total, two on each hand. One ring held the largest diamond Charlie had ever seen; another had a green stone, and a third a blue one. The man introduced himself as Gary Jones, though Charlie couldn't help but wonder if that was his real name. Shortly after leaving the Chicago station, Mr. Jones revealed that he was a professional gambler.

He moved over to their seating area and asked the Pullman porter for a table that hooked into a slot below the picture window. For the next four days, the three of them played card games, taking only breaks for meals in the dining car and to sleep.

Mr. Jones taught them Pit, Hearts, Blackjack, and several variations of poker. The boys quickly grew fond of a three-handed game called Casino. Mr. Jones, in turn, complimented them on their card skills, claiming he was lucky to have found such talented young players. Charlie and Johnny had been playing cards since they were old enough to hold and shuffle a deck, so the praise made them beam with pride. Mr. Jones confided that most of his travel companions were older ladies who didn't know much about cards, making the boys' skills a welcome change.

He also shared more about his life, explaining, "I don't own anything. I don't want the government or the IRS to know I even exist. I rent my car and my house, and I pay cash for everything—no paper trail. I even have a post office box under a fictitious name. I don't pay taxes on my winnings, and I must say, I've won quite a bit in my lifetime. Mostly, I play the ponies. Have you boys ever been to the races?"

Both boys shook their heads.

"I didn't think so," Mr. Jones said. "Someday you will, and once you go, you'll want to go again and again. And knowing you two, I'd wager that you'll learn how to dope races and end up winners." He laughed heartily at his observation.

"Why do you wear those rings, Mr. Jones?" Johnny asked. Charlie had been curious too but felt too shy to ask.

Mr. Jones smiled. "Ah, you noticed. Gamblers like wearing flashy rings. They want people to see them as successful, signaling that they're good at what they do. They also use the rings to distract the amateurs—the rubes and pigeons—they play against. If your opponent is distracted, they often make mistakes. Plus, I just like wearing them. See this green one?"

He slipped off the ring and handed it to Johnny.

"Look closely. See the lines inside the green stone? That's a high-quality emerald. I won it from a man from Colombia years ago in a poker game in Kansas City. I'd taken all his money, and all he had left was this stone. He had a straight, and I had a flush. He bet the stone, and I called. It was the luckiest moment of my life—at that time. That was the winter of 1932."

"What about your diamond?" Johnny asked as they paused after a long game of Casino. Charlie, glancing out the window, saw the snow-capped mountains rising to the north of the tracks. They were approaching Salt Lake City, Utah.

"This diamond?" Mr. Jones held up his hand. "I acquired it in Reno, Nevada. It was during the war. I got into a high-stakes blackjack game at Harold's Club. The place was packed with flyboys from Stead Air Base, playing cards and pulling the slot machines."

He leaned in, his voice dropping slightly. "I bought in for a hundred bucks and had the most amazing streak of luck. Soon, I had a thousand dollars, then ten thousand. People crowded around my table, watching me play. By the time I had fifty thousand in silver dollars, Pappy Smith—the owner—came over. Pappy was a tall, lean man, dressed in authentic Western clothes. His casino was like a museum, filled with guns, paintings, and other artifacts."

Mr. Jones paused, smiling at the memory. "'Sir,' Pappy said, 'you've broken our bank. I have to ask you to leave.' I'd always dreamed of breaking a bank—like the stories you hear about Monte Carlo. Pappy pushed my chips over to the dealer, who collected everything into a canvas bag and disappeared with it."

"It was a grand moment. Everyone around us clapped and cheered. Pappy invited me into his office, where we sat in these old leather couches. He brought out this diamond. I'd never seen one so large, with such fine color and clarity. He offered it to me in exchange for all my chips. I knew enough about diamonds to realize this one was worth much more than the fifty thousand in chips the dealer took away."

"What did you do?" Johnny asked, his eyes wide with fascination.

"I walked away with this diamond and never looked back," Mr. Jones said with a grin. "As I was heading out the door, Pappy Smith told me I wouldn't be welcome at Harold's Club again. He said I was just too good."

"There has to be a reason you're so good, Mr. Jones," Charlie said, curiosity sparking in his eyes.

"There is," Mr. Jones replied. "I can count cards. In Blackjack, the odds usually favor the house, but there are times when the deck shifts in favor of the player. It all depends on which cards have already been played from a single deck. I'd wait for those favorable moments, then place my biggest bets."

"Why doesn't everyone do that?" Johnny asked.

"They could, but most don't know they can, or don't have the capacity to do it," Mr. Jones explained. "People assume any win is due to luck. One day, someone will write a book revealing the strategy, but I hope it's not for a long time—I plan to make a lot of money until then. In fact, I'm getting off in Reno on this trip."

"Don't you ever lose, Mr. Jones?" Johnny asked.

"Oh sure. There have been plenty of times when I didn't have two nickels to rub together."

"What do you do when that happens?"

"Well," Mr. Jones began, leaning back in his seat, "one night I was riding the New York Central train from New York City to Chicago. There was always a poker game on that train back before the war. I joined in, and those guys cleaned me out—took every cent I had. I got up from the table, feeling pretty low, and walked back to my berth. I didn't even have enough money for the dining car. One of the men from the game followed me. He was from Omaha, Nebraska, and I'd crossed paths with him in a few joints over the years. He staked me ten thousand dollars. The deal was, if I got back into the game and won, I'd give him half of my winnings."

"Did you win?" Charlie asked.

Mr. Jones smiled. "I gave him a thousand dollars plus his stake back."

"Wow," Johnny said, impressed.

"You see, boys, there's a sort of honor among gamblers. They stick together. At least, that's how it was before and during the war. But today, well, I'm not so sure I could count on another gambler to help me out. And I'm not sure I'd be willing to help someone down on their luck either. Times have changed, boys. They always do. You'll learn that as you get older."

LOOKING INTO MR. JONES'S EYES, a deep sense of trust overcame Charlie. Before you could bat a lash, everything that had happened to the Strubs and everything in his mother's letters came pouring out. By the time Charlie finished explaining the entire tale, they were almost to Reno. Both Mr. Jones and Johnny sat in silence, stunned by the story.

"What do you think, Mr. Jones?" Charlie asked.

"Son, you've got a real dilemma on your hands. I think you've figured out there might be a joker in your deck—someone you haven't considered yet, someone deeply involved. Remember, every deck has a joker. All I can tell you is this: follow the money. That's usually the reason behind most actions in this world."

"I had no idea any of this was happening," Johnny said. "Can't you just stay out of it, Charlie? What if the killer comes after you?"

"Listen to your brother," Mr. Jones advised. "In cards, and in life, you have to know when to stay and when to walk away. Sometimes you need to hold 'em, and sometimes you need to fold 'em. I'm not the first person to feel this way."

THE TRAIN BEGAN TO SLOW as they approached Reno. Mr. Jones had his suitcase on the floor beside him.

"I want to tell you boys something before we reach the station. I don't think I've ever met such nice, polite young men. You two made this trip special for me. And, don't let this go to your heads, but you may be the smartest boys I've ever known."

Charlie felt a warmth spread through his chest. He'd always known Johnny was smart, but Charlie's own grades didn't reflect this. Mr. Jones must have seen something in both of them.

Mr. Jones handed Charlie a card and his Parker pen. "Would you write down your address for me? Someday, I might want to tell you what I'm up to." Charlie took the card and scribbled his address on the blank side. Mr. Jones glanced at it, then slid it into his billfold.

"Now, I want to give each of you a present." Mr. Jones removed two rings from his fingers. One was gold with an opaque, bright blue turquoise stone; the other was gold with a smaller, dark blue sapphire. "These might not fit you yet, but I have small fingers, so they just might. Johnny, you take the sapphire. It's rare and worth a lot of money. Someday you may need it, so don't part with it lightly."

"Charlie, this turquoise one is for you. It's not worth much, but it was made by Navajo craftsmen, and I know you have a feeling for Native Americans, just from the way you spoke about the Heicho people near you. Wear it and remember me, boys."

He paused, his voice softening. "You'd be doing me a great favor, just knowing that somewhere, someone is thinking about this old, washed-up gambler."

They hugged on the platform as the train hissed to a stop. Mr. Jones turned, his steps unsteady as if he were still on the swaying train, and walked away without looking back.

THE RIDE HOME WAS just like all the others. There were hugs on the train platform from his mother, Winifred, while his father, La Rue, stood aside. They piled into the Lincoln Continental, with both boys in the back.

"Your trunks arrived yesterday, and I've already washed your clothes," Winifred said, turning in her seat to face the boys. "I had to throw away some of your things. Johnny, didn't you ever wear socks? Most of yours were still balled up."

Johnny didn't respond. He hated wearing socks. So did Charlie, but he would never have dared to admit it to his mom.

"Go ahead, tell him," La Rue said, his tone resigned. Winifred shrugged, as if conceding defeat from a previous argument.

"We have some news for you, Charles," Winifred said. "Because of what happened to your schoolmate Louise Jackson, and since you mentioned in your letters that you thought it might not have been her fault, your father and I have decided to send you to a private school where you'll be safe."

"What?" Charlie exclaimed.

"It's Webb School," La Rue added. "We're driving you there tomorrow."

Nine

CHARLIE LOVED RIDING IN THE LINCOLN CONTINENTAL. He loved the feel and scent of the leather seats, the power of the V-12 engine, and the thrill of using the foot button that changed radio stations. He remembered when La Rue first saw one.

It was back in 1940 when his father took the family to the World's Fair in San Francisco. Little Johnny was only three at the time, so he couldn't go. They drove over in their Lincoln Zephyr sedan. The fair was held on Treasure Island, an artificial piece of land built in the middle of San Francisco Bay near Yerba Buena Island.

The World's Fair had originally started in New York in 1939, but it moved a year later. One of the many themes of the fair was the dirigible, which many believed to be the "airship of the future." Charlie recalled seeing little kids carrying inflatable dirigible balloons on sticks. He also remembered the miniature city exhibit, with tiny cars moving up and down its streets, and an aquatic show where divers descended from the ceiling, plunging gracefully into a pool far below.

One of the exhibition halls featured a demonstration by the Ford Motor Company, showcasing the brand-new Lincoln Continental. La Rue was immediately captivated and placed an order on the spot.

Nearly ten years later, the car was still a marvel. It was a shiny, jet-black, two-door coupe, kept under the porte cochere at the north end of their house. Every day, Winifred would go outside with a soft rag, carefully wiping down the car so that La Rue had a sparkling, pristine vehicle to drive.

They arrived back home around two in the afternoon, and Charlie immediately grabbed his Schwinn bicycle, ready to ride off.

"Where are you going?" his mother called after him. "Remember, we're leaving at four in the morning for your new school."

"I'm going to see Mrs. Jackson," he shouted back. It was four miles to Tremonton, and if he pedaled fast, he could make it in half an hour.

Charlie rode up to the Jacksons' Craftsman-style house, resting his bike on the kickstand before walking up to the front door. He rang the bell, hearing the chimes echo inside.

Debby, the next oldest sister to Louise and a classmate of his sister Carolyn, answered the door.

"Hello, Charles," Debby said flatly.

"Hi, Debby. I'm really sorry about your sister. I was hoping to speak with your mother."

"Sure, come on in." Debby led him into the house. She was a brunette, not quite as tall as Louise had been, and they didn't really look much alike.

"Sit here, and I'll get her." Debby pointed to a chair in the dimly lit living room. Overgrown house plants covered most of the windows, casting shadows across the room. Dark, stained wood accents ran along the walls near the ceiling and around the windows, and a polished wooden beam stretched over the fireplace. The wood had a warm, cozy glow that Charlie found comforting. He loved the Craftsman style.

Mrs. Jackson entered the room, wearing an apron, her face tired, and her shoulders slumped. She had clearly been cooking, but she immediately came over to Charlie and pulled him into a tight embrace. Charlie could feel her body shaking.

"Oh God, Charles. Thank you for coming. Why Weezie? Why my little girl?" She sobbed into his shoulder, and he could feel her tears soaking through his shirt. He awkwardly patted her back. Charlie had always had a somewhat distant relationship with his teacher of four years. Even when he'd spent the entire summer of 1944 at the Jackson cabin in the Sierras, she had remained aloof. This show of emotion took him by surprise, and he felt himself tearing up. He didn't know what to say. He could feel the softness of her chest against him, and for the first time, he realized she wasn't just his teacher—she was a woman and a mother. The revelation struck him deeply; maybe he was growing up after all, to recognize this. As he looked over her shoulder, he noticed black cloths draped over the lamps and the back of the leather couch.

Finally, Mrs. Jackson pulled back and placed her hands on his shoulders, looking him over.

"You must have grown an inch this summer. My, my, Charles, you're growing up."

"I know," he responded, feeling at a loss. What else could he say?

"Please, sit down. Do you have something to tell me?"

"Well," he began, stumbling over his words. "I was just wrecked when I heard about Louise's death... My mom told me in a letter. She was one of my best friends." Charlie took a breath, knowing what he was about to say might come as a shock to Mrs. Jackson. "I'm not sure Louise's death was an accident."

"I know," Mrs. Jackson said softly.

Charlie exhaled.

"I've heard the talk. I think your father asked around, didn't he? But Sheriff Blickenstaff seems so certain, so I trust his judgment." She trailed off. "What do you know, Charlie?"

"I don't know anything for sure, but I wondered if Louise kept a diary. I remember she was always writing in a notebook, and I thought maybe..."

"Yes, she did." Mrs. Jackson stood up. "I haven't had the courage to read it yet. I'm too emotional these days, and I don't think I could hold myself together reading her thoughts. But maybe you could, Charles."

"Did they ever find her binoculars? Mom didn't mention them in her letters."

"I hadn't thought about that," she said, her eyes widening. "Thank you for reminding me, Charles. No, Weezie never went anywhere on her bike without them. I'll be right back."

Charlie stood when she did, but then sat back down as she left the room. The atmosphere felt even heavier than before. He could sense the grief saturating the space, like an oppressive weight. He wondered how he would feel if he lost Carolyn or even little Johnny. He wasn't sure he could talk to anyone or even face them. He marveled at Mrs. Jackson's strength.

He heard her footsteps descending the stairs from the hall. She returned, holding a small book tightly to her chest.

Charlie stood up again as she entered. "Sit, sit," she urged. She reached past him to turn on the floor lamp, casting light over his shoulder. Then, she handed him the little blue book. Charlie saw it had a flap with a small lock, but it was already open.

"Weezie had many of these little books. She wrote constantly. She wanted to be a writer. I once told her she needed to work on dialect—most authors struggle to make their characters' speech sound real. I think she practiced that in her diaries. Oh, I forgot, I have a pot on the stove. Please excuse me for a moment, Charles." With that, she left the room. Debby was nowhere in sight. He was alone. He was grateful she had turned on the lamp, though its light was dimmed by the black cloth draped over the shade.

Charlie opened the diary. He was struck by the precision of Louise's handwriting. He had seen her school papers before, but he thought she only wrote neatly when it was for an assignment. Her penmanship here was remarkably clear and easy to read. He noticed dates at the top of the pages and quickly flipped to the last entries, feeling that reading the earlier ones would be intruding too much into her private life.

Ten

Dear Diary,

I rode my bike to spy on Mr. Overstreet. I'm sure he couldn't see me hidden in the deep shade of the walnut trees next to his farm. I used my binoculars to get a closer look.

He sure is a busy man. He was out there on his tractor, moving dirt around. I'm not sure what he's up to. A couple of times, a woman came out and brought him something to eat or drink, and then he took a break. I decided to ride into Orosi and ask around to see if anyone knew what he was doing.

It was about a mile ride into Orosi, and I eventually found a little café with plenty of cars and pickups parked outside. It's called the Old Home Place Café. I parked my bike and walked up. There were two tables out front, and a redheaded woman was sitting at one, smoking. I asked if she worked there. I'm trying to remember our conversation as best I can—her accent was so distinctive, she must be from a Dust Bowl state.

She said, "I sure do, honey. I'm jus' takin' a smoke break. Gots to have my coffin nails. These things will kill yuh, but what the heck, we all gotta go sometime."

I asked her if she knew Jackson Overstreet.

"Yep. He'd be in here all the time. You wanna see him, you best git chear 'bout six. Them farmers, they show up around six, then by seven they's out tellin' their workers what's what. Then them business guys show up. They gotta have a cup a joe afore they open them stores."

I asked her what Overstreet was doing out there.

"That Jackson boy, he's crazier than a stepped-on snake. He done built a golf course, and now he wants to make it into eighteen holes. He never did no good with just nine. These farmers 'round chear, they don' wanna play golf. They jus wanna go fishing, shoot somethin', or if they git a bit ahead, they take their wives to the city. Nope, that Overstreet man is plum nuts."

I asked her if he ever brought his wife into the café.

"He ain't got no wife, honey. He got a Mexican woman who keeps house for him, but no wife. I don't think they's a woman crazy enough to marry that cracker."

Then she said, "Now I'm gonna git my butt in a sling if I don't git back in there. Ole Sanchez, he don't smoke, and he don't want any of his hep smokin' neither. Come on in, and I'll buy yuh a cup of that black stuff."

I told her I don't drink coffee, but I followed her in anyway and sat at the counter. A big man was sitting next to me, having breakfast.

She bustled around, taking care of the customers, and finally came over, leaning on the counter. I asked her if anyone had ever paid her with a twenty-dollar gold coin.

"You bet'cha, honey. That Overstreet feller did a couple a times."

I took out the coin Charlie gave me and asked her if it looked like the one I had.

"That's it fer sure. I hain't never seen one afore Jackson's. She sure is purty, ain't she?"

Then the big man next to me reached over and picked up the coin. He turned it over in his hand and asked where I got it. I said a friend gave it to me. He asked if I could get more. I said if I had to, I could. He handed it back and kept on eating.

I got up and waved to the redhead. She said, "Name's Velma, honey. Ya come in again, an look me up, you hear?" I told her I would and rode home.

Could Charlie have taken those gold coins from Overstreet and claimed they came from Strub? I need to remember to tell Charlie about the gold coin at the Old Home Place when he gets back from Vermont.

CHARLIE TURNED TO THE LAST ENTRY IN HER DIARY. He sucked in a breath and began reading again.

Saturday July 10th, 1950

Dear Diary,

My mother asked me to do some laundry, so it was around noon by the time I could bike over to the Old

Home Place. The restaurant was packed, and though Velma saw me and smiled, she couldn't come over to where I was sitting for quite a while. There were two other waitresses. The place was so informal that none of them wore uniforms.

When Velma finally reached me, she said, "Glad yuh could make it, girl. Sorry, I'm havin' ta hook it today. What kin I git ya?" I ordered a slice of apple pie. When she brought it, there was a scoop of vanilla ice cream on top, which I hadn't asked for. "Pie's no good 'ere if it don't have no ice cream on it," she said.

I asked again about Mr. Overstreet, if he was around. "No, he hain't, but they's a lady over there yuh might wanna talk to. She and I were talkin' gold coins, and she works at the bank. See, the one with that blue top and them brown oxford shoes? Jus' go on over and introduce yourself. Annabelle is right friendly. I gotta git."

After finishing my pie, I left money on the counter and went over to the woman. She looked about forty and was sitting with another lady. I introduced myself and mentioned gold coins. She agreed to meet me outside after her lunch.

I waited for her for a bit but she eventually came out. We shook hands before she sat down. I showed her my coin and said I was starting a collection. She examined it closely, saying it looked identical to the ones Mr. Overstreet had brought in. She noted mine was new and uncirculated, the same date as his. When I asked how many he had brought in, she said she couldn't tell me— bank security and all—but hinted that it was enough to make a very large down payment on the farm he bought. She mentioned that his coins came in a wooden box she thought might have once held ammunition, based on the labeling, though she couldn't remember the exact type.

When she asked why I was interested, I lied and said I thought mine might be rare. But now I knew it wasn't. She hesitated a little bit then. Like she had more to say but didn't want to go on. I told her it was ok, I wasn't going to say anything to Overstreet or bother him, so she kept going. She mentioned that Mr. Overstreet had brought in another batch earlier this year. He claimed he was going to expand his golf course to eighteen holes, so the bank loaned him more money. She thought, since he had a whole box, that the coins must not be rare at all.

She warned me not to share what she'd told me, that bank information was private. I got the sense that since she knew I was a kid, it was no big deal to talk. I promised I wouldn't say a word to anyone. Besides, I had no one to tell that cared... After that, she walked back toward the bank.

As I was heading over to my bike, Velma came out. "See ya, girl. That Annabelle, she real nice, ain't she? I been thinkin' 'bout you and your interest in that Overstreet feller. I don' like him. He a strange bird. You watch out, girly, yuh hear?"

When Charlie gets back this fall, I must remember to tell him that I know where Mr. Overstreet keeps his gold coins. I watched him climb up on his roof. He takes a ladder from the shed behind his house and walks across the roof to a small cupola. It has a door that looks like a louver. It opens.

CHARLIE CLOSED THE BOOK. He stood and walked to the kitchen, where Mrs. Jackson was tending something on the stove.

"I have to go now, Mrs. Jackson."

"Oh, Charles. Did you read what you needed to? That didn't take long."

"I did, ma'am. Louise wrote very clearly. I think she would have been a great author."

"I think so too. Such a shame." Mrs. Jackson dried her hands on a tea towel. "Can you find your way out? I need to keep an eye on this pan."

"I can, ma'am. Could you tell me which funeral parlor held her service?"

"Yes, it was Green Pastures. Mr. Erickson was so kind. I truly appreciate him."

"I'll be seeing you," he said.

"Charles, say hi to Winifred, and thank you for stopping by. You don't know how much this means to me." She turned back to her cooking.

HE PEDDLED AS FAST AS HE COULD, cutting corners, riding along sidewalks, his legs straining with each push. He needed to reach the mortuary before it closed, though he wasn't even sure it would be open on a Saturday. It was on the north edge of town, almost across from where he was. When he finally skidded to a stop in the driveway, he saw Morris Erickson's big black Cadillac parked beside the simple, unadorned building.

Charlie remembered the interior: the stained-glass windows, the heavy velvet curtains, the gold candlesticks, and the padded folding chairs. But instead of going to the front door, he headed to the back, knowing Mr. Erickson would be in the embalming room. It was a space he had never entered—no one had. It was strictly off-limits. Once, during a funeral, he had peeked inside, and it looked like a hospital operating room.

He knocked on the door. It opened almost instantly, and the towering figure of Mr. Erickson greeted him with a warm smile.

Charlie dearly loved this man; everyone in town did. If something needed doing, Morris was there—he was a member of the Kiwanis Club, the Chamber of Commerce, and even announced the high school football games with his booming voice. He gestured for Charlie to come in.

Charlie hesitated for a moment, then stepped inside. It felt surreal—he was in the mortuary's inner sanctum.

"Charles Holmes. To what do I owe the pleasure of your company on this quiet Saturday afternoon?" Morris said, his voice booming.

Charlie stood frozen, his eyes fixed on the scene before him. On the table in the center of the room lay a man covered with a sheet, his face exposed. Charlie didn't recognize him, but the sight of the sunken cheeks and pale, lifeless skin was haunting.

"Ah, I know what you're thinking, Charles, my boy. You may be the last person to see old Mr. Jenkins here. His children requested a closed coffin, but I have to make sure he's presentable in case they want to say goodbye before we seal it shut. Work, work, work. Everybody goes sooner or later." Morris chuckled. Charlie wasn't sure if it was a show of disrespect or if Morris was just trying to lighten the mood, to make him feel more comfortable in such an unfamiliar place.

Charlie tore his eyes away from the corpse. "Mr. Erickson, I wasn't able to attend Louise Jackson's funeral. Did you take care of her?"

"I sure did, Charlie, my boy. That was a real tragedy. Such a pretty girl, and so young. It almost made me want to quit this profession, seeing her like that. I cried the whole time I was working on her."

Charlie knew that Morris had a son, Richard, who had been a talented football player and an outstanding basketball center. He thought Richard might be attending Berkeley, but he wasn't sure. He also knew how much the Ericksons loved their son; he'd seen them together at games, parades, and around town, always showing their pride and support.

"Do you think Louise drowned?"

Morris paused, looking at Charlie with a strange expression. "Sit down, boy." He motioned to a chair against the wall, and they both took a seat. "Why do you ask?"

"I don't know. I heard somewhere that the police can tell if there's water in the lungs."

"There was water in her lungs, alright. She had been in the river for several days. But there was no way to tell if she drowned or if the trauma to her head killed her. She must have hit that bridge railing going lickety-split."

"So, the rocks killed her?"

"Son, there was a bash on the back of her head—a small hole in her skull. No one could've survived that."

The vivid description overwhelmed Charlie, and he started to cry. Morris, accustomed to comforting grieving people, reached over, grabbed a Kleenex, and handed it to the boy, gently patting his shoulder. This simple gesture made Charlie cry even harder. He thought of how much he had loved Louise Jackson—Weezie, whom he had known all his life. Suddenly, he blurted out his fears.

"Mr. Erickson, I don't think she died at the bridge. I think someone killed her. I was up on the hill with all of us eighth graders at graduation. Weezie had never been there before. She rode her bike everywhere, but she stayed off Merchant Creek Highway because she thought it was too dangerous—too much traffic."

Charlie stood up, feeling his emotions surge. "My dad went to the sheriff and suggested it might not have been an accident. The sheriff insisted it was, and so did Joe Borgman, the Tremonton Police Chief. But I know that wooden bridge. The railing is kinda low, but it's too high for a bike to just hit it and go over. The bike would've been wrecked right there on the road. I just read her diary. She was investigating the deaths of Mr. Strub and Mr. Wilson Carter over by Orosi. If someone went over that bridge onto the rocks below, they'd be more likely to injure their forehead or the top of their head—not the back. She was the best bike rider I knew. She wouldn't have hit

that bridge. Oh, God, Mr. Erickson, I think someone killed Louise."
Charlie's tears streamed down his face.

Morris Erickson stood up and wrapped Charlie in his strong,
comforting arms, just as he had done for so many grieving people
over the years. He held him until he felt the boy start to calm down,
then gently guided him back to the chair. Once they were seated
again, he handed Charlie another Kleenex.

"Well, son…" Morris paused. "Now that you mention it, I have
some questions myself. You might be right. I remember thinking that
was a strange place for a skull fracture. There was no trauma to her
hands either. If someone fell into the river, wouldn't they put their
hands out in front to brace themselves? And I heard her bike was
unscathed. There wasn't a single thing wrong with it. I would've
expected at least the front wheel to be bent or some scrapes if it had
hit that bridge railing. But I didn't think much of it at the time."

They sat in silence for a moment, Charlie still hiccupping as he
tried to regain control of his emotions.

"What are you going to do with this information? I'll back you up
if you want to go to the authorities. You should get your father
involved. La Rue Holmes carries a lot of weight around here."

"I can't do anything, Mr. Erickson. Tomorrow, at four in the
morning, my folks are taking me down to a private school in Los
Angeles."

PART III

MEN GET TOGETHER

Eleven

NOBODY REALLY NOTICED JACKSON OVERSTREET. Not his grammar school classmates, not anyone at Orosi High, not his teachers, and certainly not his parents. Jackson had a way of blending in—or just being ignored. His stepfather barely tolerated him, and his mother hardly spared him a thought, too busy with long shifts and her own troubles. But Jackson liked it that way; he enjoyed the freedom it gave him.

Jackson, a quick witted, intelligent boy, had been a small-time thief for as long as he could remember. Born in 1925 on a struggling farm near Orosi, California, his parents had once been sharecroppers trying to make ends meet selling tomatoes. The Great Depression wiped them out, though, and by the time Jackson was eight, they were living in Radford's Trailer Park on the edge of town, just off the road to Stockton.

He'd started by stealing small things—gum from his mother's purse, coins left around the trailer. At McKinley Grammar School, he'd wait until the teacher turned away, then rummage through lunch sacks in the cloakroom, filching chicken legs, half-sandwiches, or cookies when he found them. In winter, he'd fish a few pennies out of coat pockets, careful to take just enough so no one would suspect him.

Jackson's mother, Blanche, worked tirelessly in the packing houses seven days a week during the harvest season, sorting fruit with quick, practiced hands. Her skill allowed her to make a dollar or two a day, just enough to cover food and rent. For Jackson's lunch, she barely gave it a thought, often tossing in a piece of bread with peanut butter or leftovers, trusting he could find water at the school fountain if he got thirsty.

Whitcomb Overstreet, Jackson's stepfather since he was a year old, had no patience for the boy. A mean-tempered drunk, Whitcomb spent his days at the town bar, The Office, from opening until dinner. He saw nothing in Jackson to be proud of. The boy's disinterest in school or sports left Whitcomb with no stories to boast about to his drinking buddies. As for Blanche, Jackson had never been a charming or affectionate child, and she preferred to let him fend for himself, paying him little mind as he roamed the trailer park or scavenged through the day.

The family's home was a battered, abandoned trailer, barely big enough for three. They had no car, no lawn, and few belongings. Blanche caught rides with coworkers, Jackson walked to school, and Whitcomb staggered his way to and from town. All three were thin, living on scant meals that left little room for indulgences.

At school, Jackson was practically invisible. He took little interest in school work. Because of this, his teachers had no idea how smart the boy actually was. They seldom called on him, and classmates rarely noticed him. After school, he'd roam the trailer park, listen to radio serials, and slip away into the night without question. His parents barely knew what he was up to, and if they did, they certainly didn't care.

In truth, he was up to a lot. Jackson had the power of careful observation. He knew every trailer, its history, and who lived there. He knew who had jobs, who had lost them, and who was searching for work. He understood which families were content and which were struggling. But most of all, he knew what the men thought.

The men gathered, as men do everywhere, outside their trailers at dusk, talking after dinner. Sometimes they had full bellies, and for a moment, they could relax. Jackson would find a spot nearby—maybe leaning against a trailer or sitting on a spare chair if one was offered. He watched them, and he listened.

The men formed groups based on ethnicity. There were the Okies, Arkies, and West Texans; the Italians and Spanish men; the Armenians, Portuguese, and Asians (mostly Japanese), who always offered him tea and a chair. No one seemed to mind the boy hovering nearby, and they soon spoke freely, as if he wasn't even there.

And Jackson listened. He might have appeared half-asleep or disinterested, his eyes wandering, but his mind was sharp and focused. He absorbed everything. Listening to the men became his prime source of entertainment, and he relished those evenings spent among them.

Almost every group passed a bottle at some point. The Italians, in particular, always had wine, as did the Spaniards and Portuguese. The Okies preferred bourbon, while the Mexicans drank beer. Sometimes Basque visitors joined the Spanish group, and they drank a mixed drink called Planter's Punch. Occasionally, someone would offer the bottle to Jackson, and though he would take a sip, he never really liked anything they gave him. He pretended to enjoy it, then passed it along.

Later, when Jackson was in high school and the war was raging, he continued to circulate around the trailer park. By then, most of the discussions centered on the war—who they knew that had been killed, who had just been drafted, and who seemed to be winning. He noticed small flags with stars appearing in many trailer windows and homes throughout Orosi. As the war dragged on, some of those stars turned gold, marking the loss of someone who had once lived there.

AT OROSI HIGH SCHOOL, Jackson found his place. Even before his freshman year began, he knew exactly what he wanted to do. He immediately applied for and secured the position as manager of the football team. Later, he managed the basketball and baseball teams as well. He became invaluable to the coaches and players, ensuring they had towels for showers, the right equipment on hand, and a clean locker room after every practice. On game days, he made sure the balls were ready, water was available, mitts, gloves, and bats were set out, and that everything in the gym was prepared for visiting referees and umpires. He made sure the coaches never had to worry about anything being left undone.

Jackson performed these duties faithfully for all four years. As the manager, he had special keys that granted him access to every locker, and he took advantage of this, just as he had planned. He stole, but he kept his thefts small—nothing that anyone would notice. A penny here, a nickel there, but over time, it added up to a little more than a dollar a day, which, during the war, was a significant amount of money.

His mother never questioned where her son got his money, and his stepfather didn't care enough to notice. To the coaches and the boys, Jackson became practically invisible. They only saw his hands handing out towels, and he moved around like a ghost, always in the background, never causing any controversy. It was exactly how he wanted it, and it worked for him.

JACKSON ALSO HAD A LOVE LIFE during high school. The girl's name was Shirley Doran, and she lived in another travel trailer at Radford Trailer Park. He had started watching her back in grammar school during the nights he wandered the park. By his freshman year in high school, he was beginning to explore his sexuality, in his own way. It finally happened when he gathered enough nerve to ask Shirley for a favor.

Shirley Doran was not a pretty girl, but she was full-figured and tall—just the way Jackson liked. Jackson knew all about the Doran family. He knew what they ate, who they spent time with, that they went to church every Sunday in their Model A sedan, and that Shirley sometimes wore her mother's clothes.

Shirley was aware she was being watched. Like Jackson, she knew almost everything about everyone in the trailer park. She had seen him lurking, sensed when he was peeking through her windows. He was just another element of their hard-scrabble life.

In the spring, Shirley and her mother would sit outside their Aljo trailer in the evenings, drinking lemonade and talking. One warm night, after her mother had gone inside, Shirley wasn't surprised when Jackson slid into the chair beside her. They knew each other, had spoken over the years, but this time felt different.

"Shirley," he whispered, almost hesitant. "Let's go sit in the Model A." The black sedan was parked on the street in front of their trailer.

"No, Jackson. We're fine right here."

"But your mom can hear us."

"So what? She doesn't listen. She has better things to do."

"Let's go sit in the back seat. Can we 'do it' in there?"

The boldness of the question surprised even Jackson; he couldn't believe he had the nerve to ask outright.

"Nope. Never. Don't even think about it again. I'm saving myself for when I get married, and I'm not marrying you, buster."

The truth was, Shirley's mother had caught her stepfather making advances a few years earlier. She had confronted him, threatening to call the police if he ever so much as touched her daughter again. She told him if he wanted sex, he could come to her, but if he touched Shirley, he was going to jail. She made it clear she knew what happened to sex offenders in prison. As soon as the war began, her stepfather enlisted in the Navy and was gone.

Shirley's mother had told her that good girls never let boys touch them. "Who knows where those hands have been," she'd say. "What they've touched, scratched, or what animals they've petted." Before, during, and after the war, this was a speech most mothers gave their daughters.

Jackson slunk away that night, and for days afterward, he could still hear Shirley's laughter echoing as he disappeared into the darkness. He'd also heard Shirley's mother's voice from the open window above the chairs. She had been listening to everything.

"Good girl."

But Jackson wasn't deterred. Somehow, someday, he'd get what he was after.

Twelve

IN 1940, THE BURKE-WADSWORTH CONSCRIPTION ACT was passed, requiring every man aged twenty to sixty-five to register for the draft. Then, in early 1942, just after Pearl Harbor, the registration age was lowered to eighteen. In 1943, when Jackson turned eighteen, he went down to city hall and registered. It was summer, and he was set to start his senior year that fall. In September, he received his draft notice. He returned the form with a request to meet with the Draft Board to seek a deferment.

The local Draft Board for the Orosi area was located in Tremonton, and Jackson caught a ride with the football coach and math teacher, Mr. Downey. Although the drive was only fifteen miles, it took them about an hour because Mr. Downey strictly adhered to the wartime speed limit of thirty-five miles per hour.

The Draft Board met in the red brick Tremonton City Hall. Four members sat behind a long table at the front of the room. The board consisted of six volunteer citizens, rotating in shifts of four. Mr. La Rue Holmes, the chairman, led the proceedings.

With Mr. Downey's support, Jackson argued that he needed to stay in school and delay his draft. He explained that he only had one year left before graduation and, more importantly, was responsible for his family's welfare, as his stepfather had recently been classified as

"4-F" (unfit for service). Mr. Downey emphasized Jackson's role as the indispensable manager for all the sports teams and how difficult it would be to replace him.

Jackson remembered the look of skepticism on Mr. Holmes's face as he handed over the student deferment paper. He knew Mr. Holmes didn't buy his story but relented anyway. Jackson was told he would need to report again after graduation. He fumed all the way home, but Mr. Downey reminded him he was lucky to get a deferment; many of his students had been drafted straight out of school.

Jackson completed high school, graduating near the bottom of his class. The only courses he excelled in were math, which he found easy; the rest he couldn't care less about.

One evening, while sitting with the old men in the trailer park, Jackson overheard the Italian group talking about working in the shipyards near San Francisco. They mentioned that many of their friends had received deferments to work in that critical industry. Someone remarked that Kaiser Steel was producing nearly one Liberty Ship a day—cargo vessels that bolstered convoys headed for Europe and the Pacific.

Just before graduation, Jackson went back to the Italian man to ask if he could get more information. The man said he could arrange papers declaring Jackson a shipbuilder, but it would cost him two hundred dollars. Jackson, who had much more than that saved from his years of pilfering, agreed. The papers looked official, with stamps and language consistent with his supposed job. When his next draft notice arrived, Jackson presented himself once again to the Tremonton Draft Board.

And once again, he faced La Rue Holmes, the chairman. The committee reviewed Jackson's papers, passing them around the table. Unbeknownst to Jackson, La Rue had done some independent investigation.

Charlie's father had been absent from the family for six weeks back in 1943, just after Christmas when the farm was quiet. One Sunday at dinner, he had mentioned to Winifred and the children that he was concerned about the number of draftees being granted deferments for shipbuilding work.

"But La Rue," Winifred said, "I read how desperately they need ships. The Germans have sunk so many. They're sending war materials to the Russians."

"Yeah, but we're granting at least five deferments a week. That's two hundred and fifty men avoiding the draft in a year. And that's just our Draft Board—there are hundreds of others in the state."

"So, what's your plan?" she asked.

"I've asked Sid Schilling to take over as Chairman for six weeks. I'm going to Richmond to get a temporary job in the Kaiser shipbuilding division."

"But Dad," asked Carolyn, "what do you know about building ships? What will you do?"

"I don't know yet, my girl, but I'm sure they'll train me for something."

IN RICHMOND, THEY ASSIGNED HIM as an electrician's assistant. This gave him the freedom to move around the massive shipyard, exploring all areas—even along the edge of the Sacramento and San Joaquin River estuary.

The shipyard was filled with ships in various stages of construction—some just beginning with their keels laid, while others were nearly complete, preparing for launch. Almost every day, there was a launching ceremony, with a dignitary smashing a bottle of champagne on the bow as the ship slid into the river.

La Rue wandered through the yards, scrutinizing the operations and searching for any signs of misconduct. Eventually, he made his way into the darker sections of the ship's holds. Feigning "electrical upgrades", he took control of the lighting and would blast the area with luminescence. *He was astounded at how many men were sleeping down there, apparently hiding out.* They would yell at him to turn off the lights.

La Rue resolved then and there that his Tremonton Draft Board would never issue another deferment for shipbuilding again.

JACKSON WAS DENIED HIS DEFERMENT, and a week later he received his draft notice with the ominous note, "Greetings, you are classified I-A." He was directed to report to an induction station near Sacramento by noon the following Monday. A week later, Jackson boarded a train heading north. Only Coach Downey and a few men from the trailer park came to see him off at the station. His parents were absent; both his mother and stepfather would barely notice he was gone.

He was issued his uniforms and a duffel bag to carry his belongings, then put on a train bound for Georgia. The war in Europe was consuming men at an alarming rate. All the way east, Jackson nursed his growing resentment toward La Rue Holmes, whom he held responsible for his predicament.

JACKSON KEPT TO HIMSELF IN THE ARMY. He didn't extend any effort and failed to make friends during basic training in Georgia. He did, however, excel at marksmanship and no one could fault his stamina—he was exceptional at hiking long distances. When he was finally shipped overseas in early 1945, he was assigned to General Patton's Third Army as a supply soldier.

Jackson caught up with Patton's forces after they had crossed the Rhine River and were making a rapid push across Bavaria. That's when the real work began. The tanks were advancing through Germany at a staggering pace of about thirty-five miles a day, and the rear echelon had to keep up. It was an endless cycle: load the trucks, drive, unload, set up camps, erect tents, organize kitchens and ammo dumps, then tear everything down and move again. The sergeants in charge were seasoned veterans who had been with the Third Army since shortly after D-Day. They were experts in the logistics required to support an army moving faster and farther than any in history.

For Jackson, the routine was grueling—work in the evening, travel at night, set up camp again in the early morning, and snatch sleep during the day whenever possible.

Then, suddenly, on May 8th, everything stopped. The war ended, and for the first time, Jackson felt like he could take a deep breath.

It was not so.

The veterans—those who had fought the longest—were sent home almost immediately. But for soldiers like Jackson, who had only been in uniform for a year or less, the high command had other plans. The Allies, now the occupiers, faced the monumental task of rebuilding a shattered Germany, and Jackson knew he was one of the men who would have to stay behind to help put the pieces back together.

To self centered Jackson, it was hardly a victory. Soon, he found himself in a small convoy of trucks heading back into Bavaria. Their destination was a region west of the Austrian border and north of Switzerland, covering roughly one hundred square miles with the village of Berchtesgaden at its center.

Jackson and about fifty other men were quartered in concrete barracks set in the countryside. The barracks, he learned, had been built for Hitler's Waffen SS guards to protect the nearby Berghof, Hitler's alpine retreat.

He arrived in the evening and was given a quick meal of K-rations. After dinner, he selected a bunk and was instructed to unpack his duffel into a Nazi footlocker, still marked with the swastika and eagle emblem on its lid. His orders were simple: get some sleep and be ready for a briefing at 0650.

Thirteen

"WELCOME, GENTLEMEN, TO THE NEW WORLD." All fifty American G.I.s stood in a Nazi-reinforced concrete assembly room, a space so fortified that even a bomb dropped outside wouldn't breach its walls.

"I am Major Gerald Boccioni, your commanding officer during this operation. That man sitting over there is Master Sergeant Raphael Peña. It is Sergeant Peña who really runs this outfit." Boccioni stood on a raised platform at the front of the room, his presence commanding attention. A lectern was positioned before him, and off to his right sat Peña, leaning forward with a stern expression as he surveyed the men.

"If there are any issues you cannot resolve within your detachment, bring them to the Sergeant. If he can't handle it, then you both come to me. My job is to make things run smoothly and to ensure our mission is carried out with precision." He paused, letting the seriousness of his words sink in.

"Before I explain our mission, understand how fortunate we are to be stationed in these quarters. The Nazis spared no expense in making these barracks comfortable for the elite Waffen-SS guards who protected Hitler. Somehow, this complex escaped bombing during the war. Besides your thick mattresses and well-sprung bunks, you have tiled washrooms and showers—luxuries compared to the trees you were peeing against just days ago." A ripple of laughter spread through the men.

"We also have the latest German washers and dryers in the laundry room," he continued. "And, here's the best part—each barrack has its own orderly. We've employed three German women to maintain your living quarters. You will make your own beds and keep your uniforms inspection-ready, but you will not have to clean the latrines or mop the floors. The orderlies will handle that. You will address them as *Fräulein* and treat them with the utmost respect."

An arm went up in the crowd.

"Yes, soldier, you have a question?"

"Sir, can we shtoop the *Fräuleins*?" The uproar of laughter was deafening. Boccioni waited patiently for the noise to subside.

"No. That is a court-martial offense. And the fact that you even asked that question means I'll be keeping my eye on you, soldier. " Boccioni clenched his jaw and continued. "In a moment, I'll explain your leave schedule and what is permitted. Men, this is serious information. Please pay attention and remember that nothing discussed here should be repeated outside this room. When you write home, you will only mention that you are part of the occupation forces here in Germany." The Major shuffled his notes as the room quieted. A blend of anticipation and unease was written on the soldiers' faces.

"Our mission: We are here to carry out a peaceful and, we hope, just occupation of a defeated nation. Remember, only days ago, they were engaged in a total war against us. There will be hard feelings. Almost everyone you encounter has likely lost someone close to them—perhaps every man in their family. Put yourselves in their position and imagine how you might feel in their place.

"Our mission has three main objectives. First, we will locate and confiscate every item in our area that could be used to wage another war. We will thoroughly search the region. Every truck, gun, ammunition dump, tank, howitzer, anti-aircraft gun, and even every uniform must be secured and rendered useless. Nothing can be left that could be turned against us if the Germans—or even the Russians—decide to take up arms again."

"Two. We are to locate and apprehend any individuals involved in war crimes," Major Boccioni continued, his voice steady and commanding. "When you go among these people, you'll notice a scarcity of men and boys—most are either dead or displaced. Toward the war's end, the Germans pressed young boys and old men into combat. Understand that nearly every person here may have been a Nazi, as membership in the party was practically mandatory. However, we're not here to detain every former party member. Most German soldiers served in the Wehrmacht, the regular German Army. They are not our targets.

"We are specifically seeking members of the infamous Waffen-SS units. These were the soldiers responsible for the worst atrocities— rounding up Jews, executing dissidents, and conducting ruthless campaigns across Europe. They pledged allegiance to an ideology that would have seen the war last a thousand years. Many of their leaders have already been captured and are on their way to Nuremberg for trial. But for every commander, there were hundreds of soldiers who carried out their orders. While some have fled to other countries, others remain here, hidden among civilians, hoping to return to normal lives."

"Not on our watch," an angry soldier shouted from the back of the room. A few whistles could be heard beneath the rumbling din.

Boccioni cocked his head and continued. "Our task is to uncover these men and bring them to justice. We have witnesses—many who survived and saw firsthand the atrocities committed. They will help us identify these war criminals. This, gentlemen, is the second of our objectives." The Major paused, surveying the room. The tension was palpable; every soldier focused on his words.

"Third," he continued, "and perhaps our most critical mission of all, is to win over the hearts and minds of these people. Let's consider some history. Germany has withstood invasions and wars since before the Roman Empire. The Romans couldn't conquer these lands; neither could the Moors, Russians, Poles, French, or British. Despite attempts from every direction, Germany has remained, for the most part, intact. Now, we are here to ensure its stability and to foster a peaceful alliance. Our mission is not just to occupy but to rebuild trust and respect between our nations. This task may ultimately define the peace that follows."

"Now, how do we accomplish this?" Major Boccioni paced, looking each man in the eye. "First, by showing them that we deserve to be the victors. Present yourselves with confidence and professionalism. Your uniforms will be spotless, shoes polished, everything immaculate. You'll show them that it was a miscalculation to go up against us. Each of you will carry a sidearm while on duty. When performing searches, always work in pairs to ensure safety. However, we are here to be more than enforcers; we're here to become allies. Some among us speak German, and we will all begin to learn it. Show respect to individuals, honor their customs, and find admiration for their villages, farms, and homes.

"We'll extend a hand and shake theirs, we'll smile, and we'll help the elderly cross the street. Accept their invitations to dine, share their tables, and meet them in their pubs and restaurants. Try their food, learn their songs. We will become '*die amerikanischen Freunde*'—the beloved Americans. And we will show them that, in their darkest hour, they are fortunate to be occupied by us and not by those they have learned to fear. Mainly, the Russians."

Sergeant Peña stepped forward. "If anyone here feels they cannot fulfill this mission, now is the time to step forward. We understand that some of you may have lost family or friends on these very lands. There will be no repercussions for anyone who opts for a different assignment."

The Major's gaze swept over the room. "For those who stay, the task will be demanding. You'll be sharp, spit-and-polish, every moment you're out there. But make no mistake—this work will be worth it. You will feel pride in what we accomplish. After all, you're Americans." Boccioni paused.

"Any questions?"

A hand went up, and the Major nodded. "Sir, you mentioned the Russians. Should we be worried about them?"

"Yes," Boccioni replied. "Keep your eyes out. I was with the Third Army. General Patton has made his views on this matter clear to Eisenhower and even to President Roosevelt. He foresees Russia as a future threat to the West. They are Communists, and they want to spread that ideology. If you find any trouble, report it. Any other questions?" He scanned the room, but no other hands were raised.

"Very good, gentlemen. Today, you will remain within the compound. Most of you have come straight from the front lines and haven't had a moment to tend to your kit or uniforms. Use the laundry facilities here—have your clothes washed, ironed, and ready for inspection. Those boots of yours likely haven't seen polish in weeks. Spit-shine them to a high gloss.

"When we break up here, you will line up in front of Sergeant Peña's desk to receive your assignments. Thirty of you will be divided into ten three-man teams. Each team's ranking soldier speaks at least a little German. You will receive a map highlighting your designated area. Tomorrow, each team will be assigned a vehicle and begin recon operations in the marked region. Your goal: locate war machines, Waffen-SS personnel, and begin engaging with the local civilians. Understand, this is not a task for a single day—it will take time. Cover what you can daily. Each evening, all teams will reconvene here at 1700 hours for debriefing and a roundtable to discuss findings and exchange strategies.

"For those not in a recon team, we need hands in the compound. There are roles in administration, motor pool, perimeter guard, supply, and the kitchen. Any further questions should go to Sergeant Peña. Now," the Major's voice softened, "I want to see Private Overstreet in my office immediately after dismissal."

Peña's command rang out, "Attention!" All fifty soldiers stomped into a disciplined brace.

"Dismissed."

Fourteen

WHEN JACKSON LEFT THE ASSEMBLY ROOM, he had no idea where the Major's office was located. Spotting a group of soldiers milling outside, he called over, "Anyone know where I can find Major Boccioni's digs?"

"Head toward the mess hall," one of them replied, nodding to the right. Just before reaching the mess hall, Jackson noticed a low concrete building with a nameplate by the first door. He knocked firmly and waited.

"Come in," a voice boomed from within. Opening the door, Jackson realized why the Major had to shout—the door was thick, almost fortress-like, made to withstand any heavy bombardment. Everything in the compound seemed built to last under siege.

Inside, Major Boccioni sat behind a large, polished desk. The wall behind him displayed an array of framed photographs: scenes of tanks in action, groups of soldiers, and one particular photo with the Major standing beside General Patton, who posed with his famous ivory-handled pistol on full display. The Major towered beside Patton, his stature impressive even on film.

Jackson snapped to attention and saluted. The Major returned the gesture, standing and moving around to meet Jackson on the other side of the desk.

The Major was the tallest man Jackson had ever encountered in the military, an imposing figure with broad shoulders and a presence that made the small office seem even smaller. He wore his hair close-cropped and had a thin mustache, which Jackson found almost comically understated given the Major's large frame. Standing at only five-foot-nine and of a wiry build, Jackson felt his own smallness. Yet, after the rigors of boot camp and months of manual labor, he finally felt a bit of muscle tone beneath his uniform. This man, though, looked like he'd been built for football, possibly even West Point, judging by the framed team photo hanging on the wall.

When Jackson's eyes returned to meet the Major's, he was surprised by the warmth in the man's expression. The big man extended his hand for a handshake, and Jackson, though slightly stunned, accepted.

"I've been reading your file, Private Overstreet," the Major began, "and it seems you're something of a loner. Your records from basic training and from your time with the supply unit here both indicate you keep to yourself, avoid friendships, but you're a strong worker. Your supply officer noted that you work quickly, follow orders to the letter, and often stay late to finish up. He even mentioned your good humor under pressure."

The Major returned to his seat, which gave a slight squeak under his weight. Jackson wondered if it might give out one day under this man's towering frame.

"So, son," Boccioni continued, his tone serious, "I'm going to give you two choices. One: you can join a three-man detachment as outlined in this morning's briefing. This would mean daily interaction with the locals, engaging them in conversation, showing kindness, and working closely with your team. You'll need to function as a unit, coordinated and communicative—what I like to call a well-oiled machine."

"Given your pension for singularity and organization, your second choice is to stay here in the compound and manage the supply depot," Major Boccioni continued. "Right now, supplies are sparse—logistics haven't yet caught up with us—but they will. You'd also be responsible for the commissary. It's nearly empty now, but I expect it will soon be stocked with toiletries, magazines, snacks, even paperback books. I'll promote you to Private First Class, which comes with a small pay raise." He paused, letting the offer sink in. "So, what will it be?"

Jackson's mind raced. In a country freshly defeated, he sensed opportunities within the current chaos. He'd heard of G.I.s stashing away prized German souvenirs—a few had hidden Luger pistols, and one even had an officer's sword with a swastika and gold eagle on the hilt. The Major said they'd be going into houses, which could mean more items up for grabs. But heading the supply depot held its own appeal...

After a moment's consideration, the choice was clear.

"I'll stay with my detachment, sir. I can be very gregarious if needed. I look forward to winning over these Germans."

"Good," Boccioni said with a nod. "You'll meet your group at noon mess call. You'll be with Group Six, led by Corporal Heinrick Strub—he speaks fluent German. Good luck to you."

Jackson snapped to attention, delivered a crisp salute, and performed an about-face, nearly bolting from the office.

Fifteen

THE MESS HALL WAS ALMOST IDENTICAL to the assembly building in both shape and size. As Jackson looked through the door, he noticed a partition about two-thirds of the way down, which he figured correctly must be the kitchen. The main room was filled with round tables, each set with three chairs.

"You're early, Private," Sergeant Peña remarked, standing near the door with a clipboard in hand. "But go on, sit down anyway."

Jackson examined the nearest table, noting its surface of highly polished, laminated wood. The chairs were unlike anything he'd ever seen; each was crafted from a single sheet of molded wood, designed to fit the contours of a seated body. Some kind of new German technology, he thought. His gaze fell to the place settings, and Peña noticed his interest.

"We're using the same dishes the SS guards used. Major Boccioni has ordered new ones from a factory near Munich, but that'll take time."

The plates gleamed white with a Nazi swastika etched around the rim, and even the ceramic spoons bore the symbol. The knives and forks were made from a shiny metal, adorned with a raised eagle and the letters "SS" on their handles.

"All iron and aluminum went to the war effort," Peña said, "but the Germans used cast-off steel and silver-coated it. For all I know, these knives and forks might be solid silver—they spared no expense for Hitler's guards."

"Impressive," Jackson noted, eyeing the set.

Peña observed his interest. "I see you eyeing those dishes, Jackson. Let me be clear: everything on this table stays here in the mess hall. If even a single piece goes missing, there'll be repercussions. In the future, Major Boccioni plans to make this tableware available as souvenirs, but until then, it's hands off—everyone's got to eat."

Jackson found table six and sat down, noticing the embroidered swastikas on the napkins. Those damn Nazis sure were obsessed with their symbols, he thought.

Almost instantly, an elderly German man in a white apron and neatly pressed shirt approached. Jackson noted the man's frayed pant cuffs and the wear on his shirt sleeves, though his white hair was meticulously combed and his shoes were polished to a gleam.

"What would you like to drink, sir?" the old man asked, his fleshy face lined with deep wrinkles and his German accent thick.

"What do you have?"

"We have coffee, tea, and water, sir."

"Can you answer a question?"

The old man gave a slight bow. "I would be pleased to do so."

"I notice you speak very good English. What did you do during the war?"

The old man straightened. "I am much too old to fight, sir. I was manager here, in these camps."

"You mean you were SS?"

"Oh no, sir. I was part of the regular army. We hated the SS."

"Then why did you work for them?"

"A person often had no choice in such matters," the waiter replied, a note of resignation in his voice.

"I see," said Jackson. "What was your specific job?"

"I was a Sturmbannführer—what you might call a major in your army. I was commandant of this entire compound."

"And you were not SS?"

"No. The Waffen-SS did not want their own people serving them. They were... above us."

"So, you were like a slave. I see. But you were higher in the ranks."

"I was."

"Why, then, are you a waiter for us?"

"I do this for you because I am grateful you have employed me. I am, how do you say... lucky to have work."

"How many of you are waiters?"

"There are six of us in the dining hall and ten in the kitchen. We have a senior chef and a baker. You should see the ovens."

"You must have seen many famous people while working here."

"Oh yes," the waiter said, his tone lowering as he recalled it.

"Did you ever see Hitler?"

"Many times. He did not come into this place, but when he was riding nearby in his automobile, we all had to line up along the road and make noise."

"Who else did you see?"

"Many times, Adolph Eichmann was with der Führer. I also saw Hermann Göring. He dined with Hitler up at the Berghof, but his soldiers ate here. Sometimes Herr Göring would stop by after and share a glass of schnapps with his men. They would laugh and sing... have big celebration?"

"A good time?"

"Yes, thank you. Heinrich Himmler was here sometimes, and so were Heydrich, Speer, even Admiral Dönitz. I saw them all." The mess hall was beginning to fill, and Jackson noticed the old man seemed eager to return to his duties.

"Do you think we could talk more sometime?"

"Yes, of course. Perhaps you could visit my house? I would like you to meet my daughter. We can have something to drink."

"What's your name?"

"I am Herr Manfred Lindsburg, at your service."

"There's a famous American with that name. Old Lindy. " Jackson looked amused.

"Yes, I know, the famous pilot." Manfred smiled. "My grandfather said we are related—Lucky Lindy is a distant cousin. You Americans dropped the 's' from his name. There are many Lindsburgs in Germany."

Jackson shook his head. He felt like he was on another planet for a moment.

"So, how will I find your house?"

"Ask anyone in Berchtesgaden. Everyone knows of me. Please come. Now I must do the work."

"I'll have the tea," said Jackson.

Sixteen

THE TWO OTHER MEMBERS of Detachment 6 arrived almost simultaneously. Heinrick Strub, short and stocky with dark hair and an easy smile, approached first. Jackson stood, and they shook hands firmly. Then came Wilson Carter, a tall, gaunt figure with serious eyes and messy blond hair. The three men exchanged introductions, hands clasped in solid, knowing grips. All wore class A uniforms, but Strub and Carter's clothes were wrinkled and grimy, remnants of battlefield wear and tear. Their tunics sported decorative ribbons, giving a nod to hard-fought victories despite the battered state of their uniforms. Jackson glanced down, realizing he probably looked no less worn.

As he looked at Carter, it crossed Jackson's mind that the tall, fair-haired soldier could have fit the image of a Nazi. But Wilson was as far from that as a person could be—an Alabama native who despised Germans with the fierce conviction of many American G.I.s.

"Would you look at this setup," said Wilson as the three sat down. "What are we now, in the frickin' German army? We just beat the crap outta them, and now we have to eat off their damn plates?"

The men laughed uneasily, their voices mixing with the low hum of the mess hall. The war had been won—humanity's most destructive conflict to date—and these swastika-laden dishes, absurd as they seemed, were a stark reminder of who the enemy had been.

As if on cue, Manfred Lindsburg appeared, asking what they'd like to drink. Both newcomers ordered coffee.

"Where'd they dig up that guy?" Heinrick wondered, watching Lindsburg disappear back to the kitchen.

"He looks like he might keel over any second," said Wilson, laughing. "This a retirement home for Nazi soldiers? Think he can manage two cups of coffee?"

Listening to the two men talk, Jackson remembered the Major's words about getting along with the locals and took it as his cue to join in. "That 'old guy,'" he began, "was a major in the Wehrmacht. Probably a captain in the First World War. For the past seven years, he was commandant of this entire compound." He lowered his voice slightly. "And believe it or not, he hated the Waffen-SS."

Strub and Carter froze, coffee cups poised mid-air.

"How the hell do you know all that?" Strub asked, his curiosity piqued. "Jackson Overstreet, right?"

"You can call me Jack."

"Well, Jack," Strub continued, eyebrow raised, "you're full of surprises. Meeting with Major Boccioni and now a full-on bio of our waiter. What's the deal?"

"I got here early and spoke with Manfred—Manfred Lindsburg, with an 's.' He's too old to have fought in this war, so they kept him in command here. He managed the place under the SS, but he despised them. He's seen every high-ranking German officer there is. All of them passed through here on their way to see Hitler. Lindsburg's thankful we've hired him, even as a waiter. Apparently, things have been rough in Berchtesgaden, even before the war ended."

"Jesus," said Wilson, shaking his head. "What was Boccioni thinking, hiring these old soldiers? Does he actually believe they see themselves as defeated? I don't buy it. They were all Nazis—they think they're destined to rule the world. They're just waiting in the wings to start up the Fourth Reich."

"I don't know," Jackson said, considering. "From what I've seen, these guys are grateful it was us and not the Russians who took Bavaria."

Strub conceded. "They might even like us if we treat them with a little respect."

"Respect?" Wilson's voice sharpened. "Were you there when we liberated that death camp? Did you see the bodies? Smell that god-awful, rotten stench of burnt flesh? See those poor souls—walking skeletons—left to die? And who do you think was responsible for that? It was this 'waiter' and his pals. There's no way I'd ever want to be friends with these bastards. They should all be dragged out and shot. Do the world a favor."

"Sounds like you've had it rough, man," Heinrick said, raising an eyebrow.

"You got to roll across the place in that mobile foxhole you call a tank," Wilson replied, forcing a laugh. "I had to slog it through mud across Germany and half of Czechoslovakia. I'm beat, I'm fed up with this place, and I'm damn sick of the Huns. What do you say we just shoot everyone we see?"

"Easy, now," said Strub, his tone softening as he noticed the strained look on Wilson's face. "I get it—you've had it hard." Jackson saw Wilson's eyes welling up, though he tried to shield his face with his hand.

"Good thing we've got the day off and maybe some real food for once," Strub added, giving Wilson a sympathetic pat on the back. "But remember the Major's orders: we're here to win over the hearts and minds of these Germans. If that doesn't sit well with you, let me know now."

"He just needs a proper American steak and a cold beer and he'll be right as rain, won't ch'a Carter?" Jackson gave Wilson a light punch on the shoulder, coaxing a reluctant nod from him, still half-hidden behind his hand. He could sense Wilson was on the edge.

"Well, then, let's eat," said Strub, his mood brightening. "Where's your buddy, the Kraut? I'll tell you, it feels nice being waited on after living in the dirt for so long. Don't you think?"

"I say, 'S'queet,'" Jackson smirked.

"Oh yeah?" laughed Strub. "'What did you do during the war, Daddy?'"

Jackson cocked his head. "I was in supply. Man, you tank jockeys sure knew how to move. We'd be hauling supplies all night to catch up to where you were at dawn. And here they go, shipping us halfway across Germany. I'm wiped out, like Wilson."

"Have you tried the beds yet?" Strub asked, shaking his head with a chuckle. "Good gravy, it's like sleeping on a cloud compared to the dirt and rocks we've been on for the last year."

Just then, a line of old men emerged from the kitchen, moving carefully but with precision, each carrying platters and large bowls. They fanned out across the tables. Manfred approached their table first, his hands balancing a large platter of boiled potatoes and a stack of hamburger patties. Holding a fork and spoon in his left hand, he served a potato and a patty to each of their plates with practiced skill. Moments later, another man came by with string beans and thick slices of bread. Another followed, leaving a small pitcher of gravy on their table. Lastly, Manfred returned, bearing a platter of golden apple strudel, and served each of them a generous slice.

Jackson looked down, wide-eyed at the feast—a feast fit for a king after the flavorless rations they'd endured. God, he thought, he was lucky to be stationed here, of all places.

"Hey Strub, you've got a ribbon I don't recognize," Jackson said, nodding toward the array on Strub's uniform. "I know two of them, but what's that blue one?"

Strub grinned, tapping the ribbon. "That's for being the lead tank when we entered Czechoslovakia. General Patton himself awarded it to my crew right after we crossed the border. Pretty wild, huh?"

"Was he wearing his pearl handled forty-five?" Wilson asked with a smirk.

"Ivory-handled, actually. And yeah, he sure was," Strub replied, chuckling. "Made sure *Stars and Stripes* was there to catch every angle. The man loves his headlines, but you've got to hand it to him—he's the best general we've got."

"Heard somewhere he slapped a soldier down in Sicily," Jackson interjected, raising an eyebrow.

"That's the story," Strub said, shrugging. "But I bet the guy needed it. Besides, the French slap their soldiers all the time, or so I hear."

"Anyone hits me, he's dead," said Jackson.

Seventeen

A FTER BREAKFAST, AT 0730, THE THREE MEN GATHERED near the motor pool. A sergeant assigned Corporal Strub a jeep, instructing him to head over to the assembly area and line up with the other vehicles. Ten men stood in a row beside six jeeps and four camouflaged weapons carriers—slightly larger, four-wheel-drive vehicles designed for rough terrain. Each soldier looked pristine, clad in a freshly pressed uniform with spit-shined boots. A parachute cord had been handed out the previous afternoon, replacing standard boot laces so that their black boots now sported the striking contrast of white laces. The pant legs were carefully bloused over their boots, adding to their precise, polished appearance. Each man carried a standard-issue .45-caliber pistol holstered on his hip.

They didn't have to wait long. Major Gerald Boccioni strode out in front of the line, his commanding presence immediately silencing the group. "Gentlemen, today is a historic moment. You will be putting the American occupation policy into action. You know your mission. Does each team leader have their map with assigned areas marked?"

A nod came from each driver.

"Good," Boccioni continued. "The most critical part of your duty is to earn the trust of the local Germans. And remember, children are key to this effort. I've added a carton of Hershey's bars and a carton of spearmint gum in each vehicle. Hand it out to every kid you see. Try to engage with them. Most of the youngsters have had some English in school and may understand you. Let your team leader, who knows German, take the lead when speaking to the adults. Now, men, off you go—and good hunting."

With a roar of engines, the line of army vehicles pulled out of the compound. A quarter mile north, they reached an intersection where six roads branched off in different directions. Strub took the narrow two-lane road leading east, cutting through farmland and patches of forest. Riding in an open jeep, the wind was too loud for much conversation, so Jackson kept his eyes on the scenery, taking in the unfamiliar landscape. His gaze swept the fields and tree lines as if looking for something he couldn't quite name.

Four miles along, Strub suddenly braked. "I think I saw something," he said, reversing the jeep about a hundred yards.

There were no fences lining the road; just open grazing land where cattle wandered freely. Strub had kept their speed down to forty-five, mindful of any livestock that might wander onto the road. He pointed toward the field on the south side. "See that?"

Jackson squinted. All he saw was a grassy field stretching to a line of forest in the distance, maybe a quarter of a mile off. "What am I looking at?"

Strub tapped the windshield. "Look at the ground. See those tracks?"

Jackson examined the faint wheel tracks stretching across the field. They were barely visible, with the grass already springing back.

"How far apart are those tracks?" Strub asked, narrowing his gaze.

Wilson looked closely. "Wider than a jeep, for sure."

"Right," Strub replied, "and what leaves tracks that wide?"

"Maybe a four-by-four truck?" Wilson guessed.

"Nope," said Strub, shaking his head. "They're wider than any truck. Those are tank tracks. Trust me, I've been in tanks for nearly a year. I know the difference—seen 'em in mud, grass, sand. That pattern's unmistakable."

"So what?" Jackson shrugged. "Germany's full of tank tracks."

"Not around here," Strub said. "There was no fighting this far out. I'm going to follow them."

With that, he turned the jeep off-road, driving over the field toward the tracks. Jackson looked back, noticing that the jeep's own tracks were much narrower than the faint ruts they were now driving on. Ahead, he could just make out a slight gap in the trees where the tracks continued. The trail led into the forest, winding left and hugging the tree line about a hundred feet in. It was clear the tank had forced its way through, crushing underbrush and snapping small trees that obstructed its path.

"Why would a tank push through the forest like this?" Wilson asked, his brow furrowed.

"To stay hidden," Strub replied without hesitation.

"But why hide out here if there was no fighting?" Wilson pressed, still skeptical.

Strub shook his head. "No idea. But notice—there aren't any tracks heading back out. If they'd come back, the ground would be more worn. We're following two tanks, maybe more, and it looks like another vehicle's involved."

They rumbled on in low gear, carefully following the trail for about a quarter mile before they came upon the abandoned tanks. There were two of them alright, sitting silently beneath the trees, with a German half-track scout car positioned in front. Strub slowed to a stop, and the men dismounted, their boots crunching softly in the brush. Jackson noticed branches piled atop the tanks, an attempt to camouflage them from aerial view. The leaves had withered, suggesting they'd been abandoned for some time.

"Looks like someone wanted these hidden," Jackson murmured, running his hand over the dusty, neglected hull.

"Probably in a hurry, too," Strub said, his voice low.

"God damned," Wilson muttered, admiringly tapping one of the tank's imposing metal sides. "Not four miles into the operation and we've got ourselves some intact German fighting machines. That ought to earn us gold stars, eh? What luck."

Strub nodded, making a mark on the map. "I'll note this for the demolition team. They'll want to blow these up or haul them out. But first, I want to take a look inside one of these monsters. These are late-model Tiger tanks, top-of-the-line. They're as good as anything we've got—maybe better. Give me a minute."

Jackson settled back in the jeep while Strub clambered up the tank's side and opened the heavy hatch, disappearing inside. Wilson, meanwhile, circled around to the halftrack, climbing into the driver's seat. The sound of the starter choked a few times, but the engine refused to catch; the battery was nearly dead.

After a while, Strub emerged from the tank, and Wilson returned from his inspection of the halftrack.

"What's the story here?" Jackson asked.

"Looks like the halftrack's out of fuel," Wilson replied. "No maps, no papers, and no weapons left behind. It's like they cleaned house before they left."

Strub wiped his hands and shook his head. "My guess is one of their vehicles ran out of gas, so they ditched it here and took off with the rest. The tanks are probably empty too. They'd have loaded everyone up in the last vehicle and followed this trail...Let's keep going."

Strub maneuvered the jeep around the abandoned convoy and continued down the trail. Overhead, branches arched, casting deep shade. Ahead, Jackson could make out a single set of narrower tracks—a vehicle had definitely pressed on through this forest.

"What was it like inside the tank?" Jackson asked.

"Cramped as hell," Strub said, his face darkening at the memory. "Nothing's padded—seats, controls, even the gun sights. In a battle, you'd get tossed around like a ragdoll. I'd be black and blue if I'd spent any real time in there."

Wilson peered around at the dense canopy. "Strange to find a road in the middle of nowhere."

"Not so strange for the Germans," Strub replied, slowing as the trail narrowed. "Forestry here is precise, almost surgical. They've lived near forests like this for centuries; I'm betting they manage every inch. Logging, replanting, maybe even game trails. Someone has a map of this place showing every bend and creek. They're meticulous about their land."

The trees parted ahead, revealing a flood of sunlight and a small clearing. As Strub guided the jeep to a stop, they spotted another vehicle concealed beneath dried branches—a sleek, silver Mercedes with SS insignia on the doors. Jackson noted the mounts on the front fenders, where flags could have been affixed for a commanding officer's display.

"This looks like a high-ranking officer's car," Strub said, tugging at a branch. "Maybe the convoy's leader. Whoever he was, he ditched the car here and took his men on foot."

The three men stood quietly, scanning the forest's edge where the trail continued. Beyond the clearing, a vast, open field stretched out under the clear sky, and in the distance, a tiny village appeared, clustered at the base of a gentle hill. Strub pointed toward it.

"I have a hunch," he said, "that we're about to make our first official contact with the local civilians. And I wouldn't be surprised if they're hiding our Mercedes-driving SS officer, somewhere in that quiet little town."

Eighteen

"THERE COULD BE MINES OUT THERE," said Strub. "Let's see if we can locate these guys' tracks. We should walk single-file in their path if we can."

"Maybe those Huns parked back in the trees because they knew about mines," Wilson suggested.

"I don't think so," Jackson replied, eyes scanning the open field. "I think they were low on fuel and wanted to keep their convoy hidden for further use. These Hun bastards don't think the war is over—they're probably itching to start up again."

"If that's true," Strub said thoughtfully, "we need to find their leader and corral him. Let's go check it out." Stub gestured toward the town just ahead.

"I'm not walking," Jackson replied, heading toward the jeep. "I'm taking the jeep."

"Jack, you're asking for it," said Wilson, casting a wary look over the field.

"I don't think so. Look at that village—it has zero strategic importance. There wasn't any fighting here. Why would anyone waste time mining this field? I'm driving." Jackson climbed into the driver's seat and started the engine. Strub and Wilson exchanged glances. Jackson had a point. They joined him, giving a reluctant shrug.

Jackson eased the jeep forward, cutting slowly across the field toward the town. Up ahead, they saw villagers walking along narrow streets and, closer, a group of young boys kicking a worn soccer ball around near the town's edge.

The terrain rolled gently, and as they got closer to the village, they noticed a small river bordering its north side, with the village itself on a slight rise, almost like a natural fortress. Whoever had chosen this location centuries ago likely understood the military advantage of this elevated ground.

The jeep jolted as they hit a paved road winding in from the left. It curved toward an old stone bridge crossing the river, its weathered stones telling of ages past. The soccer-playing boys were on their side of the river, right in the jeep's path to the main street.

"Why are you stopping here, Jack?" asked Carter, looking curiously at Jackson as he slowed to a halt.

Jackson glanced at the boys, who were now eyeing them with a mix of curiosity and caution. He'd seen enough wariness in kids' faces to know that rushing in without thought could backfire.

"I want to ask these kids a question. Corporal Strub, can you grab some of that gum from the back and invite the boys over?"

Strub turned and called, "Kinder...," and said something in German that Jackson couldn't quite catch.

The boys approached hesitantly but huddled together on the left side of the jeep. Strub tossed several sticks of Spearmint gum their way, and instantly, their guarded expressions melted into grins as they eagerly unwrapped the familiar treat.

"Kinder," Jackson began, doing his best with the German he knew, "Spreken sie Deutsch?"

Several boys nodded and replied, "Yes."

"Vunderbar. Good," he continued, "Do you know about the tanks back in the forest?"

The boys exchanged glances before a few of them nodded cautiously.

"Where did the men who came in those tanks head?" Jackson pressed.

The boys hesitated, looking at each other before one of the taller boys started shaking his head, prompting the rest to follow suit.

"Alright then, can you tell us where the Gauleiter of your village lives?" Jackson asked.

"Yes," the tallest boy answered, glancing over his shoulder toward the village, "He lives in the Gasthaus."

"What's the name of this village?"

"It's Ravengersberg, sir."

"Thank you, boys," Jackson said, revving up the jeep. The children stepped aside as he pulled forward onto the paved road and crossed the bridge into the village.

"Good work, Jack," said Strub, nodding approvingly. "We might get more truth out of the kids than their parents."

Ravengersberg was like countless other farming villages scattered across rural Germany, only smaller and quieter. The main stretch had about six buildings that made up the town's center: a pharmacy, a post office, a notions and curio store, and a shop for tobacco and basic goods. At its heart stood the Gasthaus, akin to a village pub or inn where locals gathered for food, drink, and news. The shopkeepers probably lived above their businesses in modest quarters.

A few houses dotted the surrounding area, homes for perhaps a handful of families. Serious shopping—farm equipment, vehicle repairs, and larger provisions—would have required a trip to Berchtesgaden, a mere seven miles away. Jackson had also noticed a tiny, barely functioning filling station at the edge of town as they'd driven in, a reminder of the country's dwindling resources as the war had drawn to a close. The village's layout nestled within a bend of the river on slightly elevated ground, where centuries ago, a small castle might have once stood. Now, its stones had long since been repurposed into the humble buildings of Ravengersberg's unassuming center.

A modest town square anchored the village, with a stone war memorial at its center, adorned with bronze plaques listing those who had fallen in World War I. A few benches circled the square, places where old men could sit in the sun, reminiscing—a group Jackson imagined was now scarce in the village. World War I had decimated millions of men, and World War II had likely taken most of the young ones here.

It was obvious which building on the square was the Gasthaus. They pulled up in front of the yellow-painted building, which had no other cars parked nearby. Anyone coming here for lunch would likely be close enough to walk.

The men stepped out, and with Strub leading, they headed toward the front door. A few hardy red flowers bloomed in boxes along the front, their color a bright contrast against the building's worn facade. Jackson spotted a bench off to the side and veered toward it.

"Aren't you coming in, Jack?" asked Strub.

"No, I just want to sit here and keep watch. You go on."

"We might eat lunch inside. I don't want any more of those C-rations."

"Bring me a sandwich if they have anything." Jackson nodded toward the door.

"Sure thing. Watch our back."

With his eyes half-closed, Jackson let himself sink into the bench, the subdued sunlight filtering through the clouds warming his face. He drifted in and out of a light doze, only to notice, on waking, that the tallest of the boys from the soccer game had approached and now sat quietly on the other end of the bench.

"Hello," Jackson greeted.

"Hello," the boy replied, his English surprisingly fluent though accented.

"Which one's your house?" Jackson asked.

The boy pointed down the street. "We live in the one with the yellow door."

"Your family—how many are there?"

"It's my mother, my brother, and me," the boy said, his tone brightening with the familiarity of home.

"And your father?"

"We don't know. It's been six months since his last letter. He was somewhere in Italy. Maybe he'll come home soon."

Jackson paused, considering how to ease into his next question. "I think an important soldier passed through this village a few days ago. Did you see him?"

"Yes," the boy answered openly, with the simple honesty of youth. "He's very important. A general. He lived in the house next to ours."

Jackson leaned in, lowering his voice slightly. "Was he part of the SS?"

The boy hesitated, shifting uncomfortably.

"What's your name?" Jackson asked, softening the line of questioning.

"I am Peter. My brother's name is Helmut."

"Peter, was your neighbor in the Waffen-SS?" Jackson pressed.

The boy avoided his gaze. "I don't know. I must go now."

"Wait," Jackson pulled out another stick of spearmint from his pocket, offering it to the boy. "Can I visit your house sometime, Peter?"

Peter nodded, glancing quickly toward his home, and grabbed the stick of gum. "Yes, sir. That would be very nice. Goodbye." Then he turned, hurrying down the street toward the house with the yellow door, his small figure soon lost among the narrow lanes of Ravengersberg.

Nineteen

"WAKE UP, YOU WORTHLESS PILE OF CRAP." Wilson Carter shook Jackson's shoulder, jerking him awake. "We've got rabbits to hunt." Jackson, who had slumped on the bench, straightened, immediately alert.

"What did you guys find in there? Or did you just get blotto?" he asked, rubbing his eyes.

"Nope. Not blotto," replied Strub, settling beside him. "But we did some talking. Turns out the kid was right—the Gauleiter of this village runs the gasthaus. He's an old war relic with a limp from the First World War. Claims there used to be a general who lived here, but says he probably died—either in North Africa or Normandy. His widow and daughter still live here."

"Well, that's a dead end. I thought we had ourselves an SS bastard for sure," said Jackson, deflated.

Wilson sat down, handing Jackson a wrapped sandwich. "We got you a sausage sandwich. Hope you like German mustard."

Jackson took the sandwich, biting into it as he listened.

"While we were eating, a group of about four young guys sat down next to us," Wilson continued. "They're farm workers who rent rooms here in Ravengersberg. Said there are farms all along this river up to Berchtesgaden. One of the farms lets them borrow a tractor with a trailer to haul themselves to work."

"So they're not locals," Jackson said, chewing thoughtfully. "Were they soldiers?"

"They were, but I couldn't catch the whole story," Strub answered. "One's recently back from Berlin, another from Yugoslavia. The other two fought at the Rhine."

"Nothing unusual then," said Wilson with a sigh. "Seems nobody here knows anything useful. Maybe we head to the next town, see if anyone there knows about those tank drivers."

"Yeah, let's blow this joint," agreed Strub.

Jackson swallowed the last of his sandwich. "One of those kids we met earlier—Peter, the tall one—came by while I was dozing. He lives with his mom next door to where that general used to live. There's something strange about that house."

He paused, glancing at Strub. "Do we have permission to go into any house we want?"

"That's what old man Boccioni said," Strub replied with a smirk.

"Then let's check it out. I'll visit Peter and his mom, and maybe you two can look around the general's place. Who knows? We might pick up some interesting souvenirs."

Strub shrugged, exchanging a look with Wilson. "Whatever you say, Jack. Might be good to poke around."

They decided to leave the Jeep parked where it was and proceed on foot. It was only a few yards to the general's house, where Strub and Carter headed to the front door. Jackson made his way to the house with the yellow door, which seemed almost too small to hold more than a single room. There was nothing out front—just paving bricks forming a narrow path from the road to the door, wide enough to park a car if needed. He knocked, and almost immediately, the door opened to reveal Peter, smiling.

"Come in," Peter said, stepping aside. Jackson entered the house, adjusting to the dim interior. It wasn't dark, just subdued, with shutters partially closed on the windows, letting in just enough light to see by. None of the lights were on. The living room was smaller than he'd expected—almost as compact as his mother's trailer—but neatly arranged. Two cushioned chairs faced a small stone fireplace, while padded window seats lined the walls. The wooden mantle above the fireplace held an assortment of trinkets and mementos. Jackson recognized a few as intricately decorated beer steins, but most were unfamiliar, likely keepsakes with personal significance.

A warm glow appeared from the doorway on the other side of the room as a woman stepped through, drying her hands on an apron and offering him a polite smile.

"This is my mother," Peter said.

She was tall like her son, her blonde hair arranged in two tightly rolled buns on either side of her head, reminiscent of a style that Jackson expected German women to wear. She filled out a frilly blouse and her patterned skirt fell almost to her patent leather shoes. Though not classically beautiful, she had an air of grace and purpose, her demeanor calm and inviting. She gestured toward one of the easy chairs, and Jackson took a seat.

She murmured something to Peter in German, and he nodded, quickly turning one chair to face the small room. He took his seat, while his mother adjusted the other chair, smoothing her dress as she sat. Peter settled into the window seat, watching them with an open, curious expression.

"My mother does not speak English," Peter explained. "I will translate for you."

"Please tell her that I'm an American here to make friends with the German people," Jackson said. "Let her know we'll try to make things as comfortable as possible now that we're here." Peter relayed this in German, and his mother nodded, though her expression remained tense.

"Could you ask if she's noticed any soldiers passing through the village recently?" Jackson continued. Peter spoke to his mother, but her response was clear even before he translated; her face betrayed worry, her brow furrowing as she shook her head.

"Are there just the two of you living here?" Jackson asked.

"No, there are three of us. My mother has taken in a man who rents a room to help with expenses. I think you saw him in the gasthaus—he works with three others for a farmer down the river."

"Where is he from, and why wasn't he in the war?"

Peter's eyes flicked toward his mother before answering. "He was in the war. He came here recently from Berlin."

"What about the other three? Do you know where they served?"

"I think one was in Italy, and the other two were stationed along the Rhine." Peter's mother interjected, speaking quietly to him in German.

"She wants you to know that the man is staying in my room and that I sleep with her for now," Peter translated. "When my father comes home, the man will have to leave." He paused, glancing at Jackson. "Would you like some coffee or hot chocolate?"

Jackson shook his head. "No, thank you. I should be going." Standing, he reached into his pocket and handed out two Hershey's bars—one to Peter and one to his mother. She rose as well and, with a slight bow, accepted the chocolate. Jackson noticed her hands, strong but worn, and the slight crease of a smile that softened her otherwise guarded expression.

Peter moved quickly to open the door. As Jackson stepped outside, he turned back.

"Peter, may I visit again sometime?"

The boy looked back to his mother, who gave a subtle nod. "Yes," he answered. "Please do."

Jackson walked out, now certain the mother understood English far better than she let on.

JACKSON WALKED UP TO THE HOUSE NEXT DOOR and, not seeing his partners outside, tried the front door. As he stepped inside, the pair appeared, seemingly on their way out. The room was brightly lit, and he was struck by the intricate woodwork everywhere—carved mantels, stair banisters adorned with designs, and window frames detailed with animal effigies. From outside, he'd noticed the house was a picture of Germanic craftsmanship, with elaborately cut boards on the upper balconies, patterned red shutters, and vibrant flower boxes overflowing with red geraniums. It had the kind of charm that bespoke money and heritage.

"Hey, Jack," Strub greeted him. "We were just finishing up here." Behind Strub, a young woman stood—about twenty-five, with long, tightly braided blond hair, wearing an apron that suggested she'd been in the middle of work. She introduced herself as Gertruda.

"Let's step outside," Strub added.

The three men moved out, and Gertruda closed the door behind them.

"We didn't find a thing," said Wilson, shaking his head. "Gertruda here says her father was killed in Normandy, and her mother's out working. She speaks English pretty well. We scoured the place but didn't find anything linking her father to the Waffen SS."

"We're probably at a dead end in this town," Strub said, glancing around the square. "Might be time to hit the next village."

Jackson thought for a moment. "Why don't you two go grab the Jeep?" he suggested. "I'd like to take a more thorough look around inside. Give me a few minutes. You can stop by the pub for a cold one if you like. This General had money, clearly. Who knows what I might find?"

Strub chuckled. "Alright, have fun. She's a looker—might be worth a second pass."

JACKSON KNOCKED AND THEN ENTERED before Gertruda could open the door. She was still standing in the entryway, her eyes widening slightly in surprise.

"Is your mother home?" he asked casually, gauging her English.

"She's at work, sir." Her tone was cool, and he noted her English was fluent.

"If you don't mind, miss, I'd like to look around," he said, glancing around the room with mild interest.

She hesitated, clearly disturbed. "Your men have already been through our house. Everything has been checked."

"Yes, I know. But I need to see it for myself. As an occupying force, we're authorized to enter any building, any home, to ensure security." He paused, holding her gaze. "Resistance to our work could mean a trip to a camp."

She nodded and stepped back, allowing him to continue his inspection. Jackson went straight to the mantelpiece, where a row of steins and mugs had been carefully arranged. Each seemed to represent some memory or milestone from the past. None bore swastikas or obvious symbols of allegiance. The collection felt more personal than political, though he doubted the sentiment. Next, he examined the bookshelves on either side of the fireplace, even sliding a few books aside to check if anything was hidden behind them. Nothing out of the ordinary, just spines in German that could've been anything from Goethe to Goebbels for all he knew.

His eyes swept the room, finally landing on an ornately crafted piano in the corner, its wood as polished and intricate as the banisters. It struck him that, despite the carefully arranged items, there were no photographs displayed—an unusual absence, especially in a family home like this.

"Would you show me upstairs, miss?" he asked.

Without a word, she nodded and led the way, her shoulders tense as she ascended the carved staircase. They reached a narrow hallway lined with several closed doors. He gestured toward them. "Please show me your father's room."

She pointed to the first door on the left and then stepped back. He opened it, stepping into a dim, modestly furnished bedroom. Dominating the space was a tall double bed, its headboard adorned with a painting of snow-capped mountains he guessed were the Alps.

Flanking the bed were two small nightstands, each with items carefully laid out. On one, a book with a pencil marking a page looked like it could be a diary; the other held a jar of ointment, a glass of water, and a package of cigarettes.

Jackson opened the drawer of the right nightstand, finding a neat stack of cloth handkerchiefs and a pair of reading glasses with delicate gold frames. The left drawer held only a small towel, but as he felt beneath it, his fingers brushed something cold and hard. He pulled out a German Luger pistol, its ivory handle gleaming faintly. He turned and held it up for her to see. Her face flushed, her eyes betraying a flicker of unease before she averted her gaze.

Pocketing the Luger, Jackson exited the room. He took a quick look through the other bedrooms and a bathroom, noting again the lack of personal photos. The walls held only innocuous landscapes and decorative patterns. He returned to the main floor.

"WOULD YOU SHOW ME TO THE BASEMENT, please?" he asked. She silently led him down the stairs, past the kitchen, and opened a door leading to the cellar, flicking on the light as they descended.

The basement was cramped, dominated by a massive oil heater and stacks of sporting equipment—skis, a toboggan, several leather balls, and a set of golf clubs leaned against the wall. In the far corner were some stacked boxes, which he quickly began to sift through.

Most contained winter clothing—sweaters, woolen socks, and mittens—but a smaller box near the bottom revealed something more interesting. Inside were six framed photographs, each in sturdy wooden frames with glass. As Jackson lifted them, he noticed the girl hovering nearby, wringing her hands.

He held up the top photo, which showed a middle-aged couple in traditional Bavarian attire. Behind them loomed a castle against the backdrop of rugged mountains. He glanced at her. "Are these your parents, miss?"

She nodded, her eyes clouded with a mix of tension and resignation.

The next photo showed the same man, now standing with three others in hunting attire. Two held shotguns resting on the ground, their hats adorned with tiny feathers in the brims. But it was the fourth figure who arrested Jackson's attention: a large, round man he immediately recognized. Reichsmarschall Hermann Göring. Jackson turned to the girl, and a single tear was tracing a path down her cheek as she looked away, caught between shame and defiance.

Standing there with a German Luger in his pocket, holding a photograph that tied this family to a reviled Nazi leader, something clicked within him. He felt a surge of confidence and an understanding that the war had changed him in profound ways. Jackson Overstreet, once a scrawny kid from nowhere, now had a certain power in this foreign basement, a power he hadn't sought but now felt sharply.

"Miss," he said softly, steadying his voice, "I won't tell anyone what I found here. But I need you to do something for me." She met his gaze, her expression unreadable, her body beginning to shake.

"Let's go up to your bedroom."

Twenty

IT WAS ABOUT 1400 HOURS when Jackson entered the gasthaus. He spotted Strub and Wilson on the left side of the room. Across from them, the four farmers were just finishing their meal, while the elderly bartender polished glasses behind the bar. Jackson made his way over and sat down with his team.

"Well," Strub remarked, "you took your sweet time, Jack."

"Just enough time, as it turns out," Jackson replied, a hint of arrogance in his voice.

"Want a beer?" asked Wilson.

"No, listen up," Jackson said, lowering his tone. "We've got things to do, and we don't have much time."

"Well, look who's taking charge," Wilson muttered, raising an eyebrow.

Without a word, Jackson reached into his pocket and pulled out the ivory-handled Luger, resting it discreetly on the table under his hand so that the Germans at the other end of the room wouldn't see. It was out of sight from the bartender.

"Jesus," Wilson said, eyes widening. He reached for it, but Jackson kept a firm hold, then pocketed it again, buttoning the flap.

"Where'd you get that?" Strub asked, his voice barely above a whisper.

Jackson smirked. "In the General's house. It was tucked away in a drawer under a towel."

Strub's eyes narrowed with intrigue. "That's an officer's Luger from the First World War—worth a fortune."

"Maybe it is," Jackson replied. "If you want one, pay attention." He glanced meaningfully at the four men. "Follow my lead, keep your hands on your .45s, and just back me up." He stood up.

"Wait, Jack—" Strub started, but Jackson was already moving. Strub and Wilson rose and followed, their hands ready. Jackson strode confidently to the four men, who looked up, surprised. A waitress nearby froze, her tray hovering mid-air.

"Gentlemen," Jackson ordered, his voice low and steady, "on your feet. Now."

The men hesitated, one reaching toward his jacket pocket. Wilson's .45 was drawn in an instant, its barrel aimed directly at the man's chest. Slowly, the four stood, their chairs scraping across the floor.

"Stay very still," Jackson warned, drawing his own .45. With his free hand, he patted down the man who'd reached for his jacket, retrieving a Luger from the pocket and dropping it on the table. He moved to the next man, finding another Luger. Within moments, two German pistols lay on the table.

"Now, sit back down," Jackson said evenly. "You made the right choice. We're here to make sure no one else gets hurt in another war. You holding onto these weapons doesn't help anyone. "

The men sat, their eyes flashing with anger. Jackson could feel their seething resentment as if it were radiating off them.

"Alright, guys," Jackson said to his teammates, "each of you has a Luger now. These farmers won't be causing any trouble. Let's head back to the Jeep."

THE THREE BACKED OUT OF THE BUILDING and climbed into the Jeep, Strub at the wheel. He fired up the engine, and they retraced their route. No one followed them out.

"Man!" Wilson exclaimed from the back seat. "What got into you, Jack?"

Jackson nodded toward the field. "Just keep heading back across that field toward those tanks. I think I may be on to something that'll keep us busy the rest of the day—and maybe well into the future. Stop when we reach the Mercedes."

Within half an hour, they were back in the forest, parked beside the sleek SS staff car.

"Alright, Jack," said Heinrick Strub. "What's come over you? I thought you were this quiet, rule-following soldier. Now you're out here taking charge and giving orders. Not that I'm complaining—just fill us in on what's going on!"

"Is this how a guy acts after finally getting his ashes hauled?" Wilson chimed in, chuckling. Strub winced.

"Here's what happened," Jackson began, his voice low and serious. "I found that Luger, sure, but there's more. Did you notice there were no photos in that house? Not on the piano, the mantel, nowhere in any bedroom. But I found a box of pictures in the basement. One of them shows that 'old General' standing with, get this—*Hermann Göring.*"

The three men paused under the weight of the significance.

"God damn," Strub whispered, his face showing a mix of disbelief and admiration. "So, he *was* some big shot from the First World War and maybe a top player in this one. No wonder he had that pistol. By the way, thanks for the Lugers. I've always wanted one to bring home."

"Glad you like it," Jackson said, leaning forward, his tone sharpening. "But listen carefully: this convoy and those men back in the village aren't here by coincidence. Those four guys posing as farm workers are the same ones who drove these tanks here. I'll bet my life on it. And look at this village—remote, of no strategic importance. So why are they here? I think they're keeping an eye on something, guarding it. Which means there's something valuable nearby. And, gentlemen, we're going to find it. Just follow my lead."

They climbed back into the Jeep.

"Where to, glorious leader?" Strub remarked sarcastically.

"Take us back down the road a bit. I saw something when we passed through earlier," Jackson replied.

With practiced ease, Strub maneuvered the Jeep around the parked vehicles and back onto the trail. They hadn't gone more than a quarter of a mile when Jackson motioned for Strub to stop.

"There it is—a trail branching off to the left. Looks wide enough for a Jeep."

Strub squinted. "This heads straight into the hills. What's the plan?"

"Let's just follow it and see where it leads."

The overgrown track was a bit narrower than the main trail, with young saplings and wild undergrowth springing up around them. Here and there, Jackson noted faint signs of an old path—likely used months, maybe even years ago, as thick grass and undisturbed leaves had since reclaimed the ground. The terrain gradually inclined.

"I hope you know what you're doing, Jack," muttered Wilson, glancing around at the thickening woods. "Feels like we're driving right off the map."

Jackson chuckled. "That's what they wanted."

"That's what WHO wanted?" Wilson shot back, exasperated.

"The people who hid something up here."

Wilson shook his head. "So, what—someone dragged valuable stuff up into these hills just to stash it out of sight?"

"Exactly."

"Jesus, you're nuts. Totally off your rocker," muttered Wilson, though his eyes were fixed ahead, curiosity tugging at him.

They continued on in silence, the Jeep creeping forward at a cautious pace barely faster than a walking man. After ten minutes of steady climbing, Jackson spotted something unusual in the landscape.

They approached a subtle but unmistakable rise that flattened out into a small plateau.

"Stop here," he said.

"What are we looking at?" Strub asked, squinting.

"See that flat area crossing the trail and stretching out to either side? It's man-made. Notice how level it is, and narrow."

Strub leaned forward, following Jackson's gaze. The flattened area stretched to the left, partly obscured by a growth of young trees, while on the right, it continued as a clear, straight path along the hills.

"Jack, what is this?" Strub asked, intrigue evident in his voice.

Jackson nodded. "I think it's an old, abandoned railway bed. See how it's slightly elevated and straight? Likely left over from before or just after the First World War. Look at those trees to the left—they're about twenty-five years old. Germany's economy tanked after the last war, so it'd make sense if they abandoned smaller railway lines and dismantled the tracks."

"So why isn't there any new growth on the right side?" asked Strub.

"Someone's been using this side as a pathway. Let's follow it, see where it leads. Up for a little exploring?"

"I say let's go. Jack, you might have really stumbled onto something," Strub said, shifting the Jeep down onto the old rail bed.

The path was unexpectedly smooth, and they quickly noticed they were approaching a narrow valley entrance cut through the hills. Passing over a tiny ridge, they entered another rocky cut, which deepened until they found themselves facing what looked like the entrance of a tunnel. Strub braked to a halt.

Before them lay a massive pile of rocks, blocking the tunnel entrance. It looked like a cave-in, as if the hillside itself had sloughed off, filling the opening completely. The three men got out of the Jeep and stood there, gazing up at the rocky debris.

"So, what now, hotshot?" Wilson asked. "Planning to just stand here and wish the rocks away?"

Jackson ignored him, stepping forward to examine the pile more closely. He scrambled up the heap, noticing tiny shrubs and fresh grass sprouting from crevices—signs that the rockslide was recent, probably within the past year. As he reached the top, he bent down, clawing at the rocks and shoving them down the slope.

"Look at him, going all mountain goat on us," Wilson muttered. "Jack's on a mission."

Jackson disappeared, swallowed up by the rock pile with a shout that echoed into the tunnel beyond. Strub and Wilson exchanged a glance before scrambling up the fallen rocks themselves, their hearts pounding.

Twenty one

"SOMEONE BRING THE FLASHLIGHT!" Jackson's voice echoed from within the hidden cavity.

"I'll get it," Strub said, hurrying back down the rockpile to the Jeep. He rummaged under the back seat, finding a steel box with emergency supplies—a jack, some flares, a first aid kit, and finally, a flashlight. In a minute, he was climbing back up, and he and Wilson scrambled into the small opening Jackson had created.

What greeted them was almost surreal: a vast, echoing tunnel stretching into the shadows. Carved out of solid rock, the floor was covered with gravel—a lingering trace of the railroad that had once run through it.

"What do you think, Jack?" Strub asked, his voice bouncing off the stone walls.

Jackson surveyed the space, his gaze following the tunnel's darkened stretch. "I think this rock pile was no accident. Someone purposefully blocked off this entrance. Let's go further, see what's down there."

Strub nodded, switching on the flashlight and taking the lead. The gravel crunched underfoot, amplifying the silence around them. They hadn't gone far when something pale appeared against the left wall, barely visible in the beam's sweep. As they neared, they saw a series of large, white sheets pinned to the rock. The tops of the sheets were secured somehow, while the bottoms lay draped over the gravel.

"What is that?" Wilson whispered.

Jackson stepped closer. "If I had to guess, I'd say paintings."

"Paintings?" Strub sounded skeptical. "Why would you say that?"

"When I passed through Paris on the way to the front, I overheard some G.I.s talking about how Göring had looted paintings from the French and the Jews. Word was, he'd stashed valuable pieces all over Europe. And we know the General here was connected to Göring—I saw their photo together."

Strub shot Jackson a doubtful look, then cautiously pulled back a corner of one dusty sheet. Beneath it, hidden from the world, were three large canvases stacked together. The flashlight played over their surfaces, and the soldiers stood in stunned silence, feeling as though they'd just uncovered a treasure chest. They weren't experts, but even they could see these were unlike any art they'd seen before.

Finally, Wilson broke the silence. "Alright, anyone got an idea what we're looking at?"

Strub let out a slow breath, trying to remember what little he knew. "I actually did a couple years of college before I was drafted. I took an art history class. Might be able to make some guesses here…." He focused on the first painting, one with striking red lines. Could it be? Strub stuttered a little for words. "This one…it looks like it could be by a French artist…named Picasso. See here?" He traced a shape in the air with his finger. "The outline kind of forms a bull's head. We looked at a lot of this guy's stuff in class. Picasso was known for capturing complex forms in just a few lines." Strub sucked in a breath of air. "This guy ain't just *some* painter… He's one of the biggest."

"I see it, but man that's weird," said Wilson. "I'm not sure that's art."

Strub tilted his head, admiring the bold, abstract lines in the play of the flashlight. "They say Picasso could capture the essence of something with just a few strokes. This one's special. It's gotta be Picasso."

"If this really is a Picasso, it's no wonder Göring wanted it," said Jackson, running his hand lightly over the edge of the canvas. "But it doesn't even look finished."

"That's the beauty of this guy," Strub replied. "His work wasn't about completion in the traditional sense."

Wilson's gaze shifted to the next canvas, eyes narrowing. "What about this one? Looks kind of blurry, like the guy just smeared paint all over."

Strub grinned. "Jesus...*This is incredible*...Gentleman, if I'm right, what we have here in this cave are paintings by some of the best painters of all time. I'm pretty sure that's a Monet."

"Monay???" Wilson mimicked.

"He was one of the first Impressionists—painted around the end of the nineteenth century. This style, 'Impressionism,' was all about capturing a fleeting moment, the light, and color. I remember one of his most famous paintings looked an awful lot like this one. It was called *Impression Sunrise*—it was a scene of a bridge over the Seine, but this one's got different light, like maybe the light of sunset."

"So you think it's some lost painting?" asked Wilson, squinting at the scene.

"Possibly," Strub said. "He often painted the same scenes at different times of day, capturing light in a way no one had done before. Monet created a whole series on haystacks and the Rouen Cathedral, and art historians believe he painted similar views with different lighting and times of day." Strub paused. "When this comes to light, the art world might lose it."

Wilson snorted. "A lost Monet? I don't know. It looks like a mess. I like details, something I can actually see. I wouldn't hang it in my house, that's for sure."

Jackson chuckled. "Then I bet you won't like this last one over here." He led the men to another canvas—a portrait of a man in a yellow hat, his face built with intense blue and yellow strokes that seemed to radiate from his gaze. The eyes, painted with fierce precision, felt almost alive.

Wilson squinted, mesmerized. "I don't know, Jack... I kinda like this one. The painter went wild with his brush. The guy in the painting looks a little nuts. Who painted this?"

Strub's breath caught. "That...would be Van Gogh." He shook his head, clearly moved. "A Dutch artist who went mad, cut off his own ear, and eventually took his own life. He poured everything into his work."

Wilson shrugged. "Makes sense. I don't know about the art part, but I get what he was feeling. I've felt like that myself back when we were hot footin' it across Bavaria with Patton. I was so goddamn tired and hungry and frustrated, man, when we saw those dead bodies and those starved Jews in the camp, well, I'll bet a lot of guys wanted to kill *themselves* or kill *someone*. Good thing the Germans were handy. I don't think we took many prisoners after seeing that camp."

They stood in silence, the weight of what they'd found settling over them. Finally, Jackson took a deep breath. "Alright, let's sit down and figure out our next move."

Strub glanced down the tunnel, his flashlight catching a glint off a pile of rocks that seemed too deliberately placed. "Wait, Jack. What do you think's under that pile?"

Jackson narrowed his eyes at the mound. "Let's have a look-see."

WILSON MOVED TO the pile, prying rocks off the top with the others watching intently. Strub held the flashlight steady, casting a long shadow over the pile. Wilson was soon down to what looked like a board. Clearing the remaining rocks, he realized it was a wooden box, about two feet by one foot and a few inches thick. He gripped the edges, but it wouldn't budge.

"This thing's heavy as hell," he muttered. Sliding it partway out of the pile to get a better grip, he finally hoisted it up, his muscles straining. He staggered over and accidentally let it drop onto the gravel with a deep thud. The box didn't bust.

"What's in this thing?" he panted, catching his breath. "Anyone got a crowbar?"

"Hold on." Strub unholstered his .45 and, using the butt, began banging on the side boards. After a few hard hits, the cross boards gave way, and with a bit more prying, the lengthwise planks loosened. When the boards finally came free, Strub angled the flashlight to illuminate the contents.

The three men fell silent, transfixed by the sight of gold bars glinting in the flashlight's beam. Wilson pried off the last few boards, uncovering five bars in full, each stamped with a serial number and a sinister Nazi eagle.

Twenty two

JACKSON HESITATED, gathering his thoughts. He could feel the weight of his forming plan pressing down on him, tugging at that familiar instinct he'd honed as a kid. The thrill of filching coins from school bags or pocketing an unclaimed apple from the lunchroom was nothing compared to this, but the skill of looking casual while taking a calculated risk—that he knew. What he was about to say would either bring them together or split them right down the middle. He had to be careful.

"Alright, here's what I'm thinking," he began slowly, his eyes shifting between the two men, gauging their reactions. "I'm gonna take one of these boxes, stash it in the Jeep, and drive it back to the barracks." He paused, letting his words sink in. "On the way, I'll ditch the wood somewhere in the forest. During mess tonight, I'll tuck the bars into my footlocker."

Strub's brow furrowed as he processed what Jackson was suggesting. Wilson's jaw tightened, his boots grinding into the gravel as he shifted his weight. Jackson could sense the hesitation, the silent judgment. It wasn't just a question of money now—it was trust, loyalty, the unspoken code they shared as soldiers. He steeled himself, adding a slight edge to his tone.

"Any objections?"

Wilson was the first to break the silence, but his voice was quieter than usual, uncertain. "How much... how much do you think just one of those boxes is worth?"

Jackson held his gaze, unflinching. "Gold's at least thirty-six bucks an ounce right now. A single bar, ten kilos, would be worth somewhere close to ten grand. That's at least fifty thousand per box. Easy."

Wilson let out a low whistle, his gaze drifting down to the gleaming bars. Strub's expression softened as the numbers sank in, but there was still a flicker of doubt in his eyes.

Jackson clenched his jaw, letting the tension build for a moment. "Look, this isn't just some payday. We've got a lot riding on this. If any of us cracks, the whole thing's sunk."

Finally, Wilson nodded, a glint of resolve in his eye. "Alright," he muttered, his voice steadying. "Then I want a souvenir, too." The money could change his life back home.

Strub hesitated, glancing between Jackson and Wilson, but the lure of the gold was undeniable. He had a family to feed. "Count me in," he murmured.

Jackson gave a curt nod, relief washing over him. "Good. Here's the play. After the morning briefing, we three request a private meeting with the Major. We don't spill everything right away; just hint there's something he really needs to see. We pile into his staff car—him, us, and Sergeant Pena too, if he'll come. We'll drive to the tanks, get him excited over those. Then we lead him here, show him the paintings and the boxes. When he sees the stash, we lay out our terms: immediate honorable discharges, and a ride to Paris so we can catch the next troop ship home."

Strub rubbed his chin, doubtful. "He might balk. That's a big ask."

Jackson grinned, undeterred. "If he does, we'll have a backup. There's a reporter for *Stars and Stripes* over in Berchtesgaden. He's here for coverage on Hitler's Eagle's Nest, so he'd jump at this story. We tell him enough to get him interested, and he'll want to tag along. The Major won't have much choice when the press gets a whiff."

Strub's face lit up. "You're right—this is *Stars and Stripes* front-page material. Once the brass catches wind, they'll want their own piece of this. Hell, we might be famous when we hit the States."

Jackson shook his head. "Europe can keep the fanfare. When we're home, I'm just a rancher. I'll head back, buy myself some land—twenty grand'll get me at least sixty acres with a farmhouse, maybe more. Good farmland in California, best soil around. You boys should come with me, buy your own spreads. We'll live like kings, quiet and rich."

"You know, you can't just waltz into a bank with a gold bar stamped with Nazi symbols, Jack," said Wilson, eyebrows raised.

"You're right, Kemosabe. But there's a guy in Paris—a G.I. told me about him. He's got connections, knows how to make things disappear. He keeps the bars, melts them down to sell, and trades us for U.S. Double Eagle coins. I figure we can line the bottoms of our footlockers with a hundred rolls of Double Eagles, twenty coins each. That'll be about forty thousand dollars per stash. Sure, it's less than the fifty grand they're worth, but the guy's gotta take his cut. It's worth it for clean gold."

The men were quiet, mulling over the plan until Strub finally spoke.

"All right. I'm in—all the way to California."

Wilson nodded, though his expression held a bit of fear. "Yeah, me too. Count me in."

Strub looked at Jackson. "But what's this other piece you're planning to tell the Major? What do you know that we don't, Jack?"

Jackson took a deep breath, realizing that spilling this next part would break more promises than he'd planned on. "You saw that girl at the General's house, right? She's his daughter."

"That's not news," grumbled Strub, looking unimpressed.

"But do you remember the old lady who served us drinks in the gasthaus?"

Wilson's eyes narrowed. "You're not saying…?"

"Yep. She's the General's wife."

Wilson swore under his breath. "How do you know?"

"One of the basement photos. All three of them, together."

"So?" Wilson shrugged. "Still doesn't seem like enough to bring to the Major."

Jackson's voice dropped lower. "That bartender at the gasthaus—the one who manages the place? That's the General himself."

"Jesus H. Christ," Strub whispered, the weight of the revelation sinking in. "Then he was…"

"Yes," said Jackson. "That was his staff car out by those tanks. The Mercedes. I think they're guarding this gold."

"And the paintings for Göring?" said Strub.

"No. Görings at Nuremberg ready for a war crimes trial. He's out of the picture. The paintings are theirs now. With that gold and who knows how many other hidden bunches of tanks and weapons and soldiers, these Huns could start a real takeover of their country after us G.I.s are gone. We'll tell Boccioni about this. He'll be the hero of the occupation and we'll get to go home."

"But didn't you promise that young fräulein you wouldn't tell so you could get into her pants?"

"Screw 'em all. I saw the concentration death camp, too."

Twenty three

THEY TOOK TURNS, two of them hauling each heavy crate, while the other held the flashlight, illuminating the way. Every step up the rock pile was a struggle, the crates digging into their hands, their breaths ragged with the effort. Emerging through the small opening, they scrambled down the rocky slope, sweat trickling in the cool night air, finally loading each box into the Jeep. It took three cumbersome trips; each crate weighed well over a hundred pounds.

They'd decided to take only three unopened boxes, leaving the partially open one atop the remaining stack, just as they'd found it. Carefully, they arranged the stones to obscure the cache, wanting the Major to be as stunned as they'd been by the discovery of Nazi gold.

As they worked, a grim thought passed between them. Where did this gold come from? They all knew the answer, a sickening realization heavy in their silence. Likely, these bars had been melted down from the possessions of Jews—their eyeglasses, cigarette holders, baby cups, bracelets, watches, even gold fillings wrenched from jaws, perhaps from bodies not yet cold. The cold weight in their hands carried the ghostly echoes of lives stolen and burned away.

On the narrow road winding out of the forest, Strub drove while Jackson and Wilson huddled in the back, prying open each crate and tossing the wooden slats into the trees, the fragments scattering like shards of a buried past.

They followed the road into Ravengersberg, heading northeast toward Berchtesgaden. Jackson had heard the *Stars and Stripes* reporter was staying at the Hotel Alpenhof. Strub stopped here and there, asking directions until they finally located the weathered old building.

Inside the reception hall, they learned that Ernie Malden, the lead reporter, was out. Jackson spotted a small desk in the lobby and quickly jotted a note to leave in Ernie's key box:

"Ernie, we've found a cache of Nazi gold and Göring's paintings. Meet us at the barracks at the Berghof at 0900 tomorrow. Come ready to see something big."

Back at the barracks, while the rest of the troops were at evening mess, they parked near their quarters. Wrapping each heavy ingot in their undershirts, they slipped them carefully into their footlockers.

Just in time, they joined the others, grabbing a quick bite, the heavy weight of gold—and secrets—pressing on them in the low din of the mess hall.

THE NEXT MORNING AFTER BREAKFAST, Major Boccioni held his usual briefing. When the session ended, Corporal Strub approached him, requesting a private meeting with their detail. The Major agreed, suggesting they convene in his office.

The three soldiers, dressed in crisp, Class A uniforms pressed and polished the night before, looked every bit the disciplined soldiers. As they made their way outside, Jackson noticed a man by a canvas-topped Jeep in the parking lot and broke away from the group to approach him.

"Are you Malden?"

"Yes, sir. Ernie Malden. You left me a note?"

"I did. Name's Jackson Overstreet. I think you'll be interested in what we've found. Follow me; we're meeting our Major in his office."

Malden, outfitted in a light brown jacket with deep pockets that looked stuffed with gear and a leather camera case slung over one shoulder, exuded a rugged, almost cinematic look of a war correspondent. His broad-brimmed Aussie hat, one side pinned up, added to the effect. Jackson couldn't help but think he looked straight out of Hollywood's take on the frontlines. They rejoined the others, entering the office together.

"Who's this?" Boccioni asked, eyeing Malden.

"This is Ernie Malden from *Stars and Stripes*," Jackson explained. "We think he should be part of this operation."

The Major frowned. "I'd rather he not. Mr. Malden, would you step outside for a moment?"

Strub interjected quickly, "Sir, we believe he should be in on this."

Boccioni narrowed his eyes. "And why is that, Corporal?"

Strub spoke carefully. "Major, what we're about to show you is significant—so much so that we believe you will be recognized for this discovery. We're requesting a small reward for our part in it."

The Major's face reddened. "You're stepping out of line, Corporal. You'll tell me what you have, in private, and that will be the end of it."

"No disrespect intended, sir," Strub replied, keeping his tone measured. "But this discovery could bring you recognition, even a promotion. All we're asking is a straightforward discharge, expedited by you." Jackson watched Strub, admiring his composure; it took guts to speak so directly. Malden, witnessing the exchange, looked equally impressed, eyebrows raised as he observed the standoff.

Boccioni's stare held firm, though his voice softened slightly. "Corporal, this is highly irregular. I'll consider your request, but only after I've seen what you have."

"That's all we're asking, sir," Strub replied. "Respectfully, we've served our time, fought in the war, and now located something vital for the occupation and to your success as commander of this sector."

The Major's face was unreadable as he weighed their words. "Very well. I'll approach this with an open mind." He looked to Malden. "There's unlikely to be anything here the Army wouldn't want the public to know, so Mr. Malden, you're welcome to come along. But please, let's keep this off the record until I say. We'll take my staff car." And then with a deep sigh of resignation, he commanded, "Let's move out."

THE MAJOR HAD ERNIE MALDEN sit up front in the khaki '41 Dodge sedan, with the three soldiers crowded in the back. Strub directed the route, and as they reached the turnoff into the grassy field, the Major hesitated, eyeing the terrain with unease.

"Corporal, you're suggesting I drive into that field?" he asked.

"Yes, sir. You can see our tracks just over there," Strub pointed out. "We've driven the Jeep over this track twice already, and there are other vehicle tracks, too. It's pretty easy—never even needed four-wheel drive."

"I suppose this old Dodge can handle it," Boccioni muttered, pressing the gas. The Dodge, built for rough terrain, rode smoother than the Jeep as they bounced across the field toward the forest edge. But at the tree line, the Major halted again, eyeing the narrow cut ahead.

"Now you're asking us to drive through that?" He leaned forward, scrutinizing the rough forest track. "How the hell did you even find this trail?"

"Corporal Strub is a tank man, sir," Jackson explained. "He recognized the tank tracks right away. So, we followed them."

The Major shook his head but pressed forward, maneuvering the sedan through the trees. About a quarter mile in, they turned left and followed a narrow path until a heap of branches blocked the way. As they drew closer, Boccioni could see the dried leaves were covering something large. He braked, and everyone piled out. Jackson took the lead, uncovering parts of the foliage covering the armored vehicle.

Major whistled. "These are German tanks," he said, incredulous as he walked closer. "You men found these things hidden on your first day out?"

"Yes, sir," Strub answered. "It was a bit of luck—and some sharp eyes."

Boccioni walked along the length of the first tank, then the second, before spotting the halftrack scout vehicle. "Malden, snap some pics, would ya?"

Jackson flashed Strub a knowing look.

Finally, the Mercedes came into view, its SS insignias still visible on the side.

Malden, whose shutter began to click furiously, turned to the soldiers. "Why exactly were you men out here looking for these tanks?" he asked, glancing up from his camera.

Jackson replied, "Our mission is to seek out and secure German equipment that could be used to restart the war. We were doing just that."

The Major nodded thoughtfully. "When we return, I'll send a Detail out to collect these. The halftrack alone is rare—most were destroyed during the war. And that Mercedes…with a paint job, I could use it as my own vehicle. Either that or have it completely destroyed." He laughed, seemingly half-serious.

Malden raised an eyebrow. "Any idea who drove these here?"

"Yeah, that's a good question," said the Major, turning to the soldiers.

"We do," said Strub, giving Jackson a look. "So, Major…if finding these tanks isn't enough for you to consider our discharge, would knowing where the drivers are make a difference?"

Boccioni's eyes narrowed. "That's still your job, Corporal."

Jackson met his gaze, voice steady. "And what if one of those drivers is a high-ranking Waffen SS General?"

Boccioni paused, considering. Malden, clearly intrigued, muttered, "Now *that* would be a story."

"Stay out of this, Malden," Boccioni snapped, then turned back to Strub. "But if you're telling the truth about a Waffen SS General, I'll have to think about your request."

"Can you tell me, Major," Malden asked, "In your words, why is it so important to go after the Waffen SS? And what does 'Waffen' even mean?"

"I thought you war correspondents knew everything," the Major replied, his tone tinged with sarcasm. "You've been up to the Berghof right—seen Hitler's little hideaway."

"Yes, but Hitler hadn't been there since '43," Malden said, unfazed. "He set up his command in Poland after invading Russia."

Boccioni nodded. "Well, according to intelligence, which has combed through his papers both here and in the Berlin bunker, the SS was meant to be the police force of a post-war Germany, enforcing the rule of the Nazi party. 'Waffen' just means 'military' or 'armed,' so the Waffen SS was the Nazi party's military branch—dedicated soldiers, not just regular troops. Likely, this hidden task force is here so the SS could establish their control over the people after the Allies were defeated."

"Thank you, sir," Malden said, scribbling a few notes on a weathered pad. "It helps to understand more of what our role is here with the occupation. If you don't mind my asking, where were you before all this?"

"I was Deputy Base Commander at Beale Air Field near Sacramento. They pulled me out of there and sent me here," the Major said. "I never saw combat."

"Excuse me, Major," Jackson interjected. "We have something important to add."

Walden and Boccioni turned simultaneously to look at Jackson.

"You know that Mercedes? We figured it could only have been the property of an SS general. So, we worked on tracking him. He's closer than we thought, sir," Jackson said, his voice low and deliberate. "He's got a house in Ravengersberg, right past the gasthaus. It's well-known there—locals "claim" the general died in the war, even his own daughter and a young boy in the village, keep up the story. He and his wife are running the local gasthouse" Jackson paused, glancing at Strub and Wilson before continuing. "He's been hiding in plain sight."

"There were four German soldiers hanging out in the gasthaus, too. They're posing as farm workers in that same town," Strub added. "But none of them look or act like men who've worked a field. We figure they drove these tanks here. They're stationed close by, keeping to themselves, probably waiting for orders." Strub chided, "I half expected them to be here today, what with us snooping around. They must not be worth a damn."

Jackson finished, "Sir, this isn't a coincidence. They've all been living here, just below the radar, keeping up the facade while the villagers help keep their secrets."

The Major raised his brows. "Well, sounds like you men have been busy."

"Busy enough for a discharge?" Wilson asked, hopeful.

The Major shrugged. "Depends... Anything more?"

Strub stepped in. "Jackson here put two and two together and figured out the real reason these tanks are hidden here and that those soldiers are so nearby. It's not that they're ready to be a future police force... He suggested *they are guarding something.*" Strub paused for effect, knowing he was about to reveal their grand finale. "So, we followed another trail we found nearby. Major, if you're ready, we'll take the staff car and show you."

"Jesus," the Major replied. "I guess let's saddle up."

STRUB HAD THE MAJOR BACK UP a bit and then take a sharp right onto the overgrown trail, heading slightly uphill. Branches scraped along the Dodge's sides, leaving faint smears of dust and bits of foliage stuck to the windows.

"How did you find this road?" asked the Major, squinting out the windshield at the narrowing path. "No way a tank could make it up here—it's far too tight."

"Thank Jack here," said Strub, nodding at Jackson. "He kept scanning for hidden trails until he spotted this one."

The car fell silent as they bumped along the rough track, with only the sound of the engine and the occasional crackle of underbrush snapping under the wheels. Finally, they reached a turn where the trail split.

"I guess we have to follow the path to the right," Boccioni said. "This looks different. What happened here?"

"It's an old railway line, sir," Strub replied. "But it looks like it hasn't been used since before the first war."

"You'll find plenty of these abandoned railways all over Germany," Malden chimed in from the front seat. "After the Great War, the economy collapsed, and Germany's industry was nearly wiped out. The Treaty of Versailles stripped them down to the bone. When Hitler got things rolling again they started building war machines in violation of the treaty. You take up the rails of this here track and you could build a very nice battleship. Maybe this track turned into the Tirpitz. Who knows?"

"Then that metal's likely rusting at the bottom of the ocean," said Boccioni with a grim smile. "We sank that beast. At least this road's a bit smoother now."

"Whoa," he shouted suddenly, braking hard. A pile of rocks loomed in front of them, blocking what once appeared to be the entrance to a tunnel, as if the earth itself had swallowed the railway.

"That's no natural cave-in," Strub pointed out. "It's been blocked on purpose."

Jackson chimed in. "We're getting out of here."

Malden, peering through the windshield, shook his head. "You found all this just yesterday? You guys have been busy."

"And that's after a few beers at the Ravengersberg gasthaus," joked Wilson with a grin.

"Served to us," Jackson added, "by none other than the SS General himself. How's that for a twist?"

"Now that's a headline," Malden muttered, visibly impressed. "I'll be writing this up tonight, trust me."

"Not so fast," Strub chuckled. "Bring your flashlight, Major. Wait till you see what's in this tunnel..."

Twenty four

THE MAJOR, A TOWERING FIGURE with broad shoulders, had no trouble scrambling up the rock pile, squeezing through the narrow opening at the top with surprising agility. Soon, he and the others were standing in front of the shrouded canvases, bathed in dim, flickering flashlight beams.

"This," said Corporal Strub, his voice low and charged, "isn't something you see every day. Wilson, take off the sheets."

As Wilson pulled back the dusty white coverings, a stunned silence settled over the group. The Major and Malden stared, wide-eyed, before the Major finally exhaled a breathless, "My God... This must be part of Göring's stolen art collection. Gentlemen, this is... well, ten out of ten doesn't even cover it. Imagine the headlines when these are finally returned to where they belong."

"Absolutely," Malden agreed, already preparing in his mind how he'd write the story. "It's going to be front-page news. It'll shake the art world and beyond."

"Maybe not so fast," Strub interrupted quietly, shaking his head. "Sir, I don't think these were ever in the Louvre or the Jeu de Paume, or any museum, really. They've probably been hidden from the public all along."

The Major frowned, his curiosity piqued. "And what makes you so sure of that, Corporal?"

"Just a hunch, sir, but it's based on some facts. I took a few art history courses in college, and none of these were ever mentioned. It's possible they weren't even documented, probably held privately, maybe by Jewish families here in Germany or France. Taken when those families were, well… you know, sent to the camps. If they were stolen from private collections, they'll be claimed—if any relatives remain, they'll want them back."

The Major nodded slowly, a look of somber understanding crossing his face. "Either way, Corporal, what you've found here is monumental. I'd bet General Patton will personally commend you."

"Count on it," Malden said with enthusiasm. "This story's going to ripple all the way to the States. I'd wager you three will be in Paris for the unveiling, maybe even meet President Truman himself."

Strub seized the opportunity. "In that case, Major, a discharge to head stateside wouldn't be too much to ask, would it?"

The Major hesitated, about to respond when Malden jumped in.

"Hey, I'll bet they could get you a ride back on a B-17 out of England," he suggested. "They're sending them to the Pacific to bomb Japan—could be your ticket home. And gentlemen, after what you've found here, you might even get an invitation to the White House."

The Major took a final, scrutinizing look at the uncovered paintings. "Tell me, Corporal, what exactly are we looking at here?"

Strub stepped closer to the canvases, his eyes bright with excitement. "Well, I'm no expert but I think these are incredible. The first one, with the bold red lines? I'm pretty sure it's a Picasso. I think even folks outside the art world have heard of him."

The Major grunted, clearly not understanding what he was looking at. "Sorry, Corporal, but this isn't exactly my style."

"Mine either," Wilson muttered, chuckling. "Not much for these modern types."

Malden, however, was enthralled. "And that's a Van Gogh self-portrait, isn't it?" he asked, eyes fixed on the intense, haunted gaze that seemed to follow him from the canvas.

"It is," Strub confirmed, "Van Gogh did several, but this one really captures something… raw."

Malden nodded, captivated. "It's stunning. And that last one—definitely an Impressionist."

"Right," Strub said, looking reverently at the shimmering hues. "That's a Monet. Signature confirms it. We studied his 'Impression Sunrise' in class. This one looks just like it but it seems like it was painted at sunset. I think it's 'Waterloo Bridge.' If this hits the public, especially the art historians, it'll make waves like nothing else."

"Malden," the Major said, turning with a note of urgency, "let's get some photos of these paintings right here. Then we'll carefully load them into the car and take them back to the barracks."

Malden held up his camera. "Got it covered, Major. I've got a flash with me. Let's make history."

"Better wait, Major," said Jackson.

"What? There's more?"

"Let's go a little deeper in the tunnel, sir."

"This is nuts, you guys. Don't tell me there are more pictures."

"Nope, but you'll like what else we found. You won't be able to get it in your car. You'll need a truck."

"MAJOR, STAND RIGHT THERE. Ernie, just a step to the right," directed Strub, adjusting the angle of his flashlight. Major Boccioni, holding the other flashlight, looked impatient.

"Alright, Corporal, what exactly am I supposed to be looking at? I see rocks and a tunnel wall," he said, his tone edged with irritation.

"Jack, why don't you fetch one for the Major?" Strub suggested, a glint of anticipation in his voice.

"On it, Corporal." Jackson moved to the far end of the pile, shifting a few rocks aside with practiced ease. In the dim light, it seemed as though he had picked up nothing more than a small brick.

"Here, Major," Jackson said, stepping forward. "You might want to brace yourself—Ernie, take his flashlight. He'll need both hands."

Boccioni reached out, and the ingot nearly slipped through his grasp as its unexpected weight bore down on his palms. "Good God!" he muttered, steadying himself. "This thing weighs a ton. What is it?"

"Ernie, shine the light here," Strub instructed, and the beam bounced off the polished yellow surface, casting flecks of reflected light along the tunnel walls. There, stamped in stark relief, was the Nazi swastika.

"That, Major," Strub said quietly, "is pure gold—ten kilos of it. What you're holding might be all that's left of the lives of some of the six million Jews exterminated here in Europe. You're holding history in your hands, sir."

Malden, who hadn't taken his eyes off the scene, asked in a hushed voice, "Corporal, would you mind if I used that quote in my *Stars and Stripes* article?"

"Be my guest."

THAT EVENING AT SIX, Ernie managed to secure a phone link with the *Stars and Stripes* office in Paris. He read his report word for word as it was transcribed, edited, and rushed to print for the next edition. By eleven, the story went to press, and by dawn, trucks and planes began dispersing copies across Europe. A fresh bundle of newspapers was tossed off at the barracks by ten the following morning.

The headline read:

Jewish Holocaust Gold and Lost Masterpieces
Found in Berchtesgaden Tunnel
By Ernie Malden

A hidden cache, believed to be among the last remnants of wealth stolen from six million Jews during the Holocaust, was discovered yesterday in an abandoned railroad tunnel near Berchtesgaden. Leading the mission was Major Gerald Boccioni, commander of occupation forces in the area. The discovery was made by Unit Six, consisting of Corporal Heinrick Strub and Privates Wilson Carter and Jackson Overstreet, who unearthed an incredible trove: priceless works by Van Gogh, Picasso, and Monet, along with Nazi-confiscated gold bars.

The four soldiers will be awarded medals at Supreme Headquarters in Paris on Wednesday at ten hundred hours, with Generals George C. Marshall, George S. Patton, and General Charles de Gaulle slated to attend. Afterward, they will travel back to the United States for further commendation, and a much deserved release from duty.

Twenty five

THE B-17 BOMBER droned over the Atlantic, en route to New Jersey. Colonel Boccioni, newly promoted to full bird colonel after the Nazi gold discovery, was up in the cockpit chatting with the pilots. In the main body of the plane, the three soldiers—also promoted during the Paris ceremony—sat on makeshift seats where waist gunners typically stood. The noise from the engines was nearly deafening, and each man clutched his leather flight jacket tight against the biting cold that sliced through the high-altitude cabin.

A day after their discovery made headlines in *Stars and Stripes*, they'd been flown to Paris in a C-45. While General Patton had greeted them personally, neither General Marshall nor De Gaulle had attended. Instead, a senior sergeant had handed them their discharge papers, freeing them from duty. Now, their footlockers—each unusually heavy—were stowed in the bomb bay, packed with rolls of gold coins. The dealer Jackson had found in Paris had converted their shares, taking a sizable cut but leaving each soldier with over forty thousand dollars in US gold coins."Guys!" Strub shouted over the roar of the engines, looking both excited and uneasy. "They're sending us to Washington for more decorations. I don't like it—it's too much attention. Someone might just check out our footlockers."

Jackson nodded, leaning in to be heard. "I thought about that. Once we touch down at Fort Dix, I'm arranging my own transport—quietly—to Grand Central Station. Then, I'll catch a train straight to Sacramento. Time to disappear."

Wilson leaned forward, grinning. "I'm in. Soon as I get to Alabama and pick up my wife and kid, I'll head for California. You think you could find a small farm for us?"

Jackson gave him a reassuring nod. "Easy peasy."

"Count me in, too," Strub added. "My wife and kids are near New Orleans, but I'll meet you both out West. I'm not sticking around for questions I don't wanna answer."

"They'll be mad we don't show up in Washington," said Wilson, "but they can't do a damn thing. We're civilians now."

Strub grinned. "They can kill us, but they can't eat us—that's against the law." They all laughed, the tension breaking, if only for a moment.

When they touched down at Fort Dix, Strub approached a corporal refueling the B-17. For two twenty-dollar gold pieces, the corporal agreed to drive them to New York in his Plymouth coupe.

And just like that, the three disappeared into the vast hinterland of America, gold in hand, futures unknown.

PART IV

CHARLIE RETURNS TO TREMONTON

Twenty six

CHARLIE SAT ON A HILL in the shade of a eucalyptus tree, watching the boys arrive for the fall semester at Webb School. His parents, La Rue and Winifred, had dropped him off around noon, helped him settle into his small, single room, given him a brisk farewell, and driven off in the Lincoln Continental. He felt a hollow ache as he watched them leave. This might just be the worst day of his life—if not for the discovery that there would be football practice at three. That glimmer of familiarity offered some comfort as the hollow halls and towering brick buildings loomed around him.

Sure enough, at three, he made his way to the gym and was handed pads, pants, a jersey, and even a pair of black cleated high-topped football shoes. Awkwardly, he figured out how to strap on the bulky gear, and then jogged out onto the field just as the coach started barking for wind sprints. Charlie didn't know if it was adrenaline or the built-up frustration of the day, but his legs pumped like pistons, and he realized, along with everyone else, that he was the fastest kid on the field.

The tackling drills only cemented his first impression—he was a natural, bringing down even the senior running backs with unerring precision. And any ball tossed his way found a place squarely in his hands. By Friday, he was promised playing time in the upcoming scrimmage against Chino Boys Reform School. Charlie couldn't wait to get on the field.

But Monday hit him hard. The school's academic schedule was as punishing as its athletics. English, History, Algebra, and Latin droned on one after the other. After lunch came Biology, and his head swam with facts and dates and conjugations. Then, on Thursday, he found a neatly folded notice in his mailbox informing him he'd been assigned a tutoring session with Howell Webb, the headmaster's son, at four o'clock Friday—right in the middle of their first scrimmage.

Charlie dismissed the note immediately. He had other priorities. On Friday, he suited up with the rest of the team and took his place on the bench, waiting for his turn on the field. The coach had promised him a spot as soon as they got possession, and he sat, tense with anticipation.

Suddenly, a heavy hand landed on his shoulder. Charlie turned to see the campus security guard looming over him, his uniform giving him an air of false authority.

"Mr. Holmes, come with me."

"No!" Charlie shot back, bracing himself, but the guard twisted his arm behind his back, forcing him to his feet. The pain was sharp, and before he knew it, he was marched off the field, through the library courtyard, and toward a cottage covered in ivy. The guard opened the door and gave him a rough push inside.

"Ah, Mr. Holmes, you finally made it." Howell Webb, dressed in a paisley smoking jacket, an ascot at his neck, tweed trousers, and polished brown slippers, looked up from a leather armchair. The room was dimly lit, smelling faintly of old books and tobacco. Across from him, a record player spun, filling the room with orchestral strains. "Sit," he instructed, gesturing to the leather chair opposite.

Charlie sank into the seat, feeling trapped. Webb held up a finger, silencing him, and proceeded to wave his arms in time with the music, lost in the crescendo of the symphony as though directing an unseen orchestra.

Music hummed softly from the record player before him, and Charlie couldn't believe what he was seeing. The machine looked like something from a sci-fi movie—sleek, modern, with a record bigger than any he'd ever seen spinning at a slow, almost hypnotic speed. His father had a Victrola at home that played much smaller records, crackling away at 78 rpm, each record needing a new needle and powered by a hand crank. The sound came from a tiny, tinny speaker attached to the arm. But this? This machine had no crank. It ran on electricity, and the music poured from two large speakers set on either side, filling the room with a deep, rich sound.

The music seemed endless. The needle barely crept its way across the record, and Charlie squirmed uncomfortably in his football gear, the pads pressing awkwardly into the leather chair. Howell Webb, still conducting an imaginary orchestra, turned to him during a lull. "This is the latest in high fidelity," he whispered with a gleam in his eye. "Shhh. Listen—can you hear that deep string bass?" Howell looked so enraptured that for a second Charlie thought he'd laugh. But he only nodded, forcing himself to stay still. He'd heard of classical music, but it was his dad's Victrola that had shaped his ear with old tunes like "Don't Sit Under the Apple Tree" and "South of the Border Down Mexico Way." His friend Howard Flood had a tiny radio, and they would sit on his porch listening to country music, Hank Williams and the twang of steel guitars. To Charlie, those were songs with life in them. But this? This was torture.

As the music continued to drone, Charlie's mind wandered to everything he already hated about Webb School. He hated that his parents had chosen Webb over Tremonton. He hated his classes, especially Latin. He hated the chapel Vespers on Sundays, when he had to wear a coat and tie and sit in solemn rows. He hated the dining hall's blue-patterned china and the long, stiff dinners in jackets and ties. Afterward, there was the two-hour study hall where he would sit with a hundred other boys, staring blankly at his history book, half-listening to the drone of termite wings as they fluttered out of holes in the floor. It pleased him to imagine the old school building being eaten to the ground by those termites. Mostly, though, he hated that right now, a game was being played—and he wasn't on that field.

Without another thought, Charlie stood. Howell looked at him, eyebrows raised, and Charlie held up a single finger, as if to say, "Just a minute, please." Then, without a word, he walked out the door. He figured Howell had about five minutes of music left on that record before he'd come looking for him. He sprinted to the gym, tore off his uniform, leaving it scattered in his locker, and slipped into his jeans, shirt, and tennis shoes. He shot back to his room, grabbed his jacket and his mother's alarm clock, and then made his way to the bicycle rack outside. He found one without a lock, mounted it, and pedaled down the front path, out the school gate, and onto an avenue that led downhill toward the town of Upland, lined with towering palm trees.

Charlie parked the bike at the Greyhound bus stop, hiding inside until the next bus to Los Angeles arrived. By 6 a.m. Saturday morning, he was on the streets of Stockton, a thrill of freedom pulsing through him as he started his long jog eastward. Tremonton lay just fifteen miles away.

CHARLIE NEVER LEARNED what happened back at Webb School after he left. When he didn't show up for dinner, Howell Webb, rising with his usual air of authority at the faculty table, tapped his glass with a spoon to bring the room to order. His voice cut through the murmur of conversation. "Does anyone know the whereabouts of Charles La Rue Holmes?"

Silence settled over the room. None of the boys dared answer.

After a tense minute, the football coach pushed back his chair, rising from his place at the far end of the table. He walked the length of the room, coming to stand behind Howell Webb, then leaned over to whisper into his ear. "Why did you pull Holmes out of the game?"

"Sit down, sir," Howell replied, his tone clipped. "Holmes was falling behind in English. He required tutoring."

"Not during a game," the coach's voice tightened.

"Academics come first, Coach."

The coach's expression darkened. "Let me tell you something, Howell. That Holmes boy might be the best football player Webb's ever seen." The coach looked around, shoulders slumping. "I bet ya, he's never coming back."

Twenty seven

CHARLES HITCHED A RIDE FROM TREMONTON, hopping out near Howard Flood's place. When he knocked on the door, Howard himself answered, his eyes widening.

"Charlie! Man, what're you doing here? I thought you were stuck in L.A. at that fancy school!"

They stepped into the living room, which still had the fresh, polished look of a recent rebuild—new since the Floods' old house had burned down back in '44.

"Dad's out irrigating, and Mom's in the kitchen fixing dinner. You staying?"

Charlie nodded, feeling slightly cowardly. "I ran away from that caca school down south. My folks don't know yet. I figured if I hide out here long enough, it'll be too late to send me back. I can even pitch in if your mom'll let me stay. Maybe two, three weeks? What do you say?"

Howard grinned. They'd been friends since Charlie was about to start first grade, back when Howard was a big-shot second-grader at Merchant Creek School. With its mixed-age classrooms, kids there could work at their own pace, and it turned out that Charlie and Howard had ended up graduating together, becoming closer than ever.

"You know she'll let you stay," Howard said with a laugh. "She's still talking about how your dad rebuilt this place. We owe you guys."

"Where's your dad?" asked Charlie, looking around.

"He's out irrigating for old man Doffelmeyer. He's Doffelmeyer's only ditch man now, so he's working weird hours. But it's more money," Howard said, leading Charlie into the kitchen as Mrs. Flood's voice called out from the next room.

"Boys! Dinner's ready—don't let it get cold!"

They took seats at the small, crowded table. There was no dining room in the Flood house, but the kitchen was warm and filled with the smell of baked bread and stew. Mrs. Flood, draped in a wide apron over her yellow, flower-printed dress, moved with surprising ease for her size. Charlie remembered hearing how she was one of the best packers at Blue Anchor, her hands as quick and sure as any, despite her large frame.

"Thank you, Mrs. Flood. Howard told you? Can I stay awhile, if it's alright with you? My parents are really busy right now and they'd love the help."

She raised her brows but gave a nod, sitting down at the head of the table. "You're welcome to stay as long as you need, Charles. After all, your father built this house, didn't he?" She smiled, passing the bread. "About time you got to stay here a bit yourself."

Charlie managed a grin, even as memories of that summer flooded back—the stolen payroll from Beale Air Base, the soldiers who'd burned the Flood house, and how he'd finally returned most of the money to Major Boccioni. Only he and Howard knew how the rebuild had been paid for, and now, he had a safe place to stay while he figured out his next move.

CHARLIE SETTLED IN AT THE FLOODS' and caught the school bus from Howard's each morning. Monday marked the start of school at Tremonton High, and as soon as he walked into the building, word spread fast—Charlie was back. By lunchtime, plans were set for a gathering the next Sunday afternoon at their favorite spot by the Indian rock.

That afternoon, Charlie showed up for his first practice with the freshman football team, coached by Mr. Bush, who also taught math. California high schools had three football teams: the varsity team for the top players, the B team for smaller players, and the freshman team, open only to first-year students. Occasionally, a standout freshman might make B team or even varsity, but it was rare.

By the end of the week, Charlie had quickly made his mark. His speed and experience—thanks to the week at Webb and all the play at Merchant Creek—put him leagues ahead of the other freshmen. In blocking drills, he hit harder; he threw and punted farther with pinpoint accuracy. By Friday, he had secured the halfback position on the freshman team.

In the classroom, he discovered he had a head start there, too, especially in Algebra and Latin, despite barely cracking a book down south. Compared to his classmates at Tremonton, he felt like he was a step ahead.

Each afternoon after practice, Charlie hitched rides back to the Floods' in time for dinner since Howard, who wasn't into football, headed straight home on the school bus.

On Tuesday evening, knowing his parents would be out at their bridge group—this time hosted by the Cosarts—he snuck over to the house to gather some clothes and his bike. The Holmes house was never locked, so he slipped in easily.

That Monday, Charlie's sister Carolyn, who was a senior, had spotted him during morning recess. She'd wasted no time, grabbing his arm and steering him away from the crowd around the little candy shop.

"Charlie! What on earth are you doing here?" she whispered, looking around.

He grinned, half expecting her surprise. "Hey, sis! Listen, don't say a word, okay? I couldn't stand Webb. It was horrible. So I left.

Took the bus up here Friday night and now I'm staying with Howard."

Carolyn raised an eyebrow, trying to hide her smile. "So you just... ran away?"

"Exactly. And trust me, I'm not going back. Let the folks find out when they find out—but please, keep it quiet, alright?"

"Well, Webb School called and Dad knows you took off. He's mad as hell...He figured you're hiding out with some of your friends...Shoot, brother, I won't say anything," she whispered, pulling him into an unexpected hug. They hadn't hugged like that in a while, not really. But now, with this secret binding them, something had shifted. Carolyn had her own defiant streak—she smoked, and plenty of kids did too, but if La Rue or Winifred ever found out, there'd be hell to pay. He'd known she rebelled against their parents' expectations and figured she always would. It was something he couldn't fully understand; as the middle child, he was mostly overlooked, but Carolyn, as the oldest, bore the brunt of their rules. Meanwhile, Johnny, the youngest, practically had free rein, and their parents simply chuckled.

"I figure a teacher's gonna tell 'em. Or one of these kids is bound to spill it to their parents, and then I'm busted," he said, giving her a sly grin. "But the longer I stay hidden, the harder it'll be for them to make me go back to that place."

Carolyn nodded. "Got it, little brother... Hey, scratch that—you're not so little anymore. Seems like you've shot up another inch since last week." She laughed, giving him a playful shove. "Glad to have you back, baby boy. So you're out for football, huh?"

"Yep, on the freshman team," he said proudly.

"Well, Daddy goes to every game. He's in for a big surprise."

THE HILLTOP AIR WAS THICK with late-summer heat, and the dry, yellow grass prickled their skin as they lay sprawled, laughing and taking in the freedom of being together. They were a motley crew, and Charlie soaked in every moment, knowing this might be one of the last times they'd all be together like this.

"God, it's good to have you back, you bastard," Don Don said, chewing on a grass stem, his words dripping with a playful ease. "How's football?"

Charlie grinned. "I think I've got a shot at varsity."

Don Don raised a brow, his grass stem wobbling between his teeth. "No one makes varsity as a freshman."

"No one does that," said Geneva. "You're just a measly freshman. Hoy tells me the varsity team might win their league this year. He says Garner Vickers is the best triple threat man in the Valley." While Charlie was away at camp in the summer, Geneva had started to date Harold Martin. He first attracted her attention because he had a motor scooter.

"What position are you thinking you'll get, then?" Dianne leaned in, her smirk daring him.

"Triple threat," Charlie replied simply, staring down Geneva.

Don Don snorted. "Triple threat is Vickers' slot. No way he's giving that up to some 'measly freshman.'"

"Well, I think he might," Charlie said. "I'm faster, I kick farther, and honestly… I throw a cleaner pass."

"Like fun," said Geneva. "He is bigger than you and the coach loves him, so says Hoy."

Charlie looked down, pretending to consider it. "I'll just have to see what I can do to change that."

Don Don let out a bark of laughter. "Wouldn't bet against you, Chuck. Haven't you guys noticed? This man doesn't quit until he gets what he's after."

"Yeah, but he's just a freshman," Dianne protested, rolling her eyes.

"Maybe so," Don Don replied, grinning. "But he's *our* freshman." They all laughed, the sound echoing up toward the treetops.

Charlie leaned back on his elbows, clearing his throat with mock seriousness. "Now that I've got you all here, we've got some things to discuss."

"Oh, let me guess," Dianne said, feigning shock. "You wanna talk about how you can't feel up Geneva anymore! Hoy would beat the living crap out of you."

Don Don laughed. "You even try and I'll tell Harold, and we'll all see if you're as fast as you say you are."

Charlie forced a laugh but felt a pang. His eyes drifted to Geneva, who looked away with a faint smile, a flicker of their past unspoken. It stung more than he'd thought it would. He'd been crazy about her—maybe even loved her, as much as a fourteen-year-old could. That was a question for another day.

"I KNOW IT'S NOT FUN TO THINK ABOUT, but in all seriousness, I want to talk about Louise. I have some new information," Charlie said, breaking the easy flow of conversation. His voice was low, almost hesitant, as if he were still struggling to say her name aloud. "I didn't have much time before my folks shipped me down south, but I managed to talk to Mrs. Jackson and to Morris Erickson, the mortician who took care of her body."

Geneva's voice quivered. "I cried. I cried for a month straight. She should be here with us right now. She was my girl…she was going to be someone, you know?"

"She would have been," said Diane, a touch of fierce pride in her voice. "Louise was brilliant. She knew everything. She would've gone to Stanford, maybe even been president one day. Someday she was going to write a book, paint a masterpiece, discover a new species—heck, she'd probably have raised a general for the country." Diane's voice grew soft, like she was saying goodbye all over again.

"And she was a hell of a jock," added Don Don. "She could ride circles around us on her bike, beat us all at Fresher, always won at Kick-the-Can."

Charlie nodded. "That's exactly what I wanted to talk about. Her bike riding."

Diane's voice barely broke above a whisper. "It's what got her killed."

Charlie shook his head, his gaze steady. "No, I don't think so. Morris told me he was there when they brought her bike out from under the rocks on the north side of that bridge. He said you could've ridden away on it right then and there—no bent frame, nothing damaged. The front tire was in perfect shape."

Geneva frowned, her voice trembling. "If she didn't crash into the bridge, then how did she end up in the water?"

Charlie's voice hardened. "I think someone killed her. Threw her in the river afterward—and her bike, too."

They all fell silent, the weight of his words pressing down like the heat of the late summer sun. Finally, Don Don spoke, trying to add some levity but failing. "That's why we're here, isn't it, Charlie? You've got some crazy plan up your sleeve. You're gonna rope us into something that could get us tossed off that bridge, aren't you?"

"I don't have a plan yet," Charlie said, his jaw set. "But I'd bet anything that guy near Orosi, that Jackson Overstreet—the one she was watching—he's the one who did it."

"Then," said Diane, "We should stay away from him, never go near his place, shut up about our suspicions. If he can kill the Strubs and that family over there near Orosi then what about a bunch of meddling high school kids? Nope, don't get us killed too, Charles Holmes."

Charlie's gaze was unyielding. "I think he's also the one who tried to kill my father. I can't just stay quiet."

Don Don shook his head, a wary smile on his face. "And that tells you what, exactly?"

"It's why I asked you all to come here. But don't worry, this is my fight—I'll take care of it."

THEY TROMPED DOWN THE HILL AFTERWARD, the tension melting away in the heat as they frolicked toward the road. The scent of dry grass filled the air, and Charlie felt a pang of longing for his friend Louise and his old girl, Geneva. They vaulted over the fence, mounting their bikes, everyone but Charlie turning north as he continued west. Soon he was riding past his family's house, pedaling on until he reached the Floods' place.

His heart beat hard as he remembered what he'd said on the hill. He'd put himself out there, talking big. Not only about football but about taking care of the entire Overstreet situation. Deep down, he didn't know how he'd pull any of it off, or even if he could. For now, he could only hope he'd find a way.

SCHOOL AND FOOTBALL PRACTICE soon filled Charlie's every waking moment. Balancing it all—avoiding his parents, hiding out at the Floods', and tackling the heat and grit of practice—was exhausting, but he didn't mind one bit. Football felt like a natural rhythm to him, and he loved every second of it: the crunch of tackles, the camaraderie with the other boys, the respect for the coach, and the thrill of learning new plays.

The following Monday brought an unexpected surprise. After Friday's scrimmage, Coach Bush had pulled Charlie aside to share some exciting news.

"You're moving up to varsity, Charles," Coach Bush said with a grin.

"But…what about B Class, Coach? Isn't that where freshmen usually head?" Charlie asked, wide-eyed.

Coach's expression was serious. "I had a long talk with Coach Terry this weekend, and he believes you've got what it takes. You'll be backing up Garner Vickers at tailback. He's seen how you pass, how you run. You're varsity material."

That meant a new playbook—and a steep learning curve. Tremonton High ran out of the old Ohio State single-wing formation, a bit of a throwback, even for the early fifties. Up at Berkeley, the University of California had just started using the T-Formation, but for now, that innovation had mostly reached the bigger Bay Area schools.

Practice with the varsity was intense. Charlie spent hours running single-wing formations, scrimmaging against the first string, learning to anticipate their every move. And it didn't take long for his teammates to take notice. When Charlie ran the ball, he had a natural, elusive stride that made him hard to catch, slicing through the defense for big gains. And even with limited experience and less reliable receivers, he was completing passes with surprising accuracy.

Time blurred in the haze of school, practice, and the anticipation of game day. Soon enough, it was Friday, and Tremonton High's season opener was upon them. They were set to face Tracy High, a formidable team from Modesto County. It wasn't a league game, but Tracy was a regional powerhouse, and Tremonton was expected to be outmatched.

Charlie, though, was ready. This was what he'd been waiting for.

SUITED UP IN HIS FRESH, clean game jersey, Charlie joined his teammates outside the gym, adrenaline coursing through him. Together, they burst onto the field, greeted by scattered applause. The evening air hung warm and still.

Garner Vickers led the team in a lap around the field before guiding them through drills. On the south end, Tracy's squad—last year's league champions—moved through their own routines, their players looking big and focused. As the stadium filled with family, friends, and loyal fans, the stands buzzed with anticipation. The Tremonton team ran a final drill, settling into rhythm, while the Tracy squad eyed them carefully.

Charlie, the only freshman on the team, settled onto the bench beside Pat Berry, his fellow Merchant Creek alum, fully expecting to watch from the sidelines. He knew small-town boys from outside the main town were rarely seen as varsity material, especially freshmen. But he was just happy to be part of it, watching his first high school game from the sidelines, the sounds of the crowd and the thrill of the game filling the air around him.

Charlie spotted his father, La Rue, on the sidelines among the other Tremonton men. La Rue, a former Nebraska captain and triple threat as well, was likely offering his detailed play-by-play to his friends. In years past, Charlie had sometimes stood by him, taking in his father's confident analysis. Mostly, though, he'd spent games tackling other town boys in scrimmages by the north end zone—a testing ground for speed and skill where he'd held his own.

By halftime, Tremonton trailed 14–10. As the fourth quarter began, they managed to narrow the gap to 21–17, with Vickers scoring a crucial touchdown. Tremonton forced a punt, getting the ball back with two minutes left on their own twenty-yard line. They opened with a sweep left, resulting in a pile-up near the twenty.

When the boys unpiled, Vickers was still, lying flat on the turf. The coach ran out as did the team doctor. Vickers hobbled off holding a limp arm. He had a shoulder separation and would most likely be gone for the season.

"Goddamn it, Tynse," muttered Coach Terry. "We're really screwed now."

"Maybe not. You've got that Holmes kid."

"Holmes? He's all we've got, but…"

"Send him in. You might be surprised."

"Holmes!" Terry shouted down the line of subs.

Pat Berry nudged Charlie, who seemed taken aback. "Your big chance, kiddo."

Charlie jumped up, jogging toward the coach but quickly turned back to grab his helmet from under the bench.

"Alright, Holmes. You've been running halfback the last two weeks. Get out there and try not to embarrass us in the last two minutes. Now git."

"Coach, I need Pat Berry out there at quarterback. We've been running plays together all week."

"What the...? Kid we ain't got time for this."

"Coach, trust me. Please." Charlie earnestly stared toward the coach.

After a moment, Coach Terry resigned. "You make a mockery of me, kid, and you'll be back on the freshman team. Berry, take Rasner's spot."

"Smart move," murmured Bush approvingly.

As they continued helping Vickers off the field, Charlie dashed to the huddle, where the team stood silent, watching their star limp away.

"Alright, huddle up," Charlie commanded as the crowd clapped for Vickers. "We've got eighty yards and two timeouts. Let's move this ball." Some of the boys looked at him, half-shrugging, as if to say, *Who are you?*

"Be ready the second the whistle blows. We're going to catch them off guard. Here's the play: Berry, I'm passing to you. Slip past the center, go ten yards, then hook left. Everyone else, block for the pass. Center, snap on the third hut and hold steady—they might jump."

The whistle blew. The plan was barely in motion.

"Break!" Charlie shouted. The team rushed into formation. The Tracy defense scrambled, clearly unprepared.

"Hut..." Just before Charlie could finish the count, a Tracy lineman jumped offside. The ref advanced the ball five yards.

"Stay in your stances!" Charlie ordered. "Same play."

As soon as the ref signaled ready, Charlie called, "Hut... Hut... Hut!" The center snapped the ball directly into Charlie's hands. Standing tall, he spotted Berry break past the line, hook, and turn just as the ball arrived in his hands. Berry sprinted forward two more yards—first down.

"That was slick," said Terry, watching intently. "The kid's got them moving fast and rattled. Did you see him draw that offside call?"

Bush was grinning. "Coach, Holmes was pulling stuff like that every freshman practice. Just keep watching."

Charlie signaled for a timeout.

"What the—? Jesus, Bush, he's crazy. It's too soon for a timeout."

"Crazy like a fox," said Bush. "He's teaching the boys a new play."

"Teaching?" Terry nearly groaned. A former Washington State receiver, Terry knew his football inside and out, and this felt more like improvisation than strategy.

"Kids from Merchant Creek played six-man touch football. They're fast and think on their feet," Bush explained. "And that Holmes kid? He's lightning quick."

As the boys gathered, Charlie knelt and outlined his plan.

"Alright, here's the play."

He sketched in a patch of dirt. "Tom, line up five yards wider than usual. That'll throw them off. Bobby, from fullback, take down their end hard. Carl, hit the tackle. Jack, run ten yards, then cut left. Pat, you're headed toward the right sideline. I'll follow the hole Bobby makes, and if they close in, I'll lateral to you. Everyone else, hold blocks for three counts, then push downfield for Pat."

When the ref whistled, Charlie called, "Break!" and the team lined up fast.

"Hut… hut… hut!" The center snapped the ball to Charlie, who tucked in behind Bobby's block as Pat sprinted wide. Carl pushed back the tackle, and Charlie spotted his path. The halfback was following Jack's cut left, leaving Charlie space on the right. As the linebacker closed in, Charlie pitched to Pat, who caught it in stride and bolted down the sideline.

Pat managed fifty yards before Tracy's safety brought him down, and the Tremonton stands went wild.

"Jesus H!" shouted Terry. "Coach, I've never seen a play like that. Vail was out five yards!"

Bush grinned. "Classic six-man football. Now just watch."

The ball was on the Tracy twenty-yard line. It took the ref a few seconds to start the clock, waiting for the linemen to bring up the chains. Charlie had the team already in a huddle. Just as the ref started the play clock, Charlie signaled for a timeout.

"Okay, Coach," Terry shouted over the crowd noise. "That was our last timeout. Why?"

"He needs time to draw up one final play," Bush replied. "Only twenty seconds left."

Charlie waved the water manager back and knelt in the huddle. "Alright, here's the plan," he said, voice low but steady. "We're going to line up like the last play, but when I call hut…hut…hut, don't move. Freeze. Let them set up, and we'll get a delay-of-game. That'll show us exactly where they're going."

He looked at each teammate, pointing out positions. "Tom, split wide, ten yards. Pat, head to the sideline, then turn upfield to draw the halfback with you. Bobby, don't block the end—we'll be through before he gets there. Cut inside and block whoever I call out."

"Hoy," Charlie locked eyes with him, "I want you pulling through that hole first, lead-blocking. Their safety'll be waiting on the outside for the pass, so whichever way you go, I'll cut the opposite. You slow down, and Geneva's mine," he added, smirking.

The team chuckled, tension broken. They understood, and when the ref's whistle sounded to end the timeout, they were ready.

"Break!"

The team lined up exactly as planned, with six men on the line. Tracy's defense was spread out, prepared for a pass.

"Hut… hut… hut!" Charlie called. Not a single Tremonton player budged. Tracy's defense shifted in anticipation, but Tremonton held still as stone. The crowd murmured, confused, watching the unusual setup.

Finally, the ref blew the whistle, signaling a delay of game.

"What in the world?" Coach Terry exclaimed.

"Holmes is reading their lineup. He wanted the penalty," Bush explained, grinning. "Watch what he does next."

The ball was reset back 5 yards, and Tremonton instantly took position. Tracy was scrambling, uncertain about where to line up. Charlie was already in stance, hands out, ready for the snap.

"Bobby, outside linebacker! Jack, middle linebacker!" he shouted. The crowd noise was building, and the cheerleaders had gone silent, watching the play unfold.

"Hut… hut, hut!" The ball hit Charlie's hands. He faked a pass left, then turned, charging right. Jack and Carl burst through the hole, each taking down their assigned men. Hoy Martin, pulling from the guard, moved just ahead of Charlie, clearing the path.

Charlie took in the field, his eyes sweeping for the safety. Tracy's halfbacks had been drawn wide, leaving only the safety between him and the goal. Hoy lined up his block perfectly, forcing the safety left. Charlie cut right, blazing through the gap.

Tracy's left halfback spotted the play too late. Charlie accelerated, leaving him in the dust, and crossed into the end zone with the ball.

The stands exploded, fans and teammates pouring onto the field to celebrate. Only Coach Terry and Bush remained on the sidelines.

"Six-man football," Bush said, watching the chaos unfold. "I told you."

"That kid almost gave me a heart attack," Terry said, finally taking a breath.

Twenty eight

CHARLIE SAT UP FRONT in the Lincoln Continental. Usually, his father insisted he sit in the back, though he never explained why. Maybe from the rear, La Rue could gauge Charlie's reactions through the mirror, or maybe it was just an unspoken rule that Winifred always claimed the front seat. Tonight, though, things felt different.

When Charlie emerged from the gym, the stadium grounds were nearly empty. The lights had dimmed, the stands were cleared, and the team had showered and gone. The only car left in the lot was the Lincoln, where his father stood leaning against the rail of the music building, waiting.

"Hello, son. Need a lift home?" La Rue's voice was calm but carried a weight that Charlie couldn't ignore.

They walked side by side through the quiet lot to the waiting Lincoln, the only sound their footsteps on the gravel. The four-mile drive passed in silence, the familiar rumble of the engine filling the gaps of unspoken words. La Rue parked under the porte-cochere at the house, but neither moved to get out.

After a long minute, his father spoke, breaking the silence. "First, son…" The word "first" indicated this was only the beginning; other, tougher topics would follow. "I've never been prouder of you than tonight. I'm still sore from all the back-pounding I took from my friends. I didn't know you had that in you, not at this level. Where did it come from?"

Charlie exhaled, surprised by the warmth in his father's voice. "From you, Daddy. You showed me how to throw, how to punt; you told me about your playing days. Those stories stuck with me and made me want to play, to be like you. And from all the running we do playing fresher out at Merchant Creek—and the six-man football we've played since sixth grade."

La Rue raised his brows, intrigued. "I didn't know that. Who coached you?"

"Mrs. Jackson got us started. Then, we coached ourselves, drew up plays, and played with what we had. Sometimes we even had girls join us. We played against Outside Creek, St. Johns, even Granite Ridge. Mrs. Jackson and Miss Matchin drove us to the games in their cars."

La Rue, busy with the farm and his work on the draft board, had missed a lot of his son's upbringing.

"That explains a lot about Pat Berry." La Rue nodded to himself, impressed. "Freshmen, even sophomores, rarely make varsity, you know." Charlie didn't need to respond; they both knew. "Anyway, son, I can't tell you enough—tonight, I was proud."

"Thank you, sir."

The silence settled again, thicker now, as La Rue shifted topics. "Now—why did you leave Webb?"

"Did Howell Webb call you about tutoring me?" Charlie asked, his voice guarded.

"He did, on Thursday. Said you weren't completing any of the assignments in English and that lots of boys rely on his tutoring to get by. We signed you up. So, what happened? Why were you doing so poorly?"

It was clear La Rue wanted an answer, but Charlie's reluctance showed. Finally, he gathered his words.

"Daddy, I never cracked a book except my history book. I went to class, went to study hall, but that was it. Truth is, I didn't care."

"Didn't care about what?"

Charlie hesitated, then let the words spill. "Anything but football. I've never been so low, so full of anger. I've never been that homesick before."

"But Charles, your mother and I felt that…" La Rue began, his tone uncertain.

"I know, Daddy. I know you both want what's best for me." Charlie's voice softened but held firm. "You've been on the Tremonton High School board since Carolyn was a freshman, so you know it's a pretty tough school. That's why you wanted me to learn how to box at camp, so I could defend myself when I got to high school. But then, without even asking me, you shipped me off to Webb. It felt like you didn't think Tremonton was safe or good enough."

"Son…"

"Let me finish, Daddy." Charlie took a deep breath. "When you and Mom drove off that Sunday, I felt like I was in hell. I missed you both. I missed our home, Johnny, Carolyn, my friends… everything. I was a mess. I wandered into the gym, saw the guys suiting up for football, and it was like… maybe that was my only way through it."

La Rue went silent, the ticking of the car clock filling the stillness.

"Why didn't you call? Why didn't you let us know how bad it was?"

"I couldn't. You both seemed so set on giving me this opportunity. You looked proud of yourselves, like you were doing something important for me."

"There must have been something that finally pushed you over the edge. What was it?" La Rue's voice was steady, though softened.

"That Friday, we had a game against the Chaffey J.V.s, and the coach told me I'd get to play. I was on the bench, ready. But then the campus cop shows up, pulls me out of the game and embarrasses the heck out of me, and takes me to Mr. Webb for 'tutoring.' When I got there, Mr. Webb was so wrapped up in his new hi-fi turntable that he barely noticed me. He just sat there, waving his arms like he was conducting an orchestra. I hated that music. And I hated him."

He took a shaky breath, the memory simmering with resentment. "I walked out, left my uniform in the gym, hopped on a bike, rode it to the bus depot, and came home."

"Why didn't you come straight to the house? Why hide out at Berry's?"

"Because I didn't know what you'd say or do. I thought you'd just pack me up and haul me back down there. I couldn't handle it, Daddy. I just couldn't."

Charlie felt the weight of his words settle into the quiet, his unspoken tears welling up, needing his father to respond. After a long pause, La Rue's voice broke the silence.

"Son, your mother and I are sincerely glad you're home, but…"

Charlie looked down at the floor.

"We wished you would have called us. I spent a good while wanting to ground you for life."

"I know, Daddy."

"But, knowing you went to such a great length to come home and hide out, we just feel terrible. You must have been having one helluva awful experience. You're here now, and you'll play for Tremonton. I don't want to hear another word about it." Charlie could hear the warmth in his father's voice.

"You knew I'd come back long before now, didn't you?" Charlie ventured, a small smile creeping in.

La Rue chuckled. "I did, son. You know I go around with Claude Miller every morning to check the fields. Well, one morning, he mentioned he'd seen you at the bus stop west of Berry's house, and sure enough, when we circled back, there you were, waiting for the school bus. You could have knocked me over with a feather."

"What about Mom? Did you tell her?"

"We keep no secrets. Sure, I told her. But how'd you figure out I knew for a while?"

"When you saw me at the gym tonight and didn't yell, I knew you'd already worked it out."

"You're pretty sharp for a freshman, Charles. Honestly, I didn't like the sound of that Webb guy's voice or demands."

La Rue opened his door, but Charlie stopped him. "Daddy, can I ask you something else?"

"Sure, son." La Rue shut the door again. "Go ahead."

"We didn't have time to talk after I got back from camp. Tell me about getting shot at."

"Oh, that." He sighed, then continued, "Guess your mother mentioned it in her letter to you last summer."

"She did, but without any details."

"Well, it happened while I was sulfuring the grapes. You know that old dusting rig. We'd had a mid-summer rain—just enough to risk mildew. So, I had Claude stack up ten bags of sulfur and drove the Fordson up there one hot, still evening. I'd done half the rows, stopped to refill, and noticed a car parked nearby. Thought it might be a neighbor checking things out.

"I climbed up, poured sulfur into the steel hopper, and as I was up there, balancing on the pedals, I heard this bang to my right and felt the lid clang. Thought the lid must've been hit by something, but then I saw a guy running back to the car."

"Did you realize what happened?"

"Not at first. I dropped the bag, watched him drive off, and noticed a fresh dent on the hopper lid. That's when it hit me—I'd just ducked, and a bullet had barely missed me. Found the bullet buried in the sulfur, a bit flattened on one end. I gave it to Sheriff Blickenstaff the next day, told him the story."

"Man, you were lucky, Daddy."

"That's what the sheriff said. But I couldn't figure why anyone would want to shoot me. The car looked like a Ford, but I'm still not too sure."

"Gee, Daddy, aren't you worried it might happen again?"

"I was, for a while. But life goes on—I can't keep looking over my shoulder."

Charlie hesitated, then ventured, "Has Mr. Blickenstaff ever compared that bullet to the ones that killed Mr. Strub and Wilson Carter over by Orosi?" Charlie paused, looking at La Rue. "My guess—he told you it came from a German Luger, right?"

La Rue's eyebrows rose. "Heavens... That's exactly what he said. He called it a Pistol Parabellum, said it was known as the Luger, a German semi-automatic from both World Wars, built for a special 9mm cartridge. He even thought it was an older model, probably from WWI."

"Maybe you could ask him about comparing the bullets next time you see him?"

La Rue studied his son. "I will. But, Charles... you've thought about this, haven't you? I'd wager you have a suspect in mind."

Charlie nodded slowly. "I think I do. And I have a plan for what we can do about it."

"We'll chat." La Rue regarded him thoughtfully before breaking the silence. "Come inside, son. I want your mother to see you."

They entered the house and ascended the stairs. The familiar scent of polished wood and aged Persian rugs filled Charlie with warmth, each step stirring memories of countless hours he'd spent bounding up and down, sliding in cardboard boxes, turning the stairs into a playground.

At the top, they turned into the master bedroom. La Rue switched on the reading lamp and gently shook Winifred's shoulder. She stirred, her eyes fluttering open, and instantly focused on Charlie.

"Oh, Charles," she whispered, relief flooding her voice. "Thank God. You've come home."

Twenty nine

"**D**ADDY," CHARLIE SAID as his father was saying goodnight, "I think it's important for Sheriff Blickenstaff to go with us and check out Orosi. Tomorrow, could you head down to see him and make sure he'll meet us on Sunday? Ask him to bring along the bullet that was fired at you—and, this is crucial, his kit to compare it."

La Rue, sitting on the edge of Charlie's bed, responded. "Charles, you never cease to amaze me. You've got this all planned out, haven't you?"

"If things go as I think they will, you'll never have to worry about being shot at again—and we'll finally know for sure if the Strubs and Carters were murdered."

La Rue's expression tightened with resolve. "I'll get Jeff there, even if I have to hog-tie him to do it."

"Tell him to come armed," Charlie whispered, aware of the danger ahead.

CHARLIE WOKE UP EARLY and rode his Schwinn into Tremonton that morning, surprised by the stiffness from the previous night's game. Only three plays, he thought, but they'd been great ones. He pedaled straight to the Tremonton Sun newspaper office, where he knew folks would be buzzing on a Saturday. Sure enough, Mrs. Iris Pease was at the front desk.

"Well, hello, La Rue Holmes! I hear you were the star last night. Joe wants to interview you. Go on in."

Charlie slipped through the hall into the copy room, where Joe Medico sat at his desk, cigarette dangling, green shade over his eyes, his typewriter clacking away.

"Charles Holmes," he boomed, "take a seat, boy! Man, we need to talk. Three plays—three plays that made that game. It's my headline for Wednesday. I'm sending it over to the Sacramento Bee. They might just print it, finally get them to notice Tremonton. Want a Coke?"

Charlie leaned forward, seizing the moment. "What are you doing at noon tomorrow, Mr. Medico? Come with me and Dad, and we'll buy you lunch. If you don't, you'll miss being on the ground floor of the best story of the year. What do you say?"

Joe raised an eyebrow. "I've never turned down a free lunch. Where do we meet?"

"Carl's."

"And where's lunch?"

"Orosi."

"Who's driving?"

"La Rue."

"What's this all about?"

"The Strub murder."

"Goddamn it, Charles. You sure know how to get into things. Didn't you fight a war with some soldiers behind your house a few years back? People died, if I remember."

"Well, more folks may die tomorrow, so you'd better be there."

"Alright, now—about last night. I'm writing up that game right now. Did you really draw those plays in the dirt? Because it sure looked like you did."

"Yep, but the light was too low for anyone to see clearly. That was more to throw the Tracy team off. Worked, didn't it?"

"Hell, you had everyone in the stadium confused!"

Joe reached over and patted Charlie on the shoulder. "I talked to Coach Terry after the game. He said he had no idea you were as good as you are—might even be his best player. Coach Bush told him about you, but he hadn't believed it. Well, he's a believer now."

"That's sure nice of you to say, Mr. Medico. Thank you." Charlie blushed. "I've got to go, sir," Charlie said, rising from the chair. "See you tomorrow?"

"Knowing you, kid, it'll be a humdinger of a day. Bye now."

As he headed out, Charlie stopped at Mrs. Pease's desk. "Mrs. Pease, can I ask you something?"

"Anything, La Rue."

"Do you remember last summer when Mr. Medico wrote about the Strub killings?"

"Sure do," she said, leaning back in her swivel chair. "One of his best pieces. Got lots of folks talking."

"Did anyone call in asking about it?"

"Let's see," she thought. "We had quite a few calls, if I remember."

"Did anyone specifically ask about the mention of gold coins?"

She looked off into the distance, then nodded after a beat. "Yes. One man asked how Joe got the idea about gold being involved. He seemed particularly interested."

"Did you catch his name?"

"I don't think I asked," Iris replied, somewhat embarrassed.

"Did you happen to mention my name?"

"Oh, I sure did! It was a big story, and you were part of it."

"Do you know if you said La Rue Holmes suggested the coin idea? I know you always call me by my middle name."

"Always," she replied warmly. "I think of you as La Rue, Charles. I admire your father so much—he's done a lot for this town. You're a chip off the old block." Iris looked proud.

"Thank you, Mrs. Pease. My father's a good man. Goodbye now."

As Charlie stepped outside, a chilling thought hit him: *That bullet wasn't meant for my father; it was meant for me.*

Thirty

THEY DROVE INTO TREMONTON in the Ford station wagon. La Rue had hurried Charlie out of the pool, where he was practicing holding his breath, got him dried off and dressed.

"Shake a leg, son," La Rue had said, steering him toward the car. Charlie climbed into the front seat, guessing they'd be taking the Ford. He knew his dad wouldn't want to risk his precious Lincoln in anything dangerous. A ding on the Woody wouldn't matter much—his father drove it when there was work to be done on the ranch or hauling that needed doing.

"I thought about asking Don Don to come along," Charlie said, "and maybe Diane Fleming too. But I figured there might be trouble, and I didn't want anything happening to them."

"Smart thinking," La Rue nodded. "Jeff's all we need. He told me he never goes anywhere without his thirty-eight."

"Oh, I talked to Mr. Medico," Charlie added, "and he'd love to tag along. He thinks it could be a great story for the paper."

"Did you two talk about the game?"

"Yeah, he was typing it up when I went by the Sun office. He had some good things to say."

"High time, son. You had us all fooled."

LA RUE SWUNG THE FORD into a parking space in front of Carl's. Joe Medico and Sheriff Jeffords Blickenstaff were waiting outside. Joe, still wearing his green visor, looked his usual self: like he'd stepped out of a smoky newsroom. Sheriff Blickenstaff, though shorter than expected for his reputation, had a presence that more than made up for it. A former M.P. during the war, he'd built a reputation that naturally carried him to the sheriff's office. Even his cowboy hat, resting squarely on his head, seemed to add a few inches, reinforcing his image as a modern-day lawman. Charlie noticed how the sheriff's holster, slung low on his hip, looked as much a part of him as his badge.

"Let Jeff sit up front," La Rue directed, gesturing for Charlie to hold the door. Charlie quickly jumped out to open it.

La Rue leaned out his window. "Jeff, toss your kit in the back," he called, nodding for Charlie to open the tailgate. Charlie ran to unlatch it, holding the back open as the sheriff placed his compact case inside. Then Charlie opened the rear door for Joe.

Once settled, La Rue backed out and turned onto the highway, heading north.

"So, what's this about, Holmes?" asked Sheriff Blickenstaff, glancing sideways.

"Ask Charlie," La Rue said with a grin. "This whole thing's his idea."

Caught off guard, Charlie cleared his throat. "Well, it all ties back to Germany, after the war." He glanced at Joe, "But maybe Mr. Medico could fill you in."

La Rue chuckled. "What do you say, Joe? Give us the lowdown?"

Everyone laughed. Joe was Tremonton's resident storyteller, often called to MC events and keep the town entertained with tales from his years in the newspaper game.

"Yep, it was back in Germany," Joe began, leaning forward to tell the story. "After Charlie and I talked, I called an old buddy from Stars and Stripes. He knew about three G.I.s who found a hidden Nazi gold stash. Major Boccioni was sent over at the war's end to organize a task force tracking down Waffen SS war criminals and locating any hidden Nazi valuables. My buddy said these three soldiers—Strub, Carter, and a Jackson Overstreet—stumbled on gold bars worth millions. They also uncovered three priceless paintings Göring had hidden. The soldiers were decorated in Paris with Patton there, not long before he died. They were discharged soon after and came back stateside. Boccioni, who was promoted to general, ended up over at Beale."

Joe looked at the sheriff. "One of those men, Jackson Overstreet, was from Orosi. He convinced the other two, Strub and Carter, to move here and buy up farms. Strub and Carter were from Alabama or Mississippi."

"Strub... right. He was the one who killed his family out near Tremonton," Jeffords nodded grimly. "I handled that case. Nice family, tragic ending."

Charlie jumped in. "Did you also investigate the Carter family deaths?"

Jeffords's expression tightened. "I did. That was a while before the Strub incident. But both were ruled suicides—sadly, not as rare as you'd think."

"We're headed to Jackson Overstreet's farm after lunch," Charlie said. "He was one of the three who found the Nazi gold."

The sheriff raised his brows, looking back at Joe. "Is that true, Joe?"

"Sure is," Joe said, nodding. "I'd bet that's why Charlie's bringing us along today. Right, son?"

Charlie turned to Jeffords. "Do you remember Louise Jackson, Sheriff?"

"The girl who went off the bridge near your place?" Jeffords replied.

"Yes, sir," Charlie confirmed. "Do you remember anything unusual about her death?"

"If I remember correctly, it was ruled an accident. She went too fast on the curve. Must have flipped and dumped on the rocks below. Why'd you ask?"

"Weesie and I were close," Charlie said steadily. "Her mom was our teacher at Merchant Creek School, and every day, Louise rode her bike all the way from town to school. She was the best rider I knew, careful and skilled. She never would have flipped on that curve."

"Well, I guess she did that day, son," said Jeffords, crossing his arms with a skeptical smirk.

"I went to the funeral parlor when I got back from Vermont. Mr. Erickson and I talked all about it. He said her bike was undamaged. No sign that she ran over the road guard."

Jeffords scoffed. "Morris is full of hot air. She was on the rocks. Could've skidded out, taken the bike over with her. She was found there, plain as day. So what's that girl's accident got to do with us heading to Orosi?" The sheriff wasn't liking where this was headed.

"Charles?" his father prompted, eyes steady in the rearview mirror.

Charlie took a breath. "I went to Mrs. Jackson's house and read Weesie's diary. Before I left for camp, five of us eighth-graders had a meeting up on the hill. I told them I didn't believe Mr. Strub or Wilson Carter killed themselves and their families, and they believed me. Louise took it upon herself to ride out to Overstreet's farm and keep an eye on him. She wanted to help, to find out if I was right."

"Now hold it," Jeffords cut in sharply. "You're telling me this girl took off to spy on someone you thought was a killer?"

Charlie met his gaze. "I didn't ask her to go. She decided to check it out on her own."

"You're suggesting something she did out there got her killed?" Joe Medico leaned forward, eyes narrow.

"Bullshit," muttered the sheriff.

"Hold on," La Rue interrupted, his voice calm but firm. "Charles has more to explain."

Charlie felt the sheriff's simmering disbelief but pushed on. "Louise stopped at the Old Home Place Café in Orosi a few times. She got to talking with a waitress who knows everyone's business around there. Weesie showed her a gold coin—one I'd given her to help prove what I suspected."

Jeffords eyed him sharply. "Why's that coin so important?"

"Because it was a coin from the Nazi stash," Charlie said evenly. "And it was the same coin I'd given Louise when I first told her my suspicions."

The sheriff's eyes narrowed. "Where'd a kid like you come across a gold coin? They're out of circulation."

"I can tell you where," Joe broke in, looking straight at Jeffords. "Charlie and I discussed it. That Nazi gold those three G.I.s found— Overstreet, Strub, and Carter—they must've smuggled some back home, didn't they, Charlie?"

Charlie kept his gaze steady. "I was at the Strub farm that day, Sheriff. I snuck in the back and saw the family lying there, dead. I hid my bike in the old mule stable. When I went back to get it, I noticed the floor had been dug up and then smoothed over. So I found a shovel and dug around myself—and that's when I found some gold coins. I gave one to each of my friends."

Jeffords narrowed his eyes. "This sounds like a load of horse shit, kid. Gold coins? Really?"

Without a word, Charlie reached into his pocket, pulled out one of the coins, and handed it to the sheriff.

"JESUS H. CHRIST," Jeffords murmured, turning the coin over in his hands. "I haven't seen one of these in years. And you found it out in that stable?" He studied the coin, his expression darkening. "So let me guess. You, a grammar school kid, found these coins and decided that those families—the Strubs and Carters—weren't suicides, but murders. You think someone killed them over this gold they brought back from the Nazi stash?"

"That's what I'm saying," Charlie replied, his voice steady.

La Rue spoke up, firm and unwavering. "And I believe him."

Joe nodded, leaning in. "So do I."

"Well, I don't see enough here to prove anything," Jeffords grumbled, gripping the gold coin tightly. "A girl with a gold coin, sure, that's unusual, but it doesn't give me cause to reopen those cases."

They were nearing Orosi now. The landscape had shifted from open grazing land to small farms and orchards that bordered the town.

"Son," La Rue's voice was low but firm. "You're going to have to tell the sheriff the rest of the story."

Jeffords let out a heavy sigh, clearly irritated. "More? What else could there be? This kid's got quite the imagination."

"Take it easy, Jeff," Joe cut in. "I'd wager he has more to say."

Jeffords threw up his hands. "Alright, kid, spill it."

"When Louise showed that coin to the waitress, it stirred up a lot of attention. She said Velma, the waitress, told her to go out to the table in front and talk to a lady there. I forget her name. She told Louise that Jackson Overstreet had paid for his entire ranch with gold coins. Apparently, he shelled out around ten thousand dollars' worth—all in coins."

Jeffords' gaze sharpened, but he remained skeptical. "And you think that means something?"

"Louise wrote in her diary that she was sure Overstreet killed those families. I think he found out she was onto him, and that's why she ended up dead."

Jeffords stared at him, unconvinced. "And what exactly do you think this Overstreet's hiding?"

Charlie met the sheriff's gaze with steady conviction. "That he murdered the Carters and the Strubs for their share of the Nazi gold they all smuggled back. And that he's willing to kill anyone else who finds out."

THE TOWN OF OROSI was like so many others scattered across California's Central Valley, with its main intersection lined with essentials: a couple of competing drugstores, a pair of banks—Bank of America across from Security Pacific, perhaps—a red-front five-and-dime, and a Western Auto. There was a barber shop, a hardware store, a beauty parlor, likely a small theater, and a pool hall. Gas stations, a feed store, and a Mercantile with farm equipment occupied the town's edges, alongside a modest used car lot. The train tracks of the Southern Pacific or Santa Fe ran through town, a lifeline that had brought it to life years ago. And in the distance, beyond the high school, there was the drive-in, a spot where teens gathered in the evenings.

Just past the barber shop and the Bank of America stood the Old Home Place Café. La Rue parked the Ford in an open diagonal space across the street, and the four jaywalked over to the entrance. Outside, a middle-aged woman with reddish-blond, peroxide hair leaned against the neighboring storefront, dressed in a pink apron, her cigarette tip glowing.

"Jus' go on in, gents," she drawled, nodding toward the café. "Table's open in the back."

Charlie, holding the door for the others, looked back. "Are you Velma?"

"That's my name, don't wear it out," she replied with a smirk. "Actually, all the tables are for you, noon rush just left. Grab yerselves some menus by the register. I'll be in once I finish this here coffin nail."

Inside, the men settled into a Naugahyde booth around a chrome-trimmed table. Charlie grabbed four menus from the stack at the counter and passed them around, noting the quiet hum of the empty diner around them.

"Is that the waitress Louise Jackson talked to?" Joe Medico asked, leaning in as he nodded toward Velma.

"That's her," Charlie replied. "I can see why Louise was taken by her. She wrote down their conversations in her diary. What a character."

Velma strolled back into the diner and came to a halt by their table, her order pad at the ready.

"What'll it be, boys?" She gave each of them a scrutinizing look. Her gaze settled on the Sheriff. "Say, haven't I seen you around before?"

"Could be," he muttered. "I'll have the chicken fried steak with fries and iced tea."

"You got it. How about you, big guy?" Velma turned to La Rue, taking in his sturdy build—over six feet and a solid two twenty-five, with hardly any extra weight even after years away from the football field.

"Veal cutlet and fries, iced tea, no lemon."

"And you, sir?" she asked Joe.

"Chicken fried steak like Jeff there, but with coleslaw. Coffee for me."

Finally, she turned to Charlie, her gaze softening. "What're you having, son?" She squinted slightly. "Say, you look like you could be kin to this big fella here." She pointed at La Rue with her elbow, jotting down their orders without missing a beat.

"That's my son," La Rue said, smiling. "Velma, is it?"

"How'd you know?" she asked, smoothing her hair under her pink cap as if enjoying the attention.

"Well, Charles here had a friend who came by and spoke about you. Seems you're famous all over the county." The men chuckled, and Velma looked pleased.

"Who's your friend, Charles?" she asked.

Charlie's expression grew serious. "Do you remember a blond girl who rode her bike out here last summer? She'd have been alone. About my age."

Velma paused, then nodded slowly. "That'd be Louise, wouldn't it? Such a sweet thing. I heard about what happened. Just so tragic."

"She and I were in the same grade, real close friends."

"Lemme guess. Y'all from Tremonton, right?" Velma's eyes narrowed as she looked over the group.

"We are, Miss Velma," replied Charlie, polite but intent. "Mind if we ask you about Louise?"

"You sure can, sugar. Lemme get these orders to the hash slinger, and I'll be right back."

La Rue leaned over, his voice low with concern. "Charles, you sure this is alright?"

"She seems like she wants to talk, Dad. Maybe we'll learn something if we're open to it."

Velma returned, balancing a tray of drinks, her face softening as she set the tray down and then pulled up a chair, settling in with a slight groan. "Hope you don't mind, boys—my dawgs are killin' me. Been on my feet since five, and I'm goin' till nine tonight. But I'll tell you—that Louise was sure sweet… Can you tell me what happened?"

"Mr. Blickenstaff here can tell you," said Charlie, nodding toward the sheriff. "He was the one who looked into it."

Velma's eyes widened as she took in the sheriff. "Oh, now it's come to me! Seen this man's face plastered on every telephone pole in the county last election. You're the sheriff, ain'tcha?" She extended her hand, still a bit star-struck. "Proud to meet ya, Sheriff. So, you found her? What happened? The papers didn't say much."

"Yes, ma'am. Looked like she lost control of her bike and went off the bridge—down onto some rocks. Happened fast, likely. I don't think she suffered."

Velma nodded, her face shadowed with sorrow. "I prayed for that baby, you know. She's with the Almighty now, no doubt." She stood, gathering herself. "Food's up, be right back."

As she disappeared, Joe muttered, "Louise made quite the friend here in Orosi."

Charlie nodded thoughtfully. "I can't think of anyone more special." He felt a pang squeeze his chest.

Velma returned, expertly balancing four plates on her arms and setting them down without a hitch.

Charlie leaned in slightly toward the waitress, his voice careful but clear. "Did Louise show you a gold coin, Miss Velma?"

The three men paused mid-bite, and La Rue's hand froze, pepper shaker in midair, as they waited for her response.

"She sure did, honey," Velma said, her voice softening. "When she dropped that coin on the counter, it drew a crowd. One big guy even picked it up like he was gonna bite it. I told her I'd only seen one other like it—Old Man Overstreet flashed a coin like that. Think the boss kept it as a souvenir. Gold like that, we ain't seen since the Depression."

"What else do you know about Overstreet?" La Rue asked.

"Annabelle at the bank said he paid for his whole farm with those coins. Came back later to cash in a few more, said he had big plans."

"What kind of plans?" La Rue pressed.

"He's tearing out his walnut trees to build a golf course. Says he's gonna make a killing when it's done. But folks think he's a bit touched." She glanced at a couple taking a seat nearby. "Well, eat up, boys. Gotta get back."

As Velma left, Joe turned to Charlie, an edge in his voice. "So, that's why you wanted us here? To have Velma back in your story? Now you're saying Overstreet killed his friends for their gold so he could bankroll this scheme?"

The Sheriff sighed, standing with his hat in hand. "I say let's finish up and get going. La Rue, you're buying? I'll be in the car."

"Well, I'm done too," Joe said, pushing back his chair.

"Sorry, Daddy," Charlie muttered, watching them go. "Didn't mean to rile them up."

"It's alright, son. Joe's on your side, and Jeff's just mad he might've miscalled those cases. He'll come around. We don't have to like him; just respect his badge."

La Rue paid the bill, but Velma caught Charlie's sleeve as he headed out, motioning him to the back of the café for a word.

When they were out of sight, she placed a hand on his arm. "Charles, you really cared for Louise, didn't you?"

"Yes, like a sister," he said, voice tight. "Our families were close."

"I could tell. And you think something bad happened to her?"

He nodded. "No way she'd crash like they said. Her bike was fine. I think she was killed."

"You think it's tied to that gold coin?"

"Yes. That coin's the key to finding out who did this."

"That why you got those men along, especially the sheriff? You're all headed out to confront Overstreet, right?"

"I don't know exactly what will happen, but yes, that's my plan."

Velma's face turned serious. She began to whisper. "Well, let me tell you—after Louise showed that coin around, folks here got real… agitated. The next day, Overstreet came in, asking all sorts of questions, trying to play it cool but clearly riled up. Wanted to know everything about Louise and that coin, where she got it, what she said. And then, just a day or two later, she was gone." Velma paused. "I believe he did it."

"There's more to it, ma'am." Charlie looked around before speaking. "I think he came over and tried to kill my father, took a shot at him on the tractor. I can't be sure why yet. It's a long story."

Velma shook her head.

"One last thing, ma'am," Charlie said. Velma leaned in.

"Whoever killed those families, took that shot at my dad, and got to Louise—he'll know you've talked to us, seen the sheriff, too. He's not gonna take that lightly. Watch yourself, keep someone with you, don't go anywhere alone until we can catch him."

Velma paled, taking a step back. "Jesus, God, son, I never thought of that. But maybe you're right." Her voice trailed off.

"You stay safe out there, Velma."

And Charlie was gone.

Thirty one

CHARLIE WAS TRULY FRIGHTENED. He'd seen the fear flash in Velma's eyes when she realized she might be in danger. Now that fear gripped him too, tightening in his chest as they drove out of town.

He wanted to tell them to turn around, to abandon this reckless plan. What business did three grown men have believing the wild theories of a kid barely fourteen? Maybe Sheriff Jeffords was right—maybe the Strubs and Carters had been family tragedies, just as the reports claimed. And maybe Louise had simply lost control of her bike, hit the railing, and fallen in an unfortunate accident. But if Overstreet really was a killer, what was stopping him from gunning them down the second they stepped out of the car?

His mind raced, panic building with each passing moment. *Turn around, Daddy. Let's go home. Forget all of this—we're walking straight into a trap.* He gripped the seat, swallowing back the urge to shout, to beg them to go back.

But just then, the station wagon turned onto the Overstreet farm road, the old ranch house coming into view. Charlie's stomach churned, bile rising as he fought down the impulse to be sick. They parked, and for a brief moment, the four of them stood silently beside the car, each with their own thoughts.

It was in that silence that Charlie knew it was too late to save them all.

THE FARMHOUSE LOOMED QUIET and still. They had driven up through a double row of towering palms, their trunks flanked by oleander bushes. The paved road led them to the house, facing north, its screened veranda wrapping around in a gentle embrace. Ivy crept up the west side, shielding the porch from the harsh afternoon light. To reach the screen door on the south-facing porch, a narrow cement path cut through neatly mowed grass, bordered by a simple bed of freshly tilled dirt running along the foundation.

The house itself was a weathered, two-story structure, its brown shingles faded from years of exposure. Two dormer windows on the second floor gazed down like unblinking eyes. Behind it loomed a water tank tower, an imposing relic of the farm's past. There were no cars in sight, but Charlie guessed one would be parked out of view, likely behind the house. From his vantage point, he spotted a small, newly built shed, probably housing an upgraded water pump for the irrigation system—essential if a golf course was truly in the works. Beyond that, he could see the corner of a modern steel building, likely sheltering maintenance equipment.

It was then he noticed the landscape beyond the structures: what should have been a dense walnut grove was interspersed with smooth, green fairways and gently sloping mounds leading to raised greens and tees. And in the distance, a man on a tractor was speeding toward them, emerging from the trees in a cloud of dust, hurrying in their direction.

CHARLIE'S INSTINCTS KICKED IN. "Daddy, you three better hide. He's going to park that tractor in the shed, grab his gun, and come right through that screen door. Let me meet him alone."

"No, Charles. I'll meet him," La Rue replied, his voice firm. "You three, go around and hide behind those bushes by the side of the house. Jeff, keep your gun ready in case he tries anything."

"Don't antagonize him, La Rue," Jeffers advised quietly. "Just ask what you need and stay calm."

Charlie refused to budge. "No, Daddy. I'm staying right here, behind you. If he recognizes you, he might try to shoot. If I'm here, he may think twice."

La Rue shot Charlie a hard look, one that usually settled any argument. "Go with Jeffers and Joe," he said, his tone brooking no dissent.

Just then, a door slammed from the back of the house. "Hurry, everyone," Charlie whispered. Joe and Jeffers melted behind the ivy-covered corner of the porch, but Charlie stayed rooted in place. La Rue scowled, but he turned to face the screen door, jaw clenched.

The silence broke as a man charged through the screen door, striding down the porch steps. He was maybe five eleven, balding, wearing striped overalls over a green long-sleeve shirt. No hat, but what sent a chill through Charlie was the man's right hand jammed in his overalls' hip pocket.

"What can I do for you gents?" he asked, his words clipped and sharp, his eyes narrowing as they met La Rue's.

La Rue stood tall, hands on his hips, holding the man's stare. "I came to ask why you took a shot at me."

The silence thickened as the man's gaze shifted, calculating, and Charlie's pulse pounded as he watched that hand in the pocket. Finally, the man broke the silence.

"You're a son of a bitch, La Rue Holmes. You finally found me. So what are you going to do about it?"

La Rue's voice was level. "I don't know why you did it … care to explain?"

Overstreet's lips curled slightly. "Sure, I'll tell you. But first, I want you to know I made a mistake. And I'm… truly sorry." Charlie tensed. The man's voice held no trace of apology.

Then, Overstreet's voice turned cold. "You drafted me, you bastard."

"What?"

"I had papers to prove I was working at the shipyards in Richmond. You ignored them and drafted me into the Army." A heavy silence fell, thick with resentment and old wounds. La Rue crossed his arms, brow furrowing as he studied Overstreet.

La Rue paused, accessing a long-forgotten memory. "Overstreet … Of course." La Rue shook his head in disbelief as it all came together. "You were that kid living out in Orosi at Radford's Trailer Park. You showed me those fake papers—ones I'd seen a dozen times from men trying to dodge the draft. Someone must have sold them to you. You even called me a son of a bitch then, didn't you?"

Overstreet's face twisted. "Might've. I was furious. And now you've got the gall to show up here, with your kid? Ain't you caused me enough trouble, buddy?"

La Rue's gaze hardened. "So, why did you try to shoot me last summer? This isn't just about the draft, is it?"

Charlie was proud of his father, facing the man and calling him out.

Overstreet looked dead at La Rue. He had nothing to hide. "You went to the paper, told them I had gold stashed away—that I stole it."

"What on earth gave you that idea?" La Rue asked, his voice steady but cold.

"I called the Sun office. Talked to a Mrs. Pease. She said La Rue Holmes was telling the editor that gold coins were somehow behind those shootings. That was you, right?"

"No," La Rue said, his voice measured, "it wasn't."

Charlie stepped out from behind his father. "He didn't say that, Mr. Overstreet. I did. I told Mr. Medico I'd found gold coins in Mr. Strub's shed."

Overstreet's confusion deepened. "But Mrs. Pease said La Rue Holmes told her."

"My name is Charles La Rue Holmes," Charlie said. "Mrs. Pease has always called me by my middle name. She has since I was little. You shot at the wrong La Rue."

Thirty two

JACKSON OVERSTREET MOVED to pull the pistol from his pocket.

Charlie caught the motion, saw the glint of the gun, and reacted instinctively. He launched himself sideways, tackling his father like a defensive lineman. La Rue, who'd once shrugged off blocks like that with ease, was no longer the man he'd been thirty years ago. The impact sent him toppling onto the grass, his weight folding beneath him.

As they hit the ground, Charlie caught a flash of movement. Sheriff Jeffords was standing behind Overstreet, knees bent, arm outstretched, pressing his revolver hard against the man's temple. Joe Medico hovered right behind.

"Don't move!" Jeffords barked. "Drop the gun, now!"

Overstreet's face paled. His hand opened, letting the Luger tumble to the ground beside Charlie.

In a quick, clear-headed moment, Charlie grabbed the Luger, sprang to his feet, and took three steps to the dirt bed beside the house. He snapped off the safety, pointed the ivory-handled pistol downward, and fired into the freshly turned soil.

The crack of the shot echoed, drawing every eye to him. Before they could react, Charlie knelt, dug into the dirt, and lifted the still-warm bullet between his thumb and forefinger.

"Sheriff," he said, holding it out, "take this and compare it to the one fired at my father—and the ones that killed the Strubs and Carters."

"Right," Jeffords said. La Rue, now standing, looked at his son in awe.

"Here, La Rue," the sheriff continued, handing his .38 to him. "Cover this man."

La Rue gripped the revolver, aiming it squarely in the center of Overstreet's back.

Jeffords took the warm slug from Charlie and moved behind the station wagon, where he lowered the tailgate and began setting up his portable projectile lab. The rest of them stood, silent and still, watching the scene unfold.

Thirty three

"FREEZE, GENTLEMEN."

All heads turned toward the screen door, where a petite young woman with shiny brown hair stood, her voice sharp and commanding. She held a Luger pistol raised beside her ear. Dressed in a bright green velvet dress with red slippers, she looked every bit as startling as her sudden appearance.

"On your knees, now. Quickly." Charlie immediately dropped to his knees in the soft dirt of the flower bed, noticing Overstreet was still standing.

"Ocho, please," Overstreet said softly, keeping his voice calm. "Go back inside."

"I heard a shot," she replied, her eyes scanning the men.

"It's nothing. Please, girl—go back in. We're fine." Overstreet started to lower himself.

"Don't move," La Rue growled, pressing the revolver firmly into Overstreet's back. The cocking sound was sharp in the tense silence, and Overstreet froze, finally lowering himself fully to his knees.

Charlie watched his father, impressed by his calm command, keeping Overstreet from moving. Recognition dawned on him as he looked at the woman on the steps. He knew her. Rising carefully, he took a small step forward.

"Down, kid!" she snapped, aiming her attention at him.

"Ocho, it's me. Charlie—from Merchant Creek. Remember?"

Her expression shifted as a faint, surprised look played on her face. "Charlie Holmes? Little Charlie Holmes? Is that you?"

He nodded, taking another step forward until he stood just below her on the steps. Gently, he extended his hand to touch her elbow, and though she flinched, she didn't pull away.

"Ocho, where've you been?" he asked quietly.

"I've been working for Mr. Overstreet all these years," she replied, her voice tinged with something between pride and sadness. "I never went back to school after we left for Arizona. Why are you here with these men?"

"We came to talk to your boss. He pulled his gun, and... well, things got a little tense. But it's alright now."

"Who fired?" she asked, her gaze sharpening.

"I did. I fired Jackson's gun into the ground. It's over there in the dirt."

She glanced toward the spot he indicated but kept her eyes on him, the pistol still in her hand. Charlie leaned in, his voice low and steady. "Ocho, please, like Mr. Overstreet said—go back inside. No one's in any danger."

She nodded slowly, lowering the pistol. She had no idea La Rue had his finger on the trigger. "I will. But if anyone comes in, I'm going to shoot."

Her voice rose as she addressed the others. "Did you all hear that? Don't anyone come in the house." With that, she opened the screen door and disappeared inside.

EVERYONE STOOD UP, each of them exhaling a collective sigh of relief. Charlie noticed Joe Medico struggling to rise; years of sitting hunched over his typewriter hadn't done him any favors, and the recent tension hadn't helped. La Rue, still holding the revolver, had lowered it to his side, no longer aiming at Overstreet.

"I'm going to ease up, Overstreet. You good?" La Rue commanded with authority.

"I think this thing's been blown way out of proportion," Jackson responded, rising up to standing.

Just then, Jeffords appeared from behind the station wagon.

"Man, that woman had me ducking. Guess she didn't see me back there. I was frozen."

"Did you check the bullet?" Charlie asked.

Jeffords nodded. "I did, son. And, La Rue, that gun—it's the same one that shot at you."

"We thought it might be," La Rue replied, eyeing Overstreet.

"But," Jeffords continued, "that gun didn't kill the Strubs or the Carters."

Charlie's eyes narrowed. "I thought you hadn't examined those bullets?"

"You were right to question me," Jeffords admitted, a flicker of regret in his voice. "I was too sure the Lugers found with the bodies were the killers. I'd never done a thorough comparison—until just now behind the car."

"So?" asked Joe Medico, his voice tense.

Jeffords shook his head in disbelief. "You're not going to believe this. I hardly do myself. I looked at the spent bullets twice under the microscope. The bullets taken from the Strubs and the Carters—they were all fired from the same Luger. But it wasn't the one that shot La Rue."

"What?" Joe's exclamation cut through the silence.

"I know," Jeffords said, his voice quieter. "Charlie was right. Someone else killed those families. Or at least another Luger. I never would've guessed it in a thousand years."

They stood in stunned silence.

La Rue turned to Overstreet. "Is that woman your housekeeper?"

"That's Ocho," he replied, his voice steady. "She's been with me since just after the war, since I bought this place."

"Man, she had me digging for the dirt," Joe muttered, shaking his head. "So, you have more than one Luger?"

"I have three," Overstreet said, a note of resignation in his voice. Charlie flashed a glance at La Rue.

"I collected them in Germany, never thought they'd be fired again." Overstreet paused, ready to unveil his entire truth. "And if we're all coming clean right now, then I'm deeply sorry I used one to shoot at you, Mr. Holmes. I was only aiming to give you a good scare, just to let off some steam. I held on to the anger that you sent me to the war. It's all I could think about, coming back to give you a what for." Jackson cast a sheepish glance at the ground. "I thought about it almost every day over in Germany."

La Rue's posture softened.

"How can I make it right?" Jackson bowed his head.

"Just make sure it never happens again."

"DADDY, YOU MADE A QUICK decision about Mr. Overstreet. I think he feels forgiven," Charlie said as the four rode back toward Orosi in the station wagon.

La Rue glanced over with a slight smile. "Son, I think it's high time you called me something else—maybe father, dad, or even La Rue. I think you've outgrown 'daddy.' What do you think, Joe?"

Joe chuckled, nodding. "It's time. Charles here's already stepped up—he may have saved your life by knocking you down when Overstreet moved for that gun. And didn't he save you in the war when that soldier had you in his sights with a flamethrower? Definitely time."

La Rue turned, still smiling. "So, Charles, what would you like to call me?"

Charlie thought a moment. "Honestly, I've thought about this for a long time. I know you liked 'daddy,' and I'll probably still call mother 'mommy.' But my first choice is 'La Rue.'"

"Then La Rue it is," he replied warmly.

Charlie turned to Joe Medico. "Mr. Medico, what are you calling me in the article you're writing about the game?"

"It's not done yet, so call the shot. What's it going to be?"

Charlie hesitated before answering, "Could you call me Charles La Rue Holmes?"

Joe raised a brow. "That's a mouthful, but sure. What's the reason for 'La Rue'?"

"Well," Charlie said with a glance at his father, "I just want to make sure people know I'm a chip off the old block."

"You got it, *Charles.*"

La Rue broke the silence. "About the other thing you asked, son— yes, I forgave Jackson Overstreet quickly, for two reasons."

Charlie looked expectantly at La Rue.

"One, I believed him. I heard regret in his voice; he's lived a summer of guilt. And two, I remembered him from the draft board. It was late '44 or '45. I know our decisions changed boys' lives—some were wounded, some were killed, and many still carry those scars. War isn't what they make it out to be. The nation might feel proud, but most of the boys I know feel only sorrow for those who didn't make it back, and maybe a dark relief that they did. Most don't even talk about it. They just want to reclaim the life they knew before. I hate to think I had a hand in that."

"Here, here," Joe murmured, admiring the quiet depth of La Rue's words. He had always known Holmes was a good man, but today he'd glimpsed a deeper wisdom.

La Rue shifted his gaze to Jeffers. "What do you think, Jeff? Are you going to follow up on those other Lugers?"

Jeffers sighed, looking out at the road. "In California, it's legal to own as many guns as you want. Even if Overstreet owns three

Lugers, I can't legally justify another visit unless he breaks the law with them."

"But your bullet test…" La Rue pressed.

"It wouldn't hold up in court, La Rue. I doubt any judge would sign a warrant today based on what we have. I'll look into it, though. We need to run ballistics on the guns and bullets found at the other two scenes." Jeffers looked at La Rue. "Jackson *did* mention he has two other lugers."

"How about that Mexican woman?" Joe asked. "She had that Luger, too, and she was pointing it right at us."

Jeffers shook his head. "She never aimed it at us, just held it pointing up. Without a real threat or evidence, we'd have nothing in court."

"That woman isn't Mexican," said Charlie. "Ocho is Japanese."

LA RUE FROWNED. "Hold on now. Everyone's always said that family was Mexican. 'Ocho' means eight in Spanish. Are you sure, son?"

"I'm sure her name is Oko. Somewhere along the line, someone must've misheard it as 'Ocho.' Japanese women's names often end in 'o'—like Yoko or Miko."

"How'd you know all this?" asked La Rue, raising a skeptical eyebrow.

Charlie glanced over at him. "I went to school with her. When I was in the first grade, Oko was in sixth or seventh. She had an older brother, too, though I can't remember his name. She was one of the few older kids who would talk to me. I really liked her."

"Well, I'll be…" murmured La Rue, shaking his head.

Charlie smiled, remembering. "I used to go to her house down by the creek on the Strub ranch. Her mother was always so kind, making little cakes and giving us strawberries. Oko and I would sit along

Merchant Creek, eating blackberries, talking about school. I don't think she had many friends among the older kids."

"So that's who lived in that little shack on the Strub place," said La Rue, almost to himself.

Joe chimed in, "Everyone knew of them—what with the war and all. They came to the valley back in the twenties to work the farms. Old man McQuewen had a big ranch back then. He brought in the Go family to work the berries, built them that house by the river, and piped in water. He had another group of local Indians living on the north end of the ranch, too—the Heicho family, last of their tribe."

La Rue nodded. "I remember McQuewen. He worked his land himself after the Depression hit, and later rented out his tractors. Lost a son in the war, didn't he?"

"Yep, a P-38 pilot," said Joe. "The son was an ace but never made it back. Broke the old man's heart; his wife died not long after they got the news."

La Rue glanced at Charlie. "You remember that, too?"

"I remember going to Stockton with you to see the Go family off when they were forced to leave. You said we should witness it and support them."

La Rue's face softened, and he looked out the window as they drove. "After Pearl Harbor, Roosevelt signed that order, and they rounded up all the Japanese families, shipped them off to those camps. I knew it was wrong. I wanted you kids to see what was happening. That day felt... heavy. It wasn't right, and I didn't want you to ever forget that."

"Did Mom go along with you on that?" Charlie asked.

La Rue nodded. "Winifred's always had strong opinions, son. She couldn't stand Roosevelt, but rounding up those folks—that she thought was the worst. She was fond of the Japanese lady who came around in her truck with fresh vegetables before the war. She was the one who pushed me to take the family to Stockton that day."

"Good for her," said Joe Medico. "I was there to report. I don't remember seeing you, but there were so many people. I'll never forget it."

"It was only late April," Charlie said, "but I remember it felt like the hottest day of the year. I got to talk with Oko for a bit. She was sad, but she held her chin up. Her parents, too. They told her it would be an adventure, that they'd try to think of it that way, as something they'd get through together. Father, those people were amazing. I'm glad they came back to their land."

Joe spoke softly. "I wrote a piece on it back then, but I never had it printed. Folks were still raw over Pearl Harbor, scared of what might come next. It just didn't feel right, so I tucked it away, and there it stayed."

"Maybe it's time to bring it out," Charlie suggested.

"Maybe," Joe said, his voice heavy. "It was a terrible thing to witness. Do you remember how dignified they looked? They all wore their best, like they were heading to church."

La Rue's face grew somber. "I remember that train—a weathered old thing. The cars were stifling, like ovens. It was tough just getting the windows open, and then they had to board that blistering train, packed in on that unbearable day. I'll never forget it..."

"What sticks with me is the sound," Charlie said. "When that train finally lurched forward, a sound started up from the crowd abord—a low wailing, like the wind through a forest. I'd never heard anything like it. It wasn't crying or singing. It was like they were reaching for something—"

"Like they were trying to hold on," said La Rue quietly. "It was the saddest sound I've ever heard."

Charlie glanced at his father in the rearview mirror and saw something in his expression that struck him—a depth of feeling he'd rarely glimpsed. In that moment, he felt a wave of love and respect for him, unlike anything he'd felt before.

AS THEY ROLLED INTO TREMONTON, La Rue turned to Jeff. "So, what's your plan for Overstreet?"

Jeff sighed. "Monday, I'll start looking at the guns and bullets from the first two murders."

"But it's Sunday," Joe pointed out. "You must have deputies on duty."

Jeff chuckled wryly. "Sunday's the worst, Joe."

"Come on," Joe teased. "Everyone's at home or in church."

Jeff shook his head. "That's just it—nobody's working. The Portuguese are grilling lamb and having a few drinks. The Spanish are busy with the grape harvest. The Basques are sitting down to family meals and their planters' punch. And the Anglos? They're all hungover and cranky. Meanwhile, my deputies hate being dragged out of bed. It's chaos."

He added with a shrug, "I'll have Billy in Dinuba check on Overstreet's place. His beat's quiet, so it'll give him something to do. Happy now?"

Joe raised an eyebrow. "I don't trust that man, not with gold coins and German Lugers lying around."

PART V

THE MEN EXIT

Thirty four

LA RUE AND WINIFRED HOLMES HAD AN UNBREAKABLE RULE for their children. It applied to Carolyn, now to Charles, and would eventually be Johnny's turn: no one could go anywhere on a school night. But on Fridays and Saturdays, they could stay out until twelve-thirty—as long as they came upstairs afterward to wake their parents and let them know they were home safe.

That Friday night, after Tremonton's second game of the season, Charles rode home with Carolyn. They both went straight up to their parents' bedroom. Carolyn gave a quick "hi" and slipped off to her room, but Charles could tell his father was waiting for a talk.

The bedroom sat on the southeast corner of the house, with wide-open windows that let the breeze flow in. La Rue liked to see the first light on the Sierra Nevada each morning, a far cry from his Nebraska roots.

The soft light cast shadows over his bedside floor, where a small mountain of paperbacks—mostly Westerns and mysteries—lay beside scattered magazines like The Atlantic, National Geographic, and a few car periodicals.

"Sit down, son," La Rue said, propping himself against the headboard.

"Winifred, are you awake?" La Rue asked in a quiet voice.

"Of course I'm awake. Who could sleep with you two crashing about?" She rolled over, propping herself up beside him. Even after resting, her bright red hair stayed perfectly set in neat, wavy swoops held in place by a net. To Charlie, those waves looked like something from a Hollywood film.

"Hi, Charles," she greeted. "What time is it?"

"It's a bit after midnight, Mom," he replied.

"How'd you get home? Did you go to the dance?" Winifred asked, knowing the gym dance followed every home game.

"Yeah, I went," he nodded. "I caught a ride back with Carolyn."

"Did Glenn drive her?" she asked, with a hint of curiosity.

"Yes."

"I wish Glenn didn't smoke," Winifred muttered.

"He doesn't when I'm around," Charlie replied.

"Well, he would if you weren't there. Dang it anyway. I'll sure be glad when Carolyn heads off to Stanford." Charlie knew his sister was set to attend Stanford, a school that had only recently begun admitting women alongside men.

"Winifred," La Rue interjected, his voice brimming with pride, "you should have seen Charles tonight. He was the star out there."

"I know you told me he made varsity, but I didn't really believe it," she admitted, glancing at Charlie with a surprised smile. "I wish I could have been there."

Charlie knew his mother had once been a good athlete herself, playing basketball at Wellesley. She often told stories of those days back in Massachusetts, how girls had to stay in one of three sections of the court, and how, at five-two, she played center. He remembered when she and La Rue would play badminton on the court north of the house, their laughter carrying well into the night.

"Charles intercepted two passes," La Rue continued, "and ran one back for a touchdown. Tremonton beat Turlock, twenty-one to zero. He was on the field every minute, and he was the best player out there."

Winifred looked over with a smile. "Well, then, he must be exhausted. Why don't you let him get to bed?"

"In a second—just one last thing." La Rue swung his legs over the side of the bed, standing up in his pajamas. "Charles, when you played halfback on defense, I noticed you moving up to the line when you read the run around. That was smart. Anticipation's half the battle. But you need to work on getting around the blocker." He took a stance nearby. "Get up, let me show you. You be the blocker; I'm you. Come at me."

Charlie got up, stepping in to mimic the move, and La Rue pressed his hands against his son's shoulders, pushing slightly to the side. "See how I angle my hands? You push the blocker off-center, just enough to force him one way and make the runner hesitate. He won't know where to go."

"Got it, La Rue. This is good stuff." Charlie's eyes lit up as he processed the advice.

La Rue grinned. "Practice it next week. Great game, son. Wini, you wouldn't believe how fast this kid is."

"Then let's see how quick he can get to bed," Winifred teased.

"Wait—one more thing." La Rue's tone changed, growing more serious. "I got a call from Jeffords Blickenstaff this afternoon. I didn't want to tell you before the game."

"Not now, La Rue," Winifred protested, concern shadowing her face.

"He should know, Winifred. Charles," La Rue said gently, "Jackson Overstreet is dead."

"What? That's…That's impossible!" Charlie's eyes widened in shock.

"Jeff said his deputy from Dinuba went out there a couple of times this week. Today, he noticed the place seemed deserted. He knocked, found the door unlocked, and walked in. Overstreet was on the floor, arms at his sides, a bullet hole clean through his forehead—just like Carter and Strub. The Luger was beside him. Jeff's already had the bullet analyzed. It's from a Luger, but not the one found at the scene.

It's the same type that killed Strub and Carter. Someone shot him, Charlie. It wasn't a suicide."

"I DON'T KNOW WHAT TO SAY, LA RUE." Charlie searched La Rue's eyes for answers. "I was sure Overstreet was the one who killed those families for their gold."

"Well, son, it looks like you may have been offbase."

"What about Oko?" Charlie asked, his mind racing.

"She's gone," La Rue answered. "Jeff said none of her clothes were left behind. Looks like she cleared out."

"Maybe she found Overstreet dead and panicked," Charlie suggested, though his voice held uncertainty. "Could she have been taken?"

"Jeff doesn't think so," La Rue said. "He went out there as soon as he got word. Said the place looked ransacked, like someone was searching for something."

"That must be it," Charlie muttered. "The killer was looking for the gold."

La Rue paused before speaking, his tone heavy. "Jeff thinks the killer already knew where Overstreet's gold was."

Charlie frowned, confusion mixing with dread. "How could that be?"

"Jeff thinks Oko killed him."

Thirty five

IT WAS SIX IN THE MORNING, Saturday, and still dark when Charlie straddled his Schwinn and set out. Pedaling hard, he figured it would take him around three hours to reach Orosi. The clock behind the counter read exactly nine when he finally pushed open the glass door of the Old Home Place Café and sat down at the counter, his breath coming fast, heart pounding. Biking nonstop felt so different from football, where there was always a brief pause between plays. Here, it was just relentless motion.

"Well, lookee here," Velma called, coming around the counter. "If it ain't that friend of Louise. What can I do yuh for, young man?"

"Do you have hot chocolate?" he asked, still catching his breath. Charlie loved diner hot chocolate. Even though he was panting, he couldn't pass it up.

"I sure do. Be right back, don't you go nowhere, you hear?" By the time she returned with a mug, saucer, and a spoon, Charlie's breathing had steadied. He picked up the glass sugar dispenser, poured some into his cup, and stirred it slowly.

"Want a marshmeller?"

"No thanks, this is fine."

Velma leaned on the counter, chin in her hands, looking him over with an easy smile. "What're ya doin' in these parts, young fella?"

"I want to take a look around Overstreet's place," he replied.

"Well now, you're gonna have a dickens of a time gettin' in there. They got those road blockers up, all kinds of signs." Velma caught wind of Charlie's resolve. "But I'll bet a dollar to a doughnut you ain't lettin' no itty-bitty sign keep ya out, are ya?"

"I'd do anything for Louise." Charlie flashed a look of determination.

"Boy, where'd ya go and get all that gumption? You sho is sumpthin'." Velma beamed.

"I'm not sure," Charlie said with a grin. He quickly tossed back his last sip. The smooth chocolate warmed his belly, filling him with enough courage to continue on.

"Thanks for the hot chocolate, Velma. Maybe I'll stop by again later." He left a few coins on the counter.

"Door's open 'til closing. And we don't take no wooden nickels. Take care now, ya hear?"

CHARLIE REACHED THE OVERSTREET FARM in fifteen minutes. A rope tied between two palm trees blocked the driveway, a sign on it declaring the place a crime scene. With no cars in sight, he assumed no one was there.

Inside, the dark shadow of blood still stained the living room carpet. Though he couldn't actually smell gunpowder, the scene brought back sharp memories of the Strub death room. A quick walk through the house revealed a mess—someone had clearly searched for something, likely gold coins. He lingered in a small room behind the kitchen with its own bathroom. It must've been where Oko had stayed, as it was even more torn up than the rest. Charlie wondered why her room was singled out. Had someone cleaned it out to make it look like she'd fled? Or could she have been killed and buried somewhere on the ranch?

He stepped outside to a newer equipment shed. Inside, Charlie noticed a tractor with an attached flail mower and another ride-on mower, likely for the golf course greens. Tool benches lined the walls, and nearby was a three-hundred-gallon gas tank. He found what he needed: an old wooden ladder, one used for fruit picking, with a single timber brace.

He leaned the ladder against the side of the house, climbed up, and edged along the cedar-shingled roof to the dormer window Louise had mentioned in her diary. It was then that Charlie spotted what he came for.

To the side of the window, in a tiny hidden nook, he found a wooden ammunition box fastened with a small peg. With trembling fingers, Charlie undid the latch.

"Bingo," he whispered to himself, hardly surprised. Inside, fifty shiny gold twenty-dollar coins lay stacked. He carefully filled his jean pockets, feeling the weight, then climbed down and stashed the ladder.

Charlie peddled back into Orosi, reaching the Old Home Place Café by three. As he weaved through town, it suddenly struck him—there hadn't been a car at the ranch. Overstreet's parking spot on the north side of the house had been empty.

HE PARKED HIS BIKE on the kickstand and walked to the side of the café, adjusting the coins in his pockets to minimize the bulging and clinking. With fifteen coins in each front pocket and ten in each back, he felt the weight but hoped it wasn't too obvious. Heading inside, he took a seat at the counter.

The place was buzzing—most of the customers were high school kids chatting and digging into ice cream sundaes, banana splits, and malts. Charlie felt a small thrill of kinship, blending into a crowd his own age.

Velma was at the far end of the counter, busy making ice cream orders at the soda fountain. She caught his eye and gave him a quick smile before continuing her scooping.

About ten minutes later, she came over with a dish of vanilla ice cream topped with chocolate sauce.

"Figured you could use a little somethin' sweet, huh?" she said, setting it down with a wink.

"Oh, wow. Yes, please! Could I get a glass of water, too?"

"You got it, honey. Nothin' too good for a friend of Louise." She dashed back to deliver more treats to the tables.

Before long, she returned. "Ya know, I've been thinkin'... You oughta talk to Annabelle. Louise talked to her just before..." Velma took a beat. "She works over at the bank, knows a thing or two about them gold coins of Overstreet's."

"But it's Saturday," Charlie said, surprised. "The banks are closed."

"Not here in Orosi," Velma said with a grin. "Our banker's a tiger; thinks he's gonna take over from those Giannini gents. Crazier than a bat in a bucket! Says if folks shop on weekends, why shouldn't the bank stay open for 'em? Go on, son, check it out!"

With a quick smile, she disappeared back down the counter, calling, "Gotta fly, kiddo. Adios!"

CHARLIE PARKED HIS BIKE in front of the bank, making sure his coins lay flat in his pockets, and then walked through the wide, heavy front door. Inside, it looked much like the Bank of America in Tremonton: a high-ceilinged lobby with a central island for deposit and withdrawal slips, and a couple of shiny new ballpoint pens chained to the counter. The bank had a certain smell Charlie liked - it felt familiar.

He took a moment to look around. Along the west wall was a row of teller windows, each with tiny glass doors that opened and closed.

Only one was open, where a woman was assisting an elderly customer. Charlie joined the small line of customers waiting for their turn. Within moments, he was first in line.

"How can I help you?" the woman asked with a welcoming smile. She looked to be in her fifties, with a comfortable, motherly air, her graying hair pulled back in a tidy bun.

"Are you Annabelle?" he asked.

"Yes, I am. Annabelle Applewhite," she replied, a hint of curiosity in her eyes.

"Velma sent me over to talk with you. Do you have a minute?"

"Well, I'll try to handle this rush of customers," she chuckled, glancing at the empty lobby. Charlie leaned forward on the marble counter, close enough to speak softly.

"Do you remember talking to a girl about my age last summer about some gold coins?" he asked.

"Oh, I do. That was over at the café. Velma told me that poor girl had a terrible accident."

"Louise was a good friend of mine. I have a question or two about those coins, if that's alright?"

"You people and these gold coins. They cause quite the stir." Annabelle looked at Charlie's sincere face. She nodded for him to continue.

"Louise asked about Mr. Overstreet, but did she ever ask if his housekeeper had any gold coins?"

"No, she didn't," Annabelle said thoughtfully, "but now that you mention it, Ocho—the Mexican woman—*did*. She came into the bank like clockwork every three months, always with a twenty-dollar gold coin she'd want to exchange for paper. The girls here often commented on it. She's been doing that since just after the war."

"Did she ever say where she got those coins?"

"Funny you ask—one time, Betty, one of our tellers, asked her that very question. I never had the nerve myself; felt it wasn't my place. But Betty told me the woman said Overstreet paid her two gold coins every three months."

"Two?" Charlie echoed.

"That's what Betty said."

"Forty dollars for three months. Not exactly a fortune," Charlie mused.

"Well, she probably got room and board on top of it. Who knows what arrangements they had."

"You're probably right."

"Then Mr. Watson came in this morning and told me Overstreet was killed this week. Such a tragedy. He said the sheriff is asking around, wondering if anyone has seen that Mexican lady."

"Thank you, Mrs. Applewhite. You've been really helpful."

"I'm glad to be of service," she said warmly. "Anything else?"

"Just one more thing—did anyone else ever ask you about the gold coins?"

"Well, I remember that Louise girl showed off a coin at the café, and it did cause a bit of a stir. I think someone came by and asked me a few questions afterward."

"Can you remember what he looked like?"

"That's the trouble," she said, frowning in thought. "It's been so long, and I really don't remember much. No, I didn't know him, and his face just doesn't come to mind. Sorry."

"Had you ever seen him around the café?"

"I can't say I remember. Wasn't it soon after that talk that poor girl died? You think she was...?" Her voice trailed off, concern etched across her face.

Charlie nodded solemnly.

"My, my. What is this world coming to?"

"Annabelle? That woman wasn't Mexican," Charlie said quietly. "She's Japanese."

"Well, I'll be," said Annabelle, her eyes wide with surprise. "Who'd have thought?"

Thirty six

CHARLIE NOW KNEW WHO THE KILLER WAS. He had just enough time to ride out and prove it. Pedaling hard, he pushed back toward Tremonton, passing his house, following Merchant Creek, until he reached the Go family's five-acre berry patch. He figured he'd biked over 80 miles that day.

Instead of stopping there, he braked sharply to the left, kicking up a cloud of dust as he halted in front of the old horse stable on the Strub ranch. Just as he thought. Inside, parked over the very spot where he'd once found gold coins, was a Plymouth coupe. Bunches of dried weeds were heaped behind it, a weak attempt to hide the car's presence.

He turned his bike around, racing downhill across the highway, onto the dirt road leading to the Go family's hut. He slowed as he passed the familiar stick-and-cloth shelter where the Go's had sold strawberries for years, pulling to a stop just twenty feet from their front entry. Off to his left, he spotted Mr. Go just visible among the rows of berries.

The house itself, small and unassuming, was a marvel of Northern California cedar beams interlocked above the door and at the corners, gracefully supporting a cedar shake roof. Charlie had seen larger houses in San Francisco influenced by Japanese architecture, but none with the quiet, simple beauty of this humble home.

He lowered his kickstand, dismounted, and just as he approached, the door slid open. A tiny, very old woman stood there, smiling and bowing gently. Charlie returned the bow, his hands folded respectfully in plain view.

"Charles," she greeted him in perfect English. "You have come to see Oko."

"Yes, Mama-san."

"She is not here."

"Then the car in the stable is someone else's?"

"No. That car belongs to Oko. Mr. Overstreet bought it years ago and registered it in her name. He didn't want the state of California knowing he lived in Orosi. It's her Plymouth." Typical of Overstreet, Charlie thought.

"Come, follow me. She is down by the creek in your favorite place." Mama-san led him through two small rooms—one clearly for sleeping, the other a combined kitchen and pantry. Charlie knew there was another room containing a toilet, bathtub, and a small sauna. Out back stood a square structure of red bricks—a wood-fired oven and cooking surface, with a neatly stacked pile of firewood cut perfectly to fit into the firebox below.

Charlie paused, taking the gold coins from his pockets. He stacked five piles of ten on top of the brick oven.

"What is this, Charles?" Mama-san's voice carried her surprise.

"These belong to Oko. Please see she gets them."

"I don't understand. What is this about?" Mama-san eyed the stacks of gold.

"Oko can tell you."

With a confused expression, she handed Charlie a rolled-up tatami mat tied with light green ribbons at each end. "You might need this, Charles."

"Thank you, Mama-san."

"Please stay for dinner. Papa caught a fine trout this morning, and I have your favorite cakes."

It was tempting.

"I'm so sorry. I think Winifred is expecting me."

"Then you should go home," she said gently.

"I'll miss your cooking, though. Poor mother, she never quite mastered it. Her own mother passed when she was six, so we make do. When we have a salad, she just walks around the table with a head of lettuce, tears off a leaf, and drops it onto each plate."

Mama-san smiled softly. "She tries, Charles. Remember that."

"Yes, she does try, and hard." Charlie laughed, "Look at me—do I look like I've missed many meals?"

Then he walked on while the mother stood and marveled at the coins.

CHARLIE COULD SMELL the soft, earthy scent of the creek as he neared their special spot along the bank. The delicate form of Oko sat still, her back to him, absorbed in thought. He stopped, unrolled his tatami mat nearby, and waited. She remained lost in her reverie for a moment longer, then turned, looked up, and smiled.

"Please sit, Charles. I have been waiting for you." He gently touched her shoulder for balance as he lowered himself onto the mat, knowing the touch was welcome—a reminder of their old friendship, from a time before the war.

They sat in comfortable silence, listening to the gentle murmur of water winding through the drooping willow branches and blackberry bushes.

"The creek is quiet now," Oko murmured. "With no rain, it's half its usual flow. It's the best time for my father to wade in and catch trout. Did Mama invite you to stay? One fish is enough for three."

"She did, and thank you, but I must go home."

"No, I thank you, Charles. It was you who started to sort out this whole mess."

"But someone was killed, Oko," Charlie said, his voice weighed down with guilt. "I can't help feeling it was because of me."

"Mr. Overstreet explained it all," Oko said softly. "He told me how he took the German gold bars and had them changed to coins in Paris. No, this wasn't because of you. It was because of the gold."

"Yes, the gold."

"I was so surprised to see you that day after so many years," Oko continued. "You're so grown up now, Charles, no longer the little first-grader who once made friends with a Japanese girl."

"You certainly surprised us when you came out with that Luger," Charlie said. "You took charge of the whole scene. It was…impressive."

"I was terrified," she admitted. "I knew Mr. Overstreet had a quick temper. He often talked about the foolish young man he once was and the mistakes he'd made. He told me he used to steal as a boy, that the gold was his theft, too. But that was his past. Everything changed for him the moment he shot at your father. He realized then how wrong he'd been. We spoke about it at length—he was truly, deeply sorry."

"Well, I'm sorry too, Oko. When we came out last week, I was certain Overstreet had not only shot at my father but had also killed the Wilson and Strub families."

"He didn't," Oko said quietly, "and now it seems he's the victim of the same killer. I never believed Strub or Wilson Carter killed their families. I knew them a little; sometimes our families gathered, and the men would reminisce about their time during the war. They were good men, Charles, and they loved their wives. When I read the papers saying it was murder-suicide, I knew it couldn't be true."

"So, how did you end up working for Overstreet?" Charlie asked, stretching out beside her on his mat, looking up through the willow branches.

Oko leaned back, her gaze drifting upward. "My parents came here in 1926 with my baby brother, traveling by train. My father found work with Mr. Paul McQueon, helping him with his berry farm, and Mr. McQueon let my father build our little house here by the river. I was born here in 1928. One of my earliest memories is of my father, Mr. McQueon, my brother, and Mr. Heicho—the Indian man who lived nearby—digging a trench so we could have water piped from the ranch house tank to our hut. Before that, we had to haul water from the river. They even dug a trench up to Mr. Heicho's place. Paul McQueon was a good man."

"When we were sent away to the detention camp, he promised to keep our house for us until we came back. And he did. Most Japanese families never got that chance. But in 1946, he died, and Mr. Heinrick Strub bought the ranch. He asked us to stay on and work with him, and we did. He was generous, and his family was kind. I adored his little children. There's no way he would have harmed them."

Charlie lay back on his mat, resting his hands behind his head, feeling the comfort of her calm presence.

"Do you remember that day at the train station when you were deported?"

Oko nodded. "I do. I was so touched that you, my friend Charles, came to say goodbye. No one else did. I remember thinking that somehow, someday, our paths would cross again. And now, here we are."

"What was life like in the camp?"

"We were sent to Ocotillo, Arizona. It was unbearably hot, but my mother always says those were good days. There was enough food, we kids went to school, my brother played baseball, and we had access to a doctor and dentist. We were so poor before that, in a way, it felt like an improvement. I can't say the same for everyone. Others had a different experience. But we always missed this little farm by the river."

"So, what now?" Charlie asked. "What will you do now that…well, now that things have changed?"

"This may sound wrong," Oko said, hesitating. "But I'm secretly relieved that Mr. Overstreet is gone. I never enjoyed the work, and whenever I asked to be let go, he'd refuse. I felt trapped. I never really liked the job, and he wouldn't let me go. I asked him over and over to fire me, but he always said no."

"Couldn't you just walk away?" Charlie asked.

"I did, once," Oko replied, her voice low. "But he came here, confronted my parents, and claimed I owed him for all the food and the room. He said I had an obligation to honor, so I went back."

"Where were you when Overstreet was shot?"

"I was up north, mowing. He'd taught me to operate the mower, adding it to my other jobs—cooking, cleaning, and doing his laundry."

"Didn't you hear anything?"

"No, the mower's noise drowns out everything. When I finally parked the tractor and went inside, the house was a disaster. Everything was torn apart."

"I saw," said Charlie. "I was there today. When I saw your things were gone, and the car too, I figured I'd find you here. But back at the Old Café, everyone thinks the 'Mexican woman' killed him."

She gave a short laugh. "They all think I'm Mexican."

"Couldn't you set them straight?"

"I didn't want to. It was safer this way. Around Orosi, people don't think well of Mexicans, but they despise the Japanese. I let them think what they wanted."

Charlie shook his head. "So when you got back from the camp, you went to work for Overstreet."

"The very day Mr. Strub moved in, Overstreet showed up with him, and they talked my father into letting me go work for him. They made it clear that if I didn't agree, my parents would be out. I couldn't let that happen, so I went."

Charlie shook his head. "Shoot, Oko. Overstreet doesn't sound like a good man. You've had a pretty rough go of it." Then, "Oko, you are really something."

"It's over now," she replied, exhaling. "And things are finally looking up."

"I walked through the house," Charlie said. "I noticed in your room, whoever was ransacking the place found a hiding nook in your closet."

"Yes. I'd saved about five years' worth of gold coins there, maybe around four hundred dollars. I don't care—I'm just relieved to be free of that house. At least they didn't find the bank notes I'd saved in my mattress. Another four hundred."

"So what are your plans?" Charlie asked.

"I've been talking with my parents. We remembered our time in Ocotillo and the acquaintances we made there. There was an old couple, Miko and Tadeshi, who farmed walnuts down near Visalia. Tadeshi passed away, but Miko returned and still sells vegetables in Tulare County. Their son, Kazu, is a baseball player at Fresno State. My parents always dreamed of growing vegetables too and selling them from a truck."

"That sounds perfect," said Charlie.

"It's a wonderful idea, but it takes money. My four hundred isn't enough, so we'll keep farming strawberries for now."

Charlie thought for a moment. "Who owns this land now that Strub is gone?"

"Well, Mr. Deveraux has been kind to us. My father rents these five acres for only a hundred dollars a year, and we keep all the berry sales. The Heicho family farms the other part of the property, and we help each other when we can."

Charlie's face brightened. "When you get home, you'll find there's enough money to fix up your parents' little truck for selling vegetables. You can start your new business alongside your strawberries."

Oko paused. She looked at Charlie with suspicion. "Charles, what have you done?" A small, knowing smile crept across her face.

"Let's just say Jackson Overstreet is finally paying you what he owes."

Thirty seven

IT WAS SUNDAY MORNING and Charlie set out on his bike to face his destiny, determined to right wrongs and confront the lion in his den. As he rode to Orosi, he mulled over all the old sayings— bet it all, put up or shut up, and even the cruder ones that made this mission feel like more than a game. Being Charles La Rue Holmes, he had to see it through.

It was two in the afternoon when he finally sat down on a stool at the counter of the Old Home Place Café. A few customers lingered over their meals, and Velma—good, dependable Velma—was on shift.

"Well, what ch'a hear about that "Mexican killer woman," Charlie, my boy?" Velma asked, leaning on the counter as she wiped it down. "Bet my bottom dollar you know something, don't cha' kid?"

"I do, ma'am. I just spoke with her yesterday evening back near Tremonton. She's never pulled a trigger in her life, and the scoundrel who killed Mr. Overstreet also took over four hundred dollars of her savings. What an ass." Charlie looked intently at Velma. "Oh, and she's Japanese."

"That's right. Yuh tol' me that before. And ye're here to do somethin' 'bout all these things. I'd bet dollars to dingleberries yuh know who done it. You somehow seem to know it all, kid. You and that Louise girl—same kind of animal, you two."

"Thank you, Velma. That's the nicest thing anyone's said to me in a long time. She was something special."

"So who is it? Who's the scum-suckin' pig killin' good folks and stealin' their gold?"

"Tell me something, ma'am. Remember when Louise showed you that twenty-dollar gold coin? Who seemed the most interested in it?"

Velma paused, her eyes narrowing as she thought back. "I reckon I do remember that day. She was here at the counter. I can still hear that clank when it hit the linoleum. Now I do recall there was this big fella, a real big guy. He picked it up and looked at it real close. What d'yuh think, son? Could it be him?"

"Do you know his name?"

"Shore do. That man's been comin' in here maybe two, three times a week."

"What's his name?" Charlie whispered.

Velma thought for a moment, then shook her head. "It's right on the tip of my tongue. Hold on—I got a table to tend to. I'll be back. Maybe I'll remember it." She left to check on the four men eating nearby. Charlie watched her sashay across the room, thinking to himself that she was one incredible woman.

She returned, brow furrowed. "Nope. Just slipped out'a my head."

"What does he drive?"

"Oh, I know that. He's got himself one of those puke-brown pre-war Fords. Looks like it might be war surplus. Say—that reminds me. I think he's a soldier. Walks like he's got a broomstick up his, you know what. His hair's always clipped short, and his shoes shine like a diamond on a goat's butt." She laughed, and Charlie couldn't help but join in.

"Is he about sixty-five?" he asked.

"Yep. Maybe a bit older, but he's in good shape. Looks like a tough customer to little ol' me."

"I think I know who it is," said Charlie. "Does the name Gerald Boccioni ring a bell?"

"That's him! My goodness!" Velma stared incredulously at Charlie. "Ya never cease to amaze me, son. How in the world...?"

"There's a story here, Velma. General Boccioni is the base commander at Beale Airfield. I met him back in '44 when some of his flying cadets tried to kill me and my father—one of my friends didn't make it out alive."

"Man, oh man. Ya sure do find yourself in a heap of trouble for such a polite, well-brought-up youngster," said Velma. "But a *General*? That's goin' way out to left field."

Charlie leaned in closer, lowering his voice so the men across the room couldn't hear. "I've got the clincher. General Boccioni was a Major in Germany at the end of the war. And guess who was under his command? Heinrick Strub and Wilson Carter—the men everyone thinks killed their own families. And the third man in his command? Jackson Overstreet. All three of them were awarded medals for finding a Nazi gold stash in a hidden railroad tunnel."

Velma's eyes widened, and she let out a soft gasp. "Well, I'll be. Now that's a story if I ever heard one." Velma looked at Charlie with reverence. "But son, that killer might just walk right in here any minute. He nearly always comes in for a chicken-fried steak on Sundays. I'd be hitting the road if I was you."

"I can't do that, ma'am. I'm certain he killed Louise last summer."

Velma's eyes darkened with resolve. "Well, I'll be sent to hell. Hand me a gun, and I'll shoot that sum'bitch myself the second his shiny shoes step in here."

Charlie let out a nervous laugh. "No, ma'am. I've got a plan. I want to get him outside and ask a few questions. I need him to admit to at least some of what he's done."

"Are you out of your mind?" Velma hissed. "Ya go outside with that cracker, and he'll shoot ya dead before ya get two words out."

"I don't think he will, Velma. He's been after gold coins, and he probably suspects I know where to find them. While he's focused on finding out what I know, I'm going to take him, as they say in football, downtown."

Thirty eight

CHARLIE SAT AT THE COUNTER, waiting. Doubts crept into his mind—was this a mistake? How could a high school freshman stand up to an Air Force General? Boccioni was strong, likely armed, and probably carrying a German Luger. Was he crazy for trying? Yet Charlie knew that if he didn't confront the General today, the days ahead would haunt him. Boccioni would soon realize that the troublemaker was Charles Holmes, and he'd likely go after him—or even his family—to silence them. Charlie gripped the counter, steeling himself.

"Hey, kid." It was three o'clock, according to the big clock on the wall behind the register. Velma walked over. "Let me get ya somethin' to eat. Ya can't just sit here doin' nothin'."

"Okay. Can you make a chocolate malt?" He nodded toward the soda fountain at the other end of the counter.

"Can I make a chocolate malt? Is the Pope Catholic? Does a bear poop in the woods?" Velma chuckled, winking. "Hide and watch."

Charlie watched as she opened the freezer below the counter, scooped ice cream into a silver canister, and slathered a thick stream of chocolate syrup on top. She grabbed a canister of malt powder and heaped in a generous spoonful, then added a splash of milk from the

Frigidaire. She snapped the canister into the milkshake mixer, lowered the arm, and turned on the machine.

"These mixers—they're a new thing, five to a bunch," Velma commented. She stayed nearby while the machine whirred. "There's this fella who drops by a few times a year, always tryin' to sell us a new one. Name's Ray Kroc. Persistent as a tick on a dog. He always asks how we do our fries. I tell him we just cut 'em up and cook 'em, like everyone else. Says some fellas in San Berdoo soak their fries out back for days before cooking 'em. Claims they're the best he's ever tasted." Velma glanced at the machine. "Well, it's done."

She poured the thick malt into a tall, clear tumbler. "Now this here is a *real* milkshake glass," she declared, tapping the bottom. "Not one of them heavy, pointy-bottomed things. Hate those."

She set the glass and the half-full canister in front of him with a satisfied grin.

"Did you use chocolate ice cream?"

"Are you nuts? No sirree. Not in my malts. It's chocolate syrup on real vanilla ice cream—that's the secret. Always order malts with vanilla, kid. Remember that." Charlie tucked away that advice. Tremonton's Rexall Drug Store made his usual malts, and he figured he was practically a malt-a-holic. He noticed this one was too thick to pour easily, so he scooped up a spoonful and took a taste.

He prided himself on being a malt expert, and with a practiced palate, he recognized this was one of the best he'd ever had.

"Ma'am, I love this," he said, wiping his lips with a paper napkin. "It's perfectly thick, perfectly blended—not too many ice crystals. You really know your stuff."

"Didn't I say so?" Velma grinned. "Ol' Velma's been around the block. Now, don't gulp it down or you'll get a headache. Take care, hon."

Charlie savored it slowly, knowing he was in a one-of-a-kind moment. He thought, *You don't talk, read, or think of anything else while you drink your milkshake—you just focus on the taste.* If he'd known about Zen, he might have called it a Zen moment.

Two and a half glasses later, he was finally done. Velma returned to pick up the empty glass, looked at him over her glasses, and when he nodded in thanks, she gave a nod back and went on her way.

He resumed his vigil, watching the front door through the wall mirror. Playing a mind game to pass the time, he bet himself the General would be the tenth person through the door. He was close.

General Gerald Boccioni was the twelfth.

CHARLIE WATCHED THE GENERAL'S GAZE sweep the room, analyzing each person before landing briefly on him. Then, as if dismissing the boy's presence, Boccioni selected a table near the front window. The man was just as imposing as Charlie remembered from the war—tall, broad-shouldered, and meticulously dressed. He wore mustard-colored corduroy pants with a dark, narrow belt, a blue button-down shirt with a striped red and blue tie, and a Harris Tweed sport coat. His shoes shone like polished mirrors. Velma appeared swiftly, setting down a cup of coffee before darting away, passing behind Charlie as she returned to the counter.

"Time to haul your freight, son. You don't want to mess with this feller." She whispered quickly, then disappeared.

For Charlie, this was a defining moment. He knew if he backed down now, he'd regret it for the rest of his life. But the risks were real, and he knew it could all go wrong. Still, avoiding turmoil was never his style; he'd made bold, split-second decisions on the football field, when he left Webb School, and in every encounter that led him here, including reading Louise's diaries.

He turned on his stool, slid off, and walked to a spot between the door and the General's table.

"Sir. Do you remember me?" He kept his tone steady, hoping he caught Boccioni off guard. The General looked him over, from head to toe, then slowly shook his head.

"Don't believe I've had the pleasure."

"We met years ago, during the war. You came to my house after the incident with your soldiers."

Recognition flickered across the General's face. "Yes. Now I know you. You're that Holmes kid—the one who saved the payroll back in '43, wasn't it?"

"It was. But I thought you went to Europe during the war."

"Sit down, son," he said, gesturing to the chair across from him.

"I'll stand, thank you."

Boccioni cocked his head.

"I did go to Germany for a time, toward the end of the war. Then came back as the commander at Beale. But you already know that, don't you? In fact, didn't you call me this spring?" The General's eyes lit with recognition.

Charlie nodded. "Yes, after Heinrick Strub was killed with his family."

"A tragic affair. Heinrick was a good man, a solid soldier. I believe I mentioned knowing him back in Germany, didn't I?"

"Yes. You also knew Wilson Carter and Jackson Overstreet. All three are dead now. Overstreet was killed this week." Charlie noticed the General's eyes narrow slightly, calculating.

"Coincidences, all of them," the General replied. "But why would a boy like you take such an interest in events like these?" Charlie could feel the tension building.

"I rode my bike here to talk to you about them." Charlie watched as the General shifted in his chair, positioning his legs as if ready to spring to his feet. His right hand moved near the left side of his coat, brushing against it lightly.

"Why is that?"

"I had a friend, Louise Jackson. She told me she came here and showed you a gold coin. She said you were especially interested in it."

The General nodded, unfazed. "I remember. You don't see gold coins much these days. Everyone was curious."

Charlie took a deep breath. "I believe you've seen more of those coins in the past few days."

The General shot to his feet, faster than Charlie expected for a man his size. Instinctively, Charlie edged a step back, positioning the table between them.

The General leaned forward, his voice low. "Let's step outside. This isn't something folks need to overhear."

Before Charlie could respond, Velma appeared between them, her tone firm. "You can't take this kid outside—he hasn't paid for his malt yet." She shot Charlie a quick look, her head tilting slightly as if to say, *Be careful.*

"I'll be right back, Velma," Charlie assured, keeping his eyes fixed on the General. "It's all fine."

"Just don't go skipping out on your bill, you hear?" she said, not moving from her place.

"I'll be back in a minute. Wouldn't want my steak to get cold." The General gave a tight smile, his posture all but forcing Charlie toward the door.

Outside, the General's expression hardened as he leaned down into Charlie's face, his voice barely controlled. "So you know about the gold coins. How the hell did you find out?"

"Louise had one. She got it from me," Charlie replied, his heart pounding.

"She told me that." The General's eyes narrowed as he processed, then—too late—realized his slip.

Charlie's blood ran cold; the General had confirmed Louise had shared that detail. But how? Louise would never have told him willingly. She must have been forced, coerced, before…

Fear and clarity surged through Charlie. This was the man responsible. He took a step back, but the General closed the gap, his large hands flexing, his frustration and anger boiling over into something unmistakably dangerous.

Thirty nine

VELMA CAME OUTSIDE, handing Charlie a piece of paper. "This here is what you owe for your drink. Come inside and pay, please." She was practically begging, her eyes wide with worry. Charlie knew she wanted to keep him inside, safe with witnesses.

Boccioni reached into his back pocket, pulling out a thin leather case, which he flipped open to reveal a badge. Holding it in his left hand, he reached into his jacket and pulled out a gun.

"Velma," he said with a snarl. "I am a deputized peace officer, and this boy is my prisoner. He's wanted for illegal possession of government gold coins. I'm taking him to the base. So go back inside, and everything will be fine."

"I ain't goin' back in there without this boy." Charlie had never seen such bravery. But the gun was now aimed squarely at Velma's chest.

"If you won't go back, then at least be useful. Here, put these on Charles." He shoved a pair of handcuffs into her hands. The pistol, which Charlie recognized as a Luger with ivory grips, pressed deeper into Velma's blouse. The waitress glanced at Charlie with a look of apology. He gave her a slight nod.

With a trembling hand, she secured the cuffs around his wrists, the click of each lock echoing louder than it should. A short chain kept his hands close together, allowing only a few inches of movement.

"General," Velma said, her voice now level and precise, "let's all go inside. I'll call the county sheriff since this is his jurisdiction. He should be involved in this arrest." Charlie noticed that she had dropped her usual dialect, speaking in clear, controlled English.

"Thank you for that offer, Velma. But I can call him myself...Holmes, which is your bike?" Boccioni asked. Charlie pointed at his Schwinn, parked near two other bikes. With the gun still in his right hand, the General lifted the bike like it weighed nothing.

"Now, walk ahead of me to that brown Ford right there." The sedan was parked diagonally next to the curb.

Charlie opened the back door and stepped aside. Velma stood there, her mouth open, helpless as she watched the scene unfold.

The bike fit snugly in the back with its front wheel turned and resting on the seat. Charlie briefly considered bolting while the General closed the door, but it seemed like his plan was still falling into place. He needed to be in that car.

Boccioni shut the door and opened the passenger side.

"Get in," he ordered, his voice carrying an unspoken threat. Charlie obeyed, the door slamming behind him. The General moved swiftly around the car, slipping into the driver's seat.

As they pulled away, Charlie caught one last look at Velma, standing by the café, her face filled with frustration and fear. He gave her a slight nod and a reassuring smile, hoping she understood. The car started. The General shifted gears, his right hand on the floor lever, the Luger steady across his lap, aimed at Charlie. They backed out and were gone.

NOTHING WAS SAID until they left town, heading down the highway toward Tremonton.

"This isn't the way to the base," Charlie remarked. The General kept his eyes on the road, driving skillfully, steering with his right hand while the Luger in his left stayed trained on Charlie's midsection.

"We're not going to the base. We're heading to your home. Maybe."

"Why maybe?"

"I need some information about the gold coins," Boccioni replied, his voice tight. "How did you find out about 'em?"

"Here's what I know," Charlie said, steadying his voice. "Your soldiers—Carter, Strub, and Overstreet—found Nazi gold, took some of it, and came to California to buy ranches with gold coins. They've all been shot, all with a gun just like the one you're pointing at me. I found a couple of coins at Strub's place, and that's all I know."

"Not enough, son."

"Why do you care about the gold?"

"It belongs to the U.S. government. We want it back."

"You're lying, sir. You want it for yourself."

The General smirked, keeping his eyes on the road. "Now why in the world would I want it? I'm a General. I get paid very well."

"Is that why you owe Pappy Smith in Reno around forty thousand dollars?" Silence fell over them, the only sound the tires humming on the macadam.

"You have no idea what you're talking about," Boccioni muttered. "So just shut up unless—"

"Unless what?" Charlie interrupted. "You know Joe Medico, the reporter? He put a few feelers out yesterday. He discovered you're quite the big spender at Harold's Club, out in Reno."

Charlie watched as Boccioni tightened his grip on the luger.

"He said you ran up a forty-thousand-dollar I.O.U. and paid back twenty last June. You still owe another twenty."

The General's face tightened, his knuckles white on the wheel. "Well, that about does it, son. We're going somewhere more private, where you'll tell me everything you know."

"Like the same place where you killed Louise Jackson?" Charlie's voice was a whisper.

Boccioni jerked slightly but kept the gun steady. As they approached the stop sign where the Orosi highway met Tremonton Road, he reached across Charlie and pushed down the door lock.

"Can't have you getting out, can I?"

Charlie was really starting to worry. He hadn't accounted for being handcuffed in his grand plan for the day. As they drove, he thought he'd at least have the chance to open the door and roll out, his best shot at escape. But now, with the door locked, there was no way he could reach to unlock it and open the door in time. He'd need another way out—and fast. His mind raced, though his body language was carefully resigned, showing nothing to tip off the General.

"I didn't kill that girl," the General said suddenly.

"Yes, you did. You bashed her head, dumped her, and threw her bike off the bridge."

Boccioni's eyes narrowed. "You think you know so much, little boy."

Charlie met his gaze, steady and unflinching. "You'd already killed Wilson Carter and Heinrick Strub—his wife and kids, too. And just this week, you killed Overstreet."

The General's sneer grew into a look of grim satisfaction. "Well, my boy, if you know so much, then you know what this means for you."

"Yeah, I figure it's curtains for me," Charlie replied, his voice low but sure. "But I just wanted you to know—you're not as safe as you think. The sheriff, my father, and Joe Medico were out at Overstreet's place just before you killed him. Velma knows you're a killer. My friends suspect you, and I think, no matter what you do to me, you're out of time."

The General's knuckles whitened on the wheel. "I'll get a lifetime of satisfaction destroying you, my little friend."

Charlie sensed he'd hit a nerve. Perfect. Now to push him even further.

"I know where there's over twenty thousand dollars' worth of gold coins," Charlie said, leaning back, feigning nonchalance.

The General's eyes darkened, and Charlie braced himself, half-expecting the man to shoot him right then. "Not possible. I found a few at Overstreet's. There are no more."

"Wrong. I found nearly twenty thousand dollars' worth at Strub's place. They were hidden in an old horse stable. You didn't look hard enough."

The General's eyes flashed with barely contained rage. "Where's the rest?"

"Louise knew about Overstreet's stash. Yesterday, I went out there and found that one too, hidden up on his roof."

"That girl couldn't have watched him that closely. You're lying. If she knew, she'd have told me to save her life."

Charlie felt the General's rage radiating. "She wouldn't have told you anything. She was tough. She'd watched Overstreet for days, saw him take a ladder from his shed and climb up to his roof. She knew you were the killer, and that's why you killed her. And now you're going to kill me. That makes ten dead—four Strubs, three Carters, Overstreet, Louise... and me." Charlie took a breath, steadying his voice. "You made stupid mistakes, General. You're going to the electric chair at San Quentin."

Charlie stared at Boccioni, like he'd never looked at anyone before.

"So, your dad knows, the newspaper guy knows, the Sheriff knows, and Velma knows. Four more to kill. What's four more?" Boccioni smiled wryly. "And when I go to your house, I'll have to kill your mother—and you probably have a brother and sister. They die too ... You could save them all if you just tell me where you've hidden the gold."

"You think I'm that stupid? You'd have to kill them anyway."

"Once again, you're so dumb, my little friend. I have an alibi for every single killing. Maybe I'll get arrested, but I'll get off. That bumpkin of a Sheriff is convinced Strub and Carter killed their own families. Ballistics back it up—the gun right there in each man's hand. Who else but the Mexican housekeeper could've killed Overstreet? If she says I did it, no one will believe her. The law won't touch a General. I'll only have to kill you, and it'll look like an accident, just like your girlfriend's. Tell me where the gold is, and they live. Don't, and I'll take your house apart. Anyone inside will die because of you."

Charlie held his breath, thinking fast. They were nearing the foothills and the bridge. It was getting dark, and Boccioni had switched on the headlights.

"Alright, sir," Charlie said, keeping his voice steady. "I'll show you. Stop at the bridge—where you killed Louise. My hiding place is nearby."

THEY PARKED AT THE EDGE of the bridge, the car angled by the side of the road. The General got out, pulled Charlie's bike from the back seat, and leaned it against the railing of the bridge. He strode to Charlie's door, unlocking it with the car key and swinging it open.

"Time to talk, Charles Holmes."

"Alright. Listen carefully." Charlie stepped out, pointing into the distance. "See that hill over there? My favorite one. Jump the fence and cross the irrigation ditch, then climb up toward that single tree halfway up. See it? Above the cliff face. There's a small cave. In the back, under a pile of rocks, you'll find your gold. Now, promise you won't hurt anyone else."

"I WON'T PROMISE YOU ANYTHING."

"But if I come up missing, the newspaper guy will call your commanding officer at Lackland in Texas and tell him about your Reno fiasco. They'll court-martial you for sure. Let me go, and you can keep the gold on the hill. I won't say a word about any of this—I promise."

Charlie knew his chances were slim, but this was his final shot at survival. If it didn't work, he feared it would truly be the end.

"Step over to the railing by your bike."

CHARLIE KNEW HE HAD FAILED. This was it. He was going to die. He took a few steps to the railing, his mind racing. Though Boccioni had shut off the engine, the car's headlights illuminated everything with startling clarity. The Luger was pointed squarely at his chest, and Charlie slowly raised his bound hands above his head. The night was eerily silent, but he could hear the river below, splashing over the exposed granite boulders.

"Turn around," the General barked, his command as sharp as an order on the parade ground.

Charlie turned, facing the dark stretch of river and the rocks below.

"Now step up onto the railing."

"No. I won't."

"Do it, or I'll shoot."

"You won't. You could never explain a gunshot. They'd catch you. Velma saw me leave with you."

Boccioni's tone shifted. "Then I'll put you up there myself."

Charlie's mind raced. If the General tried to lift him, he'd have to stow the gun. It was a thin chance, but he'd take it.

Sure enough, Charlie felt the man's hands gripping his sides, hoisting him up so his feet were perched on the wide timber railing. He knew the next move would be a shove from Boccioni over the edge, down to the rocks twenty feet below. His hands were still raised high, and he could feel the General's grip moving around to push him from behind.

In that split second, Charlie spun around and brought his arms down over the General's head, circling his cuffed wrists behind the giant man's neck. His arms slid down quickly, trapping the man's elbows and chest in a tight hold. Chest to chest, and he could feel the bulk of the Luger in Boccioni's jacket pocket. He wondered if the General could feel his heartbeat, which thundered like a jackhammer.

Before Boccioni could react, Charlie pushed off the railing towards the asphalt with the full force of his legs. They staggered a few steps into the middle of the road.

Boccioni regained his balance, but only for a moment. Charlie, his feet now solidly on the pavement, pushed again and again. The General, top-heavy and unsteady, stumbled back until the opposite railing hit him behind the knees, knocking him into a half-sitting position on the rail, Charlie still gripping him with all his strength.

Then, with a powerful heave, Charlie drove them both over the edge, and they plunged down toward the water below.

ON THIS SIDE OF THE BRIDGE was a deep river pool. Every kid in the area had come here to swim and dive off the bridge at some point, thrilling at the knowledge that just feet away, beyond the bridge, lay jagged granite rocks—the very ones on which Louise Jackson had died.

They struck the water with a tremendous splash, both kicking and flailing as they sank quickly. Charlie knew Green Hole was about fifteen feet deep, its muddy bottom strewn with waterlogged tree trunks. In those few free-falling seconds, he'd inhaled a lungful of air.

Their downward momentum drove them to the bottom, and Charlie hooked his sneakers around a submerged log, anchoring them both in place. The General's body stiffened, his arms beginning to thrash with growing panic. Boccioni's movements turned furious as he attempted to pry Charlie's arms loose, struggling to break free. But Charlie was prepared—he clamped his forearms tightly around the man's chest, holding him in place like he would an opponent on the field.

The General twisted and jerked, pressing his arm hard against Charlie's face, trying to force him to let go. With his teeth clenched, Charlie leaned into the pressure, keeping his grip steady as Boccioni's frantic efforts intensified. Then came a muffled scream—an angry, garbled sound of pure desperation as the man exhaled the last of his oxygen. Charlie felt his skin prickle as the General's breath bubbled around him, the panic and rage palpable in the water.

Charlie's chest burned, but he forced himself to remain calm, his football training kicking in as he kept his hold, feeling the General's strength wane with each passing second. The man's claw-like fingers dug into Charlie's thighs, twisting in one last frantic attempt to break free. Charlie braced himself, gripping tighter, his face pressed against the man's chest, feeling his heartbeat hammering wildly—until it faded.

At last, the General's thrashing stopped, his once-mighty form going limp. Charlie wiggled out, leaving the body to sink into the depths of the Green Hole. He drifted slowly toward the surface, knowing he could have held on for even longer if he'd had to.

CHARLIE DID A SLOW SIDE STROKE to the river bank, his hands still locked in the cuffs. Exhausted, he wasn't sure he'd make it with his waterlogged shoes and heavy clothing pulling him down. But finally, he reached the shore, grateful for the light of a waning moon cresting over the Sierra Nevada. He carefully picked his way around rocks and bushes until he found the road, then turned left and headed toward the bridge.

Reaching the General's Ford, he leaned in to push the knob and turn off the headlights, casting the area into shadow. He knew he could have waded back into Green Hole to retrieve the dead man's body, maybe even recover the car keys or the ivory-handled Luger he would have liked to keep. Perhaps he'd find the key to the handcuffs, too. But just the thought of touching that lifeless form again, of going anywhere near the man he had fought with, was more than he could bear.

Resigned, he looked down the dark road, realizing he'd have to ride his bike home in the pitch black. He took a deep breath, steadied his nerves, and headed for his bike, determined to put as much distance as possible between him and the Green Hole.

THROUGH THE PERILOUS NIGHT CHARLIE RODE. The handcuffs bit at his wrists, forcing him to lean forward and grip the handlebars with his hands awkwardly close together. Steering was jerky, the bike weaving slightly under him. But after a while, he found a rhythm—sitting upright and letting the gyroscopic pull of the front wheel carry him forward, the road stretching silently into the night.

The moonlight cast strange shadows of trees and poles across the highway, creating shifting, ghostly forms that moved ahead of him as he rode. He felt a kind of dark exhilaration out on the empty road, a quiet joy in knowing he had righted the wrong done to his beautiful Louise and his little friends, Alice and Hank Strub.

About half an hour later, he pulled into the Holmes' driveway, parking his bike by the front door. He walked up the steps, and with both hands on the knob, opened the always-unlocked door. Inside, he checked the Seth Evans chronometer in the library—it was eleven o'clock. He crossed the hall, passed through the living room, and climbed the three flights of stairs to his parents' bedroom, nearly dry from the long ride.

He woke them gently as usual. La Rue, instantly awake, turned on his reading light and propped himself on his pillows.

"Charles, where have you been? It's a school night, and we've been worried sick." Winifred, now awake, sat up as well, her red hair tucked under a net and a bit of cold cream on her cheeks.

"I'm exhausted, I can assure you that." Charlie shook his head. "I'll explain everything tomorrow if that's ok with you guys. I'm too tired to make much sense."

La Rue and Winifred searched Charlie's face for answers.

"But I do need help down in the basement," Charlie said.

"Why the basement?" asked Winifred, still blinking her eyes at the light.

"Because, Father, I need your hacksaw to get these handcuffs off of me." Charlie held up his wrists.

"Handcuffs?" Winifred gasped. In a heartbeat she was out of bed, throwing on her robe to follow them down.

As they reached the stairs, Charlie couldn't hold it in any longer. "I have to say one thing first…"

La Rue turned to him, eyebrows raised. "What's that, son?"

"The man who killed Louise Jackson *is finally dead*."

POSTSCRIPT

General Gerald Boccioni Found Dead Near Tremonton;
Investigation Raises Suspicions of Murder
By Joseph Medico

Merchant Creek, east of Tremonton—General Gerald Boccioni was found dead Monday morning in Merchant Creek, approximately five miles from Tremonton. Acting on an anonymous tip, Sheriff Jeffords Blickenstaff and his deputies conducted a search of the creek's banks, ultimately locating the General's body. Preliminary autopsy reports suggest drowning as the cause of death. Boccioni's car was discovered parked on the Wicks Road Bridge, a local favorite swimming spot, situated just off the Merchant Creek Highway leading into the Sierras.

The General was fully dressed, including a sports coat and polished shoes, and his pockets contained cash, car keys, and other personal items. Sheriff Blickenstaff noted the presence of torn and bloodied fingernails on Boccioni's hands, describing them as "unusual findings." A loaded German Luger pistol was also discovered in his coat pocket.

In a statement to this reporter, Sheriff Blickenstaff shared that the anonymous informant implicated General Boccioni as a suspect in several deaths previously ruled as suicides, including those of the Strub and Carter families earlier this year, as well as Jackson Overstreet's death. Additionally, the accidental death of Miss Louise Jackson of Tremonton, whose body was found in nearly the same location in Merchant Creek, is now under re-examination.

General Boccioni was formerly stationed in Germany after World War II, where he commanded a unit assigned to track down Nazi war criminals and seize war assets. Three soldiers under his command— Heinrick Strub, Wilson Carter, and Jackson Overstreet—were awarded a unit citation for locating a cache of Nazi gold hidden in an abandoned railroad tunnel. Sheriff Blickenstaff reported that, according to the tipster, Boccioni and his former subordinates may have possessed some of the gold, possibly melted down from items such as jewelry, gold teeth, and other valuables confiscated from Holocaust victims.

The anonymous source also alleged that Boccioni owed significant gambling debts, notably to Harold's Club in Reno. The Sheriff is investigating this lead, as well as two possible motives for Boccioni's death suggested by the informant. One theory is that Israeli Mossad agents might have retaliated against the General, believing he profited from Jewish-owned gold. The other theory suggests that his death may have been a gangland killing tied to debts owed to Nevada casinos.

Sheriff Blickenstaff stated that investigations into these deaths remain active as authorities work to uncover further details surrounding this unsettling series of events.

AFTERWARD

CHARLIE ARRANGED FOR LA RUE'S ranch manager to rig a temporary crossing over the canal at the base of his favorite hill. It was Sunday afternoon at two o'clock, and cars lined up near the wooden bridge off Merchant Creek Highway. Charlie arrived first, sending Geneva Derrick and Diane Fleming ahead.

"Find a place at the edge of the Indian grinding rock. We'll be up in a minute," he told them. The two hugged their friend tightly. They knew how close he had come to death.

Don Don showed up next, driving his father's Buick.

Mrs. Jackson arrived dressed in well-worn chinos tucked into high-top leather boots and a khaki shirt. She climbed the hill briskly, leaving Don Don struggling to keep up.

Then Oko arrived in her Plymouth. Charlie hesitated, unsure whether a hug would be welcome. But as they exchanged a smile, he knew the moment was right.

"Thank you for inviting me today," she said warmly.

"This is a celebration of the life of Louise Jackson," Charlie replied. "You knew her; she knew you, too."

"I'm happy to be here," Oko replied.

"Please head up and find a spot near the granite rock with the others. I'll introduce you when I come up." He watched her cross the bridge and walk gracefully through the dry, golden grass, her bib overalls looking as if they belonged to her as naturally as the land itself.

Next, Velma arrived in a rattling, chugging 1927 Ford Model A coupe, which sputtered even after she shut it off. She stepped out in her Sunday-best, with a cheerful yellow hat on her faded reddish-blonde hair.

"Oh, Charlie. Yur a sight for sore eyes, you rascal," Velma beamed. "I thought I'd never see yur hide again."

"Believe me, I felt the same," Charlie replied.

"Give this old woman a hug!"

They embraced for a long time, and Charlie caught the faint, familiar scent of cigarette smoke in her clothes—it seemed just right for her. She finally held him at arm's length, hands on his shoulders.

"Jus' look at you. I reckon yuh grew an inch since I first set eyes on you. Big enough to handle that killer man, that's for sure. Oh, Charlie, I was mighty sad when yuh left me."

"You were so great to try to get me back inside the café. You knew I was in for it. But now I need you to do something for me." Charlie lowered his voice.

"You just name it, honey. I'd move the world for you."

"Okay. The Sheriff's going to investigate Boccioni's death, and he'll come talk to you. No matter what, don't tell him I rode off with the General that day. You know how the law can be—they're always looking for someone to pin things on."

"Don't ya know it. I've had enough run-ins with Johnny Law. I never saw you git in that man's car, alright? Honey, yuh did us all a great big favor. Even if nobody else thanks yuh, well, Velma shore do."

"Velma, come with me. We're going for a hike up to the hillside. Can you make it?"

"Hey, buster, if I cain't, I'll jus' grab a hold a yuh, and you can pull these ol' bones up."

Charlie picked up the two folding chairs, and together, they started up the hill.

"ONCE, EVERYTHING YOU SEE OUT THERE was covered with blue and yellow in the spring—California poppies and lupine," Alice Jackson began, her voice carrying a story that wanted telling. "There were no cattle or sheep, only antelope and elk and Indians." The small crowd gathered around, students once again, hanging on her words. Charlie and Velma listened from a step back.

"This hill was full of live oaks, and the women who ground acorns here found them in abundance. There was so much food that the people never needed agriculture. Every other tribe east of California farmed, but here they had all they needed. Summers in the high places, winters down here where it was warm."

"What changed it all, Mrs. Jackson?" asked Oko.

"Perhaps not all of you know Oko," Alice said, her gaze sweeping the circle. "Oko was my student before the war. They took her away in early 1942. It's so good to see her again."

"I remember her," Charlie said. "I was in first grade; she was in seventh. She was my friend."

Alice paused, removing her glasses to rub her eyes. "I'll tell you what changed: gold. They discovered it not far from here, and suddenly the world came over those mountains or around Cape Horn. San Francisco grew from a few huts into a city. Miners filled these hills and needed to eat, so they brought pigs, then cattle. The pigs rooted up all the acorns, and the cattle ate every seedling oak. Soon, they drove the Indians out of their food, and then the miners hunted them down."

"Someday, no one will remember what this hill was like," Oko murmured.

"Everyone who's been Mrs. Jackson's student will remember," Diane said. "We'll tell our children and bring them here."

"When you said gold caused all this, it did," Charlie added. "And gold is still changing lives." He rose and crossed over to Mrs. Jackson, taking her hand. "I need to tell you—I feel responsible for your daughter's death."

Alice shook her head, her face wet with tears. "Oh, Charles. It wasn't you."

"Yes. I gave her a gold coin here on this rock. She saw it as a challenge, and I got her killed."

"No, Charles." She stood, wrapping him in an embrace. "I know the whole story. Without you and Louise, that evil man would still be out there, still killing for gold. You saved lives, Charlie. You saved Velma, yourself, maybe your parents. Who knows how far that man would have gone?"

In the silence, Charlie set up two chairs beside Alice and Velma.

"Velma, I'd like you to meet Mrs. Alice Jackson, Louise's mother. Mrs. Jackson, this is Velma Cutts from Orosi—she knew your daughter."

"Oh, my soul," whispered Velma. "Yes'em, I knew your daughter for only a short while, but we hit it off right away when she came into my café. I'm so sorry for your loss. I loved that little girl, and I'm proud to meet her mother."

"And I am proud to meet you, Mrs. Cutts." Alice took Velma's hand. "Since Charles came and read Louise's diaries, I've been reading them too. She wrote about how much she enjoyed you, Velma. She even planned to write a book someday, and you were to be one of her main characters."

"Oh my. Well, I ain't had much book learnin' like you folks here. I only made it to third grade 'fore the Dust Bowl took our farm. But you know what? I don't care. Folks is folks, no matter how they talk. And I'm right proud to be sittin' here on this hill. Thank yuh, Charlie, for havin' me here."

"Does anyone know," asked Diane Fleming, "what happened to the Strub ranch?"

"I do," said Don Don. "But first, we have a real hero among us. If I remember, there was a bet."

"I know what you're going to say," said Geneva. "I was there. Charlie won that game almost single-handedly. Even Hoy thinks he's something special."

"What's this about?" asked Alice.

"Didn't you know?" Geneva smiled. "Charlie here is the latest football phenom at Tremonton High. You should come watch him play next Friday."

"If you say I should, I will."

"Alright," said Don Don. "Enough about the star athlete. I was telling you what's happened to the ranches. My father's been keeping up on it. He looked after the Strub place up until this week. The Wilson Carter place over in Orosi was deeded to a brother in Alabama. He visited but isn't sure he wants to move here, says the area feels dangerous, what with all the murders. He might put it on the market."

"I been out there," said Velma. "He's got a fine little walnut grove. Someone's gonna get a real good deal."

"Sure will," Don Don continued. "As for the Overstreet spread, it's going to his mother, Blanche Barrow Overstreet. She still lives in Orosi, at Radford's Trailer Park. She may sell, though—she wants nothing to do with his 'death house' or golf course. After the army, he never even went to see her."

Charlie cut in. "Everyone, this is Oko Go, our neighbor. She's Japanese, by the way." Charlie gave Oko a knowing grin. "Her family has lived on the Strub ranch since just after the First World War, and you've all probably enjoyed their strawberries. Oko worked for a number of years for Overstreet. Oko, would you like to share what's happening with the Strub place?"

Oko's voice was soft, almost blending with the gentle breeze rolling up from the bay. "Last Friday, Mr. Donovan came by and gave my family the deed to the Strub's sixty acres. Someone paid off the bank holding the mortgage, and it's ours now. The only request from the donor was that the Heicho family can stay in the farmhouse, and they're happy to help with day work in our berry fields."

"I'm sure everyone here has heard the sad news," Alice Jackson said quietly. "David Heicho was killed in Korea. He was drafted and sent there. They say it happened when the Chinese crossed the Yalu River into the north of Korea."

"Oh my gosh," said Geneva Derrick. "Wasn't David the last chief of his tribe?"

"Yes, he was," Alice replied. "I was his teacher. It horrified me that he didn't get a deferment, being the last of the Southern Yana Indians. But no, they sent him to Korea."

"I remember David," Charlie added. "He could swim two lengths of the Tremonton pool underwater. He's the reason I learned how to hold my breath."

"Do you have other news about the ranch, Oko?" asked Don Don.

"Yes, actually. We've bought a flatbed truck and installed a beautiful awning and compartments for vegetables," Oko replied. "My father's already planting five acres of different varieties, and my mother will drive the truck all over the county to sell our crops. I'll help, and so will the Heicho family. But we'll still have our strawberry stand and live where we always have."

"Your family will do well with these plans," said Alice warmly.

Oko glanced around, her voice softening. "I want to thank whoever found the money to pay off the mortgage. It was very kind." She looked into the group as if one of them might step forward. Everyone glanced around, a few shrugged. Especially Charles La Rue Holmes.

"I THINK WE ALL SHOULD SAY A PRAYER," Charlie said, kneeling at the edge of the stone. "What do you say? Let's think about Louise."

"Thank you, Charles," Alice Jackson whispered.

They sat or knelt in silence. Velma and Alice held hands. Sniffles broke the stillness as Geneva quietly began to cry, soon followed by Diane, while a sudden sting of tears came to Charlie's eyes.

A gentle breeze swept through the yellow grass, brushing past their faces, soft as a whisper. Charlie knew, in that moment, that Louise—his Weezie, his lifelong friend—was there with them, a quiet presence in the warmth of that special afternoon.

THEN CHARLIE BROKE THE SILENCE. "The last time I ever saw Louise, it was here on this rock. She'd never looked more alive. Since I'll be coming here often, I wanted something to remember her by."

He rose from his kneeling position and walked across the granite rock, his tennis shoes squeaking softly in the stillness. Kneeling again before Alice Jackson, he brushed aside grass and dirt right at the rock's edge.

There, he revealed a one-foot square piece of polished gray granite, buried gently in the earth. The inscription read:

LOUISE JACKSON
Lest We Forget

THE END